THEODORA IN LOVE

After her father's death Theodora Buck-leigh's new adopted family want to give her a London season. But though she is a pretty girl, Theodora has limped from birth, and dreads exposure to the social round. She takes evasive action, accepting an invitation from Dorothy Wordsworth to stay with her and her poet brother, William, in Dorset. Here she will find love, danger and intrigue. Might Coleridge and the others be engaged in treason? Can Theodora's chaperone, Alex Kydd, rescue her from this dangerous company; and even if he does, could there ever be any more between them than friendship?

Books by Ann Barker
Published by The House of Ulverscroft:

HIS LORDSHIP'S GARDENER
THE GRAND TOUR
DERBYSHIRE DECEPTION
THE SQUIRE AND THE SCHOOLMISTRESS
THE ADVENTURESS
THE OTHER MISS FROBISHER
LADY OF LINCOLN
CLERKENWELL CONSPIRACY
JILTED

ANN BARKER

THEODORA
IN LOVE

Complete and Unabridged

ULVERSCROFT
Leicester

First published in Great Britain in 2011 by
Robert Hale Limited
London

First Large Print Edition
published 2012
by arrangement with
Robert Hale Limited
London

The moral right of the author has been asserted

British Library CIP Data

Barker, Ann.
    Theodora in love.
    1. Wordsworth, Dorothy, *1771 – 1855*- -Fiction.
    2. Wordsworth, William, *1770 – 1850*- -Fiction.
    3. Women with disabilities- -Fiction.
    4. Dorset (England)- -Fiction.
    5. Love stories
    6. Large type books.
    I. Title
    823.9′2–dc23

    ISBN 978–1–4448–0954–1

Published by
F. A. Thorpe (Publishing)
Anstey, Leicestershire

Set by Words & Graphics Ltd.
Anstey, Leicestershire
Printed and bound in Great Britain by
T. J. International Ltd., Padstow, Cornwall

This book is printed on acid-free paper

Dedication

For my dear friend Eileen, not forgetting
Dave and Gordon

PART ONE

Imagination

1

Summer 1795

'Ma! Ma! Why was that lady walking funny?'

'Ssh! She's a cripple, that's all,' was the answer.

Theodora Buckleigh turned her head away resolutely, and tried to pretend that she had not heard. Given the noise that echoed around the busy inn yard in which she was standing, this was not as difficult as it might have been.

It was not the first time that such comments had been made about her. She had been lame from birth, and this respectably dressed child and his mother, probably a farmer's wife, were not the first to have noticed the fact. For the majority of her seventeen years, Theodora had lived a quiet life, seldom leaving the village of Ripondell where she had been born. Those who also lived in the village had become accustomed to her uneven gait, and never remarked upon it. It was only strangers who sometimes stared and commented, as the farmer's boy had just been doing.

3

Truth to tell, it was not a very severe limp, but tiredness or over use tended to accentuate it. Theodora had been standing for rather a long time in order to wait for the stage to Halifax. She had only taken a few steps up and down to change her position. It had been at that point that the boy had noticed her.

Her father, The Rev'd Paul Buckleigh had delivered her to the inn yard of The Bird in Hand earlier that morning and, after asking the landlord to keep an eye upon her, had left to go about his duties. He had married Theodora's mother late in life some twenty-seven years ago, when she had already been expecting a child. A rather remote, scholarly man, he had never really understood how to be a father. His daughter had been a little surprised that his paternal instinct had been sufficiently strong to impel him to send her from the village when two cases of smallpox had become known. It was not that he did not care; it was simply that it did not occur to him that she should merit any kind of special treatment.

She had known perfectly well, therefore, that any request that he should wait with her until the stage came would be greeted with surprise and a hint of disappointment. Nevertheless, it was the first time that she had made such a journey alone, and she was rather nervous.

'I wish you could come with me,' she had said wistfully.

He had smiled austerely. '*Aequam memento rebus in arduis servare mentem*,' he had said laying a hand on her shoulder. 'Which translated means . . . ?'

''Remember when life's path is steep to keep your mind even',' she had replied obediently.

'Exactly so. We will have no foolish sentimental displays. Goodbye, then, and do not neglect your Latin.' With a brief but not unkindly nod he had gone, leaving her standing alone in the inn yard with her travelling bag. The landlord, who was very harassed due to the sudden illness of two of his staff, was far too busy to pay her any attention, particularly since The Rev'd Mr Buckleigh's request had been made without any kind of gift to ensure compliance. No doubt someone would have helped her into The Bird in Hand, but as the inn was in the small town just down the road, rather than in her own village, she had no acquaintance there and was too shy to ask.

The stage did not arrive until an hour after her father had taken his leave. By that time she was thoroughly tired of standing and very thankful to climb in and take her seat. There were already three people sitting inside, and

Theodora, together with the farmer's wife and her son, took up the remaining three places. Theodora was not tall, being a little under five feet, and she found the seats on the stage rather high for comfort. What was more, because all the other seats were occupied, there was not room for her to change her position during the journey. To add to her discomfiture, the boy continued to stare, until his mother reprimanded him. She then stared herself and muttered something derogatory about people with deformities, and how they ought to be locked away so that decent folk didn't have to look at them.

Feeling the tears prickling behind her eyes, Theodora hastily got out the most recent letter that she had received from her half-brother Michael. He was ten years older than she, and was presently serving as a curate in another parish. How she missed him! She was much closer to him than to her father, and she longed for the day when he would have his own parish and she could go and live with him. In this his latest letter, he had written very amusingly about his cramped rooms above the butcher's shop, and his supposed temptation to take a rod and line and fish out of the window for sausages. Even while she smiled, she thought about how she could never live with him whilst he was lodged in such a place. She would just have to be patient for a little longer.

Fortunately the journey to Halifax was not a long one, and as Theodora was lucky enough to be next to a window, she was able to look out at the passing scenery. She stored up everything that she saw in order to write an amusing letter back to Michael. She must let him know straight away that she was in Halifax. He would certainly write to her there once he knew her address, for he was a faithful correspondent, and she was never very many days without a letter.

From thinking about Michael, her mind turned to a pleasant daydream in which Michael's real father, whom he had never met, suddenly descended upon them all showering riches, and making it possible for brother and sister to set up house together. These and other thoughts took her mind off her fellow passengers, and in a comparatively short period of time, she was getting down from the stage.

She had tried not to worry about what she might do if her hosts failed to meet her at the end of her journey. She dreaded the prospect of another long stand in an inn yard full of staring strangers. Thankfully for her peace of mind, she had barely set a foot to the ground

7

before a booming voice declared, 'My dear Miss Theodora! There you are! Did you have a tedious wait for the coach?' A well-dressed man, with a build to match his voice, strode across the inn yard, his smile drawn in a huge bow across his rubicund face.

'Doctor Marchant,' Theodora replied, smiling in return. She was very pleased to see him, for he had been physician to her family for six years before moving to Halifax twelve months before. It must be admitted, however, that her pleasure was mingled with relief at not having to wait alone in another strange place.

'You are looking very well, if a little tired, my dear,' he said, after casting a quick professional eye over her. His attitude towards her limp had always been a robust one, making little of it, and encouraging her to do the same, and accomplish as much as she could. It was an approach that she welcomed, for the most part, much preferring it to the way in which some of her acquaintance behaved, acting as if she were made of glass.

'The coach was rather crowded, so I could not get comfortable,' she answered, as the doctor picked up her bag, escorted her to his little gig and helped her up. It was a welcome change from her father's rather distant approach.

'It's only a short drive to my house, so you shouldn't find it too trying,' Dr Marchant said reassuringly as they negotiated the bustling streets. Theodora looked about her with great interest. This was by far the biggest town that she had ever visited. Although she had read about cities such as London or Paris, that was not quite the same as witnessing such sights in real life. Once again, she made a mental note of all that she was seeing, so that she would remember it in order to put it in her next letter to Michael.

As if reading her thoughts, the doctor said, 'And how is that brother of yours? Still fit and well? Does he have his own parish yet?' Theodora was always happy to talk about her adored older brother, and in this pleasant way, the journey soon passed.

As the doctor helped her down from the gig, Theodora looked about her. She could see that his house was a handsome brick-built building in a well-kept street. Mrs Marchant's well-trained parlour maid opened the door whilst at almost the same time, the doctor boomed, 'Here she is, my dear, safe and sound!'

The lady of the house hurried past the parlour maid to greet her visitor in person and enveloped Theodora in a kindly embrace. 'My dear! Come in! Come in! What a delight to see you! Has she not grown, Hubert?'

The doctor stood back to look at her. 'You could be right, my love,' he replied consideringly. 'Now that I see you standing next to her, I have a comparison, and I believe that she may be taller by as much as an inch.'

'It is lovely to see you as well, Mrs Marchant,' said Theodora, trying to disguise her fatigue. 'It is so kind of you to have me.'

'I feel rather guilty that this is the first time that we have had you to stay,' Mrs Marchant went on as she led her visitor towards the stairs. 'It is just that life is so busy, with Hubert's practice, and four children to see to.'

'Yes, of course,' Theodora agreed. A legacy from a relative had enabled Marchant to take up a larger practice in town. No doubt the purchase of this house, considerably bigger than the one in which they had lived in Ripondell, and with fine grounds, made a welcome change for a growing family.

'I have arranged for you to have the most delightful room! It is overlooking the garden. I will take you upstairs to put off your bonnet, and then you must come down for a drink of tea. I don't know how it should be, but a journey always seems to leave me gasping with thirst.'

The room to which Theodora was conducted was indeed very attractive, and despite

10

her tiredness, she looked round appreciatively at the green bed hangings which matched those at the window and toned admirably with the carpet. It was a much larger and more luxurious chamber than the one which had always been hers at Ripondell vicarage.

'This is lovely,' she said, trying not to look longingly at the bed, for in truth she would have very much preferred a lie down to a cup of tea at that moment.

Mrs Marchant eyed her keenly. 'You look tired,' she said. 'Would you not prefer to rest for an hour?'

Theodora nodded gratefully, relieved that the other woman was so understanding. 'I confess I *am* very tired,' she agreed. 'But I do not want to disrupt your arrangements.'

'I would be a poor hostess if I were discommoded by so simple a thing as putting off a cup of tea for an hour or so,' replied Mrs Marchant. 'Rest for as long as you like. We want you to be comfortable.'

After her hostess had gone, Theodora lay down on the bed — which was as comfortable as it looked — and closed her eyes. Within minutes, the tiring journey and the poor night that she had had owing to excitement had taken their toll, and she was fast asleep.

'She is resting, poor dear,' said the doctor's

wife as she joined him in their handsomely appointed blue drawing-room. 'She looked absolutely exhausted. It may not be the thing to criticize a clergyman, but I am very surprised at Mr Buckleigh. I would have thought that he could have hired a carriage to bring her this distance. It is not at all fair to expose her to the difficulties of public travel. Her disability is slight, I know, but she is only seventeen after all.'

'I am inclined to agree with you, my love,' the doctor responded, laying aside a sheaf of papers that had been occupying his attention. 'However, I believe I understand Buckleigh's motives. He does not have a large personal fortune after all. His stepson is obliged to make his own way in the world, and everything that Buckleigh has will go to his daughter. No doubt he wants to leave her as much as possible and is making economies where he can.'

'To be making economies with regard to her comfort and safety does not seem to me to be a very good way of looking after her,' his wife replied with a sniff. 'Shall we have tea now? We can always order some more when Theodora comes down.'

2

The noisy, bustling household of Dr and Mrs Marchant was very different from the usual atmosphere that obtained in Ripondell vicarage, and Theodora welcomed it. It was very quiet at home, particularly now that Michael had gone, and any kind of disruption was discouraged, as the vicar needed to study, write or pray. Even when Michael had been at home, the house had never been a noisy one. If brother and sister had wanted to play lively games, they had taken good care to get well out of Mr Buckleigh's earshot. In any case, the ten-year gap between brother and sister, together with Theodora's disability, had meant that their games had not usually been of a boisterous nature.

The lively activity of Mrs Marchant's four children was a revelation to Theodora. They were all boys for a start, and only six years separated Tom, the eldest, at twelve, from six-year-old Stephen, who was the youngest. Theodora watched with wonder how Dr Marchant seemed to be able to enjoy a vigorous game of cricket with them at one minute, and at the next firmly send them inside to wash their hands for tea. It was a species of fatherhood that she had not encountered before.

Tom and Russell, who was ten, both went to a school in Halifax. Richard, who was eight, was due to join them in September.

'It's not fair,' said Stephen to Theodora after she had been staying there for nearly a week. 'After Richard has gone, I will be the only one left at home!'

'The time will soon pass,' said Theodora soothingly. The other three boys were climbing trees at the bottom of the Marchants' extensive garden, whilst Stephen, who had fallen and wrenched his wrist the previous day, had remained behind sitting on a rug whilst Theodora read to him.

'Two whole years,' he groaned. 'I know that it will be two, because Richard is two years older than I am.'

'Two years is not very long,' said Theodora consolingly.

'It is when you are waiting and waiting for something,' the boy answered.

Theodora opened her mouth to contradict him, and then remembered how much she was longing for the time when she would be able to live with Michael. 'Yes, you are right,' she agreed. 'You will just have to think of lots of other things to do, so that your brothers

14

will wish that they were home. Would you like me to help you make a list?'

'Yes, please.'

They had brought pencils and paper outside as well as the book that they were reading, so Theodora picked up some of the paper and resting it on the book, took up a pencil and wrote as a heading: *Stephen's interesting activities*.

Before they could write anything else down, however, Thomas came running across the grass. 'Stephen, Richard has found a bird's nest with some eggs! Come and see!'

'Oh do not disturb the poor birds,' said Theodora anxiously. 'They may desert the nest if you go too near.'

'We're being very careful,' Thomas told her earnestly. 'Father has brought his spyglass so that they will not know that we are looking at them.'

'I want to look through the spyglass,' said Stephen urgently.

'Come on then,' replied his brother.

Theodora smiled as she watched his retreating figure. Then, because there was paper to hand, she set about writing another letter to Michael. She had written to her father that morning, sending him her duty and informing him, with rather less than complete accuracy, that she had not forgotten her Latin. True, she had taken pains to write this particular letter in Latin. It was also true that her volume of Horace was on her bedside table. It had simply not been opened for several days. She resolved to remedy that later on. It was just that in the Marchants' house, there was always something happening. She had even found it difficult to write to Michael as often as she was wont to do. These minutes to herself would be a good opportunity, and she had almost filled a page when Mrs Marchant came towards her across the grass.

'There you are, my dear,' she said. 'I am very conscious that I have neglected you, and you must be finding life quite dull.'

'No, indeed,' Theodora replied truthfully. 'I could not possibly be dull in your house.'

'Well perhaps not dull,' her hostess conceded as, the bird-watching over, the boys gave a whoop as they began a boisterous game. 'All the same, I know that I have been rather dilatory as a hostess. Now that Richard's cold is better, and nurse, who passed it on to him, has also recovered, we can go out and about a little more. I thought that this afternoon, we might go shopping.'

'Shopping?' exclaimed Theodora, her eyes growing very wide. She was used to the kind of shopping where one bought things like flour, sugar, meat and soap, but from Mrs Marchant's expression, this was clearly not what was intended.

'Yes, indeed,' replied Mrs Marchant, her eyes twinkling. 'I have decided to buy you a gown.'

'No, you must not,' Theodora said anxiously. 'Papa has given me some money; five whole pounds! Besides, you have your own family to provide for.'

'Yes, I do. Have you noticed that they are all boys? I am desperate to buy an item of clothing that is not going to get dragged up a tree or under a hedge and over a fence! Permit me to indulge myself, I beg you!'

After a number of speeches in this vein, Theodora allowed herself to be persuaded. She could not deny that it would be extremely pleasant, not to say novel, to wear a garment which she had not made herself. She had been taught to sew by a seamstress who lived in Ripondell, and she was now responsible for the maintenance of nearly all of the linen in the vicarage. She reflected that if Mrs Marchant was going to treat her to a gown, then she could use some of her precious five pounds to buy material to make another shirt for Michael.

In the end, Mrs Marchant bought two gowns for Theodora, as well as new stockings, shoes, a shawl and an exceedingly pretty bonnet. When Theodora tried to protest, Mrs Marchant referred to her skill with a needle. 'I can tell you how you may repay me,' she said. 'You will have seen that fire-screen that I am working. I have been trying to complete it for three whole years! If you can only finish it for me, then it will not stand as an everlasting reproach to me, and I can abandon my ideas of sewing, which I hate, and concentrate on drawing and sketching instead.'

When Theodora accompanied Mrs Marchant only a few afternoons later in order to take tea with an acquaintance, therefore, she was wearing a new gown of light blue patterned with tiny white flowers. She was thankful to know that she was at least fashionably dressed, for the simple truth was that the idea of taking tea with strangers made her feel quite nervous.

Her father was not a particularly sociable man. It had never occurred to him that he might make an effort to introduce his daughter into society, and the biggest group of people that she ever encountered was when she went to church on Sundays. Consequently, a natural tendency to shyness had been accentuated, and she rather dreaded large gatherings.

Mrs Marchant eyed Theodora keenly as

they waited on her friend's doorstep, but she did not say anything. She had a shrewd idea of how much Theodora's social education had been neglected, and was determined to use this visit to redress the balance a little.

As they walked in, Theodora could see that the company was almost entirely female, and she breathed a tiny sigh of relief. She was very unused to the society of men. She could cope easily with elderly, scholarly men like her father. She had no idea how to communicate with young members of the opposite sex. The few that she had encountered had initially shown interest in her petite blonde prettiness. As soon as she had taken a few steps, however, her limp had become obvious, their eyes had glazed over and they had beaten a hasty retreat.

Theodora could not blame them. She hated her limp, which immediately made her feel singled out in comparison to others. Perversely, however, although she knew that to enter a wider scene would invite comments, she longed to see more of the world. Sometimes she indulged herself with dreams of meeting a man who would be able to love her for herself, and who would not give a fig for her disability. She just could not imagine how it could ever happen.

There was a brief hush as they entered.

Theodora knew that this was partly due to curiosity because she was a newcomer to this circle. A swift glance around showed her that, at seventeen, she was the youngest person there by several years. As Mrs Marchant led her forward to be introduced to their hostess, she was aware that some of those present were looking in her direction and she became very conscious of her limp. From being a slight unevenness in her gait, it became, in her mind, a monstrous deformity. It seemed as if everyone in the room was staring at her. Suddenly she felt very out of place. Not really taking in the names of anyone else present, she sat down as quickly as she could, and found herself next to another lady, who turned to smile at her.

In her own way, this other lady looked as out of place as Theodora felt herself to be. She seemed to be small in stature, with dark hair, and wide, piercing eyes. She was simply dressed, with an olive complexion, and very slender, and her manner was quick and alert, as if she might spring up from her place at any moment. She was probably older than Theodora by a few years.

'It is not as noticeable as you think,' she said earnestly, in a soft North-country accent. She looked at Theodora with keen attention. At that moment, Theodora felt that she was at

20

the very centre of this lady's world.

'I beg your pardon?' she said, half understanding the lady's remarks, but not wanting to make any assumptions. In her experience such an open and matter-of-fact approach to her disability was rarely found.

'Your limp is not as noticeable as you think,' the other lady replied, enlarging upon her original statement. 'I observed you as you came in. There was a moment, perhaps no more than a heartbeat really, when you stepped forward and looked round at the company. I could see that you were anxious by your stance and your expression. Then it was as if you became not simply worried about being on view, but aware of your own person; and that was when you thought about your limp.' She spoke rather quickly, and stumbled over the occasional word, as if her thoughts moved more rapidly than her lips would allow.

'You are very perceptive,' Theodora answered, fascinated.

'It makes me wonder if you could hold on to the idea that comes to you in the heartbeat, and not think about the limp at all. It may be your awareness of it that people notice, you see.'

'That had not occurred to me, I confess.'

'I do not mean to be impertinent. You must

forgive me. I tend to notice things, and my brother encourages me in this.'

Theodora would have liked to continue talking to this lady, but Mrs Marchant beckoned her over to meet some of her friends, and when Theodora looked around a little while later, she noticed with some regret that the lady had gone. She felt that she would have enjoyed further conversation with her.

'The tiny dark-haired lady with the olive complexion? No, I do not know her, I'm afraid. I will make enquiries,' said Mrs Marchant later, when Theodora asked about her new acquaintance's identity.

The following day, Theodora was busily engaged upon completing the fire-screen and Mrs Marchant was making a drawing of her at work, when Mrs Rawson and Miss Wordsworth were announced. Looking up, Theodora saw the lady with whom she had spoken the previous afternoon, and greeted her with pleasure.

'I am so sorry that I had to rush away,' Miss Wordsworth explained when Mrs Marchant and Mrs Rawson had their heads together. 'Elizabeth recollected an urgent errand that she had previously forgotten. We had to go in rather a hurry and I did not want to interrupt your conversation. Is this your work?' she asked, indicating the fire-screen.

'Some small part of it,' Theodora answered. 'I am finishing it for my kind hostess. She does not enjoy sewing, but I do.'

'It is not my favourite activity, but necessity obliges me to take up my needle,' replied the other lady. 'I make most of my own clothes, and sew for my brothers as well.'

'You have more than one brother, then,' said Theodora.

'I have three,' Miss Wordsworth agreed, 'but it is my brother William to whom I am closest.'

'I have only one brother,' Theodora told her, 'but we are also very close. I am making him a shirt at the moment — when I am not engaged upon the fire-screen.'

'Men's shirts need to be made in the daylight, I find. The sewing of white on white is very trying. The one consolation of the occupation is that one can sit at the window and keep looking at the scenery outside. I have sat at the same window sewing for hours, but each time I look up the world is different. The wind causing branches and grasses to undulate; the clouds with their different patterns; a shadow cast upon the ground, the change brought by the seasons.'

'You clearly notice a great deal, Miss Wordsworth,' said Theodora. 'I confess I am not so observant.'

'I look at things partly on William's behalf,' her visitor confessed. 'He is a writer, you see. One day, I hope that we shall be able to live together, then I can help him all the more. What of your brother, Miss Buckleigh?'

'He is a clergyman,' Theodora replied. 'A curate. He is in lodgings at present; but he has promised me that as soon as possible, he will have me to live with him. I mean to help him by keeping house.'

Miss Wordsworth's penetrating eyes sparkled. 'How alike are our circumstances and our plans!' she exclaimed. 'What brings you to Halifax? Are you living with relatives, as I am?'

Theodora shook her head. 'Mrs Marchant is not a relative; she is a kind friend of my family. There is smallpox in our village, so my father has sent me to stay with her until the danger is over.'

'There is not the same warmth in your voice when you speak of your father as there is when you speak of your brother,' Miss Wordsworth remarked.

Theodora straightened her spine. She liked Miss Wordsworth and found her frankness refreshing, but criticism of her father, even if only hinted at, could not be permitted. 'My father is an excellent man,' she said. 'He has done his duty.'

'That is exactly what I had supposed,' replied Miss Wordsworth earnestly. 'I did not mean to imply any criticism of him. To return to my earlier remarks, there is a likeness between our situations that commands my sympathy. Shall we write to one another? I am an indefatigable correspondent. Whichever of us succeeds first in securing an independent establishment with her brother may encourage the other.'

'I should very much like to correspond with you, Miss Wordsworth,' said Theodora eagerly. 'I don't have many friends.'

'If we are to be friends, you must call me Dorothy,' was the reply.

3

Following her return to Ripondell, life for Theodora continued much as before, save that she now had two regular and frequent correspondents — Michael, and Dorothy Wordsworth. She soon found that Dorothy had described her nature very accurately. She was indeed a tireless correspondent, and she wrote about her life and concerns in great detail. Theodora almost felt that she was living through Dorothy's excitement as the time drew near when she was able to set up home with her beloved brother William in a rented house in Dorset. Although Dorothy said nothing specific about money, Theodora gathered that there was not a great deal to go round. This gave her hope for her own situation. If Dorothy and William could manage on a pittance, surely she would soon be able to live with Michael.

Once the Wordsworths were settled at Racedown, an invitation soon came to Theodora to go and stay with them. She would have liked very much to have done so, but the winter of 1795 brought nasty colds for both herself and her father, and she could not countenance getting away. Then the following spring there was some very severe weather that made travelling impossible. She was glad of both Dorothy and Michael's letters which helped to enlarge her small world.

Michael's letters brought their own anxieties, however. His first curacy had come to an abrupt end when a young lady had become infatuated with him and her fiancé had taken exception to the state of affairs. Although he wrote cheerfully enough from his second appointment, Theodora, rendered sensitive through her love for him, could detect a note of anxiety and she longed to help him.

Dorothy's letters came as a welcome contrast. Her delight at living with William was quite palpable. He had now begun to write more consistently, and to her great astonishment, Theodora found herself the recipient of versions of poems by Mr Wordsworth, whom she had never met! Dorothy invited her comments, and anxious to say nothing that might stem the tide of his thought, she tried to be very sensitive in her remarks. She only hoped that her criticisms were not so bland as to discourage him from sending her anything ever again.

She often wondered what Mr Wordsworth

might be like. He was a poet. Would he be thin and ascetic-looking, with fiery eyes and a mane of wildly curling hair? Would the tone of his voice be deep and sonorous? She was aware that she was thinking about him rather a lot, but there did not seem to be any harm in it. It was a romantic little daydream which lifted her life above her daily chores and duties. Besides, although her romantic side might weave fantasies about him, her practical side told her that there would be set-backs to any real romance with Mr Wordsworth. For instance, she knew from Dorothy's letters that she and her brother walked through the countryside for miles and miles, sometimes in inclement weather. This was not an activity in which she could ever share. When eventually she went to stay with them, she would have to find other ways of spending her time whilst they were off on their rambles. Perhaps she might use her skills in sewing to make a shirt for Mr Wordsworth? She blushed at the boldness of her thought.

It was on a wet Tuesday in the spring of 1796 that Theodora received an unexpected visitor. Her father had gone to meet a priest from a neighbouring parish, and was not due back for a couple of hours. Their housekeeper had gone out for her half day, and would not be returning for the rest of the afternoon. So it was with a feeling of surprise that Theodora heard the front door open. This feeling soon turned to delight when her brother Michael put his head around the door.

'Thea?' he said.

'Michael!' she exclaimed, springing up from her seat by the fire, where she was engaged upon mending the household linen, and hurrying to hug him.

'You have put that needle down, haven't you?' he said, smiling, as he picked her up and swung her round. 'I don't want to turn into a pincushion.'

'Oh this is a wonderful surprise, and just when I was feeling dull,' said Theodora when she was back on her feet. 'What brings you? Father is not here, so we can be cosy for a while.' She did not apologize for this slightly critical note. They both knew that when Mr Buckleigh arrived, their relaxed ease could not continue in quite the same way.

Michael sighed and sat down, his hands clasped between his knees, his eyes fixed on the floor. 'Don't think I'm not pleased to see you, but I fear I bring no good news,' he said, lines of worry marring his handsome countenance. 'I have almost certainly been dismissed from my curacy.'

'Oh Michael, no!' she declared. 'How could such a thing occur? It is so unfair!'

He looked up at her, smiling crookedly. Despite the ash-blond hair that both had inherited from their mother, brother and sister were not really very much alike. Theodora was small and dainty, whilst her brother was tall, with broad shoulders. His features were firmly chiselled, whereas the contours of her face were softer. His brows, startlingly black in contrast to his hair, and steeply arched, were a feature that drew the observer's gaze immediately. Theodora's brows, though well marked, were softer in colour and in shape. Her eyes were something between hazel and green rather than grey like his.

'I might have guessed that you would not blame me,' he said ruefully.

'Of course I do not blame you,' she responded. 'It cannot be your fault. I know that you do the best you can.'

'My dearest Thea, where will I find a woman who thinks as well of me as you do? On this occasion, however, I fear that I only have myself to blame.'

'I don't believe it,' she said stoutly. 'Tell me what happened.'

'I have insulted my vicar beyond forgiveness.'

'Well he must have deserved it. What did he do?'

Michael laughed, despite himself. 'Oh Thea!' He paused, then glanced at her keenly. 'I don't know whether that is something that I should disclose.'

'Do you mean that the vicar was behaving improperly?' she asked, her eyes widening.

'I don't think I ought to say.'

'Then in that case, you were right to do as you did. Michael, if you don't want to tell me then I shan't pry; but if you think that this may be the end of your curacy, you must tell Father the whole story. He will understand if you have been trying to correct improper behaviour.'

'Yes, I shall,' he agreed. 'I owe it to him. But, Thea, I don't know how long it may be before I get my own parish now.'

Theodora could feel tears of disappointment pricking at the back of her eyes. For Michael's sake, she was determined not to let them fall. 'It will be very soon, I am sure,' she said with a confidence that she was far from feeling. 'It cannot be but that your merits will be recognized.'

Michael looked serious. 'I pray that it may be so,' he said.

He did not share his worst fear with Theodora. His vicar, Mr Pettigrew, had attempted to molest a young woman in his study. Michael had come in during the incident. The vicar had tried to bluster his way out of the situation, but Michael, seeing the young woman's obvious distress, had taken the law into his own hands and tanned his vicar's backside with a yard rule. Predictably enough, Pettigrew had roundly condemned Michael, saying that he had misunderstood the situation, and had demanded that he leave the parish.

'I shall be having words with the bishop about you, Buckleigh, you may be sure,' he had said, his face purple with anger.

Michael did not regret defending the girl, whose reputation he knew, and who had certainly been vigorously repulsing Pettigrew's advances. Looking now at Theodora, valiantly trying to hide her disappointment however, he bitterly regretted the dashing of her hopes. To give her thoughts another direction, he asked her about what she had been doing. She told him about some of the goings on in the village, and in this undemanding way, they passed the time until the sound of the front door opening informed them that the vicar had come home. Brother exchanged glances with sister. Much would depend upon what happened now.

★   ★   ★

32

Whilst Michael was shut in the study with Mr Buckleigh, Theodora went to the church and sat praying fervently. 'Please let Father forgive Michael. Please let Michael have another chance. Please let him have his own parish soon.' She said these phrases and others like them over and over again. It was nearly an hour before she returned home.

Her journey back to the vicarage took her past her mother's grave. She stood looking at the headstone, engraved with her mother's name, Dora Buckleigh, and the dates that marked her life, 1751–1778. Beneath were the words *Aleph mulierem fortem quis inveniet procul et de ultimis finibus pretium eius*. It was one of the first Latin sentences that she had learned to translate: 'Who can find a virtuous woman? for her price is far above rubies.' 'Oh Mama, I wish you were here,' she sighed, before going back to the vicarage.

She did not listen for raised voices. The Rev'd Paul Buckleigh never raised his voice under any circumstances. She longed to put her ear to the door to discover what was happening, but she dared not risk being found in such an embarrassing position. To take her mind off the situation, she took up her latest letter from Dorothy Wordsworth.

Sadly this did not prove to be much of a distraction.

How wonderful it is to share a home with my beloved brother! I do hope, my dear Theodora, that your joy will soon be the same as mine.

Theodora shed a tear or two. She feared that it would be long enough before she would be able to set up home with Michael.

Eventually, the door opened, and the vicar came out. His face was very solemn and Theodora thought that he looked angry. Barely acknowledging his daughter, he went into the hall and then his footsteps were heard ascending the stairs. As soon as he had gone, Theodora hurried into the study to find Michael standing next to the hearth. He looked pale but composed.

'He has believed me and forgiven me,' he said. 'He is making ready to go to Sheffield and plead my case with the bishop. God willing, I may have another chance.'

★ ★ ★

Never a very communicative man, Mr Buckleigh told Michael and Theodora very little about his interview with the bishop. 'I

34

have done my best,' he said. 'Now the matter is in the hands of God.'

They did not have long to wait, but for Theodora and Michael, the time seemed to pass with agonizing slowness. Theodora busied herself with her usual household chores, and Michael assisted the vicar in every way possible. Life in the vicar's presence had always been one of not unfriendly formality. In private, Michael and Theodora sought to conduct themselves much as they had always done, although it was difficult with this matter hanging over them. Theodora told Michael about her friend Dorothy, and he was interested to hear about the similarity between their situations.

'If I am unfrocked, then perhaps I could take to writing poetry,' he said wryly, trying to hide the anxiety he felt about the very real possibility of such a disgrace. 'Thea, I'm sorry I've disappointed you.'

'You could never disappoint me,' she answered simply.

When a letter came summoning Michael to Sheffield, he hurried off on his way after a kiss from his sister and a blessing from the vicar. For much of the time he was away, Theodora was muttering prayers under her breath. On one occasion, her father caught her doing so, and asked the meaning of her utterances. 'I am praying for Michael,' she said boldly. 'He has done nothing wrong, and he deserves another chance.' It was the first time that she had spoken directly to her father about the matter, and she was a little shocked at her own temerity.

'It was for that very reason that I went to Sheffield on his behalf,' the vicar replied calmly. 'He should not have taken the matter into his own hands, but Pettigrew was much at fault.'

Emboldened by this response, Theodora asked, 'Will the bishop pay attention to your words?'

A small smile crossed Mr Buckleigh's thin features. 'My relationship with the bishop goes back a good many years,' he replied. 'I believe that I may have been able to remind his lordship of some matters that had possibly escaped his memory.'

The vicar was being so unexpectedly communicative that Theodora dared to say 'What matters were those, Father?'

Unconsciously echoing his son's words a short time before, he replied, 'I do not think that I should say. Suffice it to tell you that I reminded him of an incident which occurred when we were at university together. Perhaps one should not remind a bishop of such things, but *audaces fortuna invat*.'

Anticipating his next question, Theodora translated ''Fortune favours the bold'. I do hope so, Father.'

Just a day later, Michael returned from Sheffield. Theodora, who was looking out for him, met him at the gate, an anxious expression on her face. 'Well?' she asked.

He smiled, his face relieved. 'I have another curacy,' he said. 'Perhaps, Thea, we may set up home together soon, after all!'

4

Spring 1797

'It is really most unfortunate,' said Evangeline Buckleigh to her husband. 'Poor Theodora will now have to wait another year for her London season. What is to be done?'

The Rev'd Michael Buckleigh looked up from the sermon that he was writing and laid down his pen in order to give his full attention to his wife. She was worthy of such attention, her charming complexion glowing with health, her golden hair becomingly arranged, and her blue eyes sparkling. If her excellent figure was looking a little more matronly since the bearing of a son just a few weeks before, that in no way spoiled the vision in the vicar's eyes.

'I am not at all sure that anything can be done,' he replied. 'Her father died at the beginning of this year. She could not possibly put off black gloves yet. Every feeling would be offended.'

Mrs Buckleigh crossed the room with a swish of her skirts. She was one of those fortunate women who could carry off wearing black to perfection. 'My love, I do not wish to sound callous, but her father was not a man who ever encouraged closeness. Why, I recall at our wedding, he looked at me in what I can only describe as a disapproving manner, and then quoted some Latin at me! As I did not know whether he was uttering a blessing or a curse, I had no idea how to respond.'

Michael laughed. 'It was a blessing, dearest.'

'I am pleased to hear it. But what I am trying to say is that it would not be at all surprising if Theodora were to feel sufficiently recovered from her grief to go to London.'

'That is just the point,' Buckleigh answered, standing, and moving round the desk in order to pull her into his arms. 'I don't think that either Theodora or her father ever really managed to stop feeling guilty because they did not mind being apart. Had they been closer, Thea might have been happier to let her instincts guide her. As it is, she will want to adhere strictly to form.' He paused. 'Will you miss going to Town for the season, my darling?' Mrs Buckleigh had been the toast of London for two seasons before she had met her future husband.

'Not in the slightest, if I am with you,' she answered promptly, which satisfactory answer encouraged him to plant a kiss upon her lips.

'Will your father still go to London?' she added, as soon as she was able.

'Can you imagine my father missing the season?' Michael had met his natural father, Lord Ashbourne, for the first time the previous year when he had been granted a third curacy in the village of Illingham, near to the earl's home. Since then, partly through Ashbourne's good offices, Michael had at last gained his own parish.

'No, indeed. Your father is nothing if not a fashionable man of the town.'

His face took on a thoughtful expression. 'Evangeline, do you think that Theodora will mind not being presented this year?'

'Mind?' she asked incredulously. 'Of course she will mind. Every young woman wants a London season.'

'I'm not so sure whether Theodora does. The subject has not yet been broached with her, has it? My suspicion is that she will try to look disappointed, but will actually be relieved.'

'I do not believe it. I was thinking about my debut for a whole year before I actually went.'

'Forgive me dearest, but Theodora is not you, is she? I very much doubt whether a single thought of going to London will have entered her head.'

Neither one of them was completely right. Theodora had certainly given the idea a good deal of thought; but most of her thoughts had been to do with how to get out of it.

She had come to live in Illingham quite soon after Michael's appointment to the curacy there. His accommodation had comprised a little cottage which had been just big enough for the two of them. By the time of her arrival, however, Michael had already fallen in love with Evangeline Granby, and although the proverbial course of true love had not run smooth, they had soon announced their engagement.

After an initial awkwardness, Michael and his father had settled into an easy relationship, and Theodora had very soon begun calling Lord Ashbourne Step-papa, to his great delight. Evangeline had shown neither excessive pity nor callous indifference to Theodora's disability, and had readily endorsed Michael's invitation to make her home with them in the vicarage. Lord Ashbourne's legitimate son and heir, Viscount Ilam, together with his wife, had also been cordial. In short, the whole family had accepted Theodora without reservation and seemed to want to lavish upon her the kind of loving care that she had never had.

One of the first things that Lord Ashbourne had done for her had been to arrange for her to see a boot-maker. This skilful craftsman had measured her very carefully, and then produced some stout footwear that was built up in such a way as to make her limp virtually undetectable. It had made walking much more comfortable, and had also given her the confidence to try riding again, with some success. Unfortunately, however, nothing could be done about indoor activities, where light slippers were the order of the day. She still dreaded occasions when she was obliged to walk into a public room in front of comparative strangers where her limp would be observed and commented upon.

When she was eight, she had begged her father to allow her to attend a picnic which had been arranged by the squire's wife. It was to mark her youngest daughter's birthday, and some visitors together with some local children, including Theodora, had been invited. Theodora would never normally have bothered about such things, but the invitation had come at a time when she had been feeling particularly lonely at the loss of Michael.

Although he had been attending Charterhouse school in London for a number of years, he had now begun his studies at university, and this had seemed subtly different. He was to read for holy orders, and he would not really be living at home any more. He had been her playmate, her guardian, and her dearest friend. She could never have put it into words, but she had felt the need to find some companion, not to replace him, for that would have been impossible, but to fill the gap.

She did not have many pretty dresses, but knowing how important the picnic was to her, her father's housekeeper had helped her to trim a plain white one with some lace, and add some pink ribbons. Unusually, her father had agreed to take her there in the gig, and she had arrived at the squire's house in good time.

Most of the other children at the picnic had been friendly and polite, but one guest, a very pretty, dark-haired girl, had made her feel awkward and clumsy, particularly when the games were being organized. 'Our team will be at a disadvantage because we have the cripple,' she had said almost under her breath at one point. 'Can we not have extra time to compensate?'

Unsurprisingly, such comments had had the unfortunate effect of making Theodora feel even more clumsy and awkward. The final straw had been when she had stumbled as she was carrying some food from the tea table and had spilled what was on her plate, not over her own dress, but, as ill luck would have it, over that of the dark-haired girl. 'You clumsy idiot!' the child had complained, bursting into noisy tears. 'Why did you have to come at all? You have spoiled the whole day!'

Everyone else had been very kind, but the damage had been done. The remarks had remained with her, and had come back to haunt her when other similar incidents occurred, such as the time when the woman and her son had talked about her on the journey to Halifax two years before.

No, she would never subject herself to the public scrutiny of the London season if she could possibly help it. The death of her father meant that London this spring would be out of the question; but what of later? And what if Evangeline concluded that Bath or Harrogate might do? She needed a means of escape, and preferably one that would lead to a permanent solution.

★ ★ ★

The following day, a letter arrived from her friend Dorothy Wordsworth. She and her brother were busy working in their garden at

Racedown. William was writing whenever he could. Dorothy enclosed an early draft of his ideas, asking for Theodora's suggestions. How wonderful it would be to see her at their home. Did she think that she would be able to come soon? It was such a long time since they had met; and, of course, Theodora had never met Dorothy's beloved William. How Dorothy longed to introduce them to one another!

Theodora put her letter down, her eyes shining. Here was the very opportunity that she had been looking for! It would enable her to escape the whole vexatious question of the season without upsetting anyone.

She had always been fascinated by Dorothy's accounts of her talented brother. She no longer dreamed about him as she had two years before, but she had not forgotten him either, and she knew that at twenty-seven he was still single. She was not going to be foolish about a man she had never met; but she did stand a chance, surely? Her income from her father — amounting to some £500 a year — together with what William already possessed would be plenty to enable a poet to continue his work, as well as to support a wife, a sister and any children that might come along. Then she need never think about London or the wretched season ever again!

'Racedown? And where might that be, my

dear?' Michael asked her, when she came to his study with her letter and her idea.

'It is in Dorset; not far from Lyme Regis, I believe,' she replied. 'Miss Wordsworth says that I would be very welcome, and I would like to see her again.'

He had stood at her entrance. Now he looked down at her. She had never grown above just under five feet. In her mourning attire, she looked more pale and fragile than ever. He knew, however, that the appearance of fragility was deceptive. When he had been going through difficult times, her support had been unstinting. Despite the limp which had been with her from birth, she was remarkably resilient. She never complained about her disability. He could only guess how much of a trial it was to her.

'You really don't want to make your come-out either this year or any other, do you?' he said, with sudden insight.

She stared at him for a moment or two before shaking her head. 'I can't think of anything worse,' she said frankly.

'Then it shall be as you wish,' he said in a businesslike tone.

'What about Evangeline?'

'You may leave Evangeline to me. Give me a little time and I will make all the arrangements for you.'

46

5

Theodora was highly educated for a young woman of the time. Her father had taught her Latin and Greek, as well as some Hebrew, and had also made sure that she had a good grounding in mathematics. He had also encouraged her to read widely. It was not as if her father had not cared for her in practical terms. She had been well-fed, and clothed appropriately for her station, and the vicarage had been a warm and comfortable place.

Emotionally, however, her needs had not been understood. She had often had no shoulder on which to weep; no one with whom to share a joke or a concern. Michael had gone to school when she was three, then to university, and Theodora had had to train herself to be quite self-reliant when he was away. She had of necessity grown accustomed to sharing things with Michael by correspondence. In between times, she had sometimes made up fantasies concerning what might happen if, for instance, a handsome stranger were to appear in the village. Needless to say, one never did.

Now, of course she was living with her

beloved brother; but Michael was married to Evangeline, and Theodora had never questioned that the needs of his wife and child must come first. Perhaps this was why her friendship with Dorothy Wordsworth had flourished, even though conducted almost exclusively by letter. It was a way of maintaining a relationship with which she was very familiar.

Observing some of the families in the village where she had grown up, notably that of Dr and Mrs Marchant, she could not but be aware of what she lacked. She had often found herself wishing, particularly on occasions such as her journey to Halifax, that she might have a protective male relative who would look to her needs in a less impersonal way.

After she had gone to live in Illingham, however, everything had changed. Michael himself was always on hand, which was a real joy. His father had treated her as an adopted daughter from the first, and considered nothing too good for her. Michael's half brother, Gabriel, regarded her with affection. Even Mr Granby, Evangeline's father, was ready to offer a helping hand. Sometimes, her world seemed to be full of tall, handsome men who were itching to protect her. Occasionally, this could almost feel stifling.

More than once, she found herself wondering with varying degrees of irritation at the perversity of her nature, and she felt very ungrateful for longing for just a little neglect.

Pointless to think in that way when there was a journey all the way to Dorset to be accomplished! Jessie, Lady Ashbourne, turned to her sympathetically as Ashbourne, Gabriel and Michael were discussing the matter. They had all gone to Ashbourne Abbey for dinner and were waiting in the blue drawing-room for the meal to be announced. 'It's of no use, I'm afraid,' she said. 'They do like to look after one.'

'Does it not make you feel a bit, well, pathetic?' Theodora asked.

'Not really,' Jessie answered after a moment's thought. 'Remember that before I married Raff I worked as a companion to his sister Lady Agatha, and often had to make such arrangements on her behalf. To have a man to deal with the mundane things leaves one's mind free for higher matters!'

The chief concern seemed to be how Theodora was to get from London to Racedown in Dorset. 'We can take her to London quite easily when we go for the season,' Ashbourne was saying. 'Then Jez can remain in London and I will escort Theodora the rest of the way.'

'There is really no need,' Theodora ventured. 'If you put me in a post-chaise in London, I will travel quite comfortably to my friends' house.'

Three male faces turned to look at her. Theodora gained the distinct impression that she had suggested something almost as shocking as driving the post-chaise herself.

'That cannot be permitted,' said Ashbourne.

'I have travelled to Halifax on my own, and when I came to Illingham I came on the stage.'

'Yes, but, my dear Thea, there were other reasons for your having to do that,' said Michael tactfully. 'Remember, too, how uncomfortable you found the journey. It will be less than helpful to arrive at your friends' house so exhausted that they are obliged to put you straight to bed.'

'Yes, perhaps,' agreed Theodora reluctantly. 'But they are not wealthy people. I do not want to appear at their front door with a show of affluence that will embarrass them.'

Seeing that Theodora was becoming rather agitated, Michael suggested that they should think further about the matter and discuss it later. His motives were good, but the consequence of his suggestion was to make Theodora feel even more cosseted than ever.

As they all walked into the dining-room, she decided that the family would not be happy until they had discussed and chewed over every last detail. No doubt the men would have the whole thing organized without any reference to her whatsoever!

With this in mind, therefore, she waited the following morning until an hour when she felt sure of finding Michael alone, then made her way to his study. As she got there, however, she discovered that the door was not quite shut. She was thus able to overhear a fragment of a conversation that was taking place between Michael and his father who, she concluded, must have ridden over earlier.

'She is clearly fond of these people, at least the lady of the family with whom she has been corresponding,' Michael was saying. 'However, her remark about their straightened means makes me realize that I do not really know a great deal about them. What if it should be damp there, or suppose the weather should turn cold? They might not be wealthy enough to be able to afford a fire. At such a distance too, it would be long enough before we could rescue her.'

'What was the name? Wordsworth?' Ashbourne said. 'It's not a name I'm familiar with. Do you want me to make enquiries among my acquaintanceS in London while we're there? I can easily delay her departure from my town house for a short time.'

Part of Theodora simply wanted to tiptoe away, but this could be her future that they were deciding between them. In the most charming way possible, Ashbourne might keep her in London until she had no alternative but to join in with the London season. She pushed the door open.

'If you want to know anything about William and Dorothy Wordsworth, why do you not simply ask me?' she said, her voice trembling slightly at thus addressing the two men in the world who meant the most to her. 'Mr Wordsworth was born in Cockermouth. He is a gentleman with three brothers and one sister, my friend Dorothy, with whom he resides. His oldest brother is a lawyer. Another is in the Royal Navy and the third is to be a clergyman. They may not be wealthy people, but they are kind, and respectable and ready to welcome me. Can this not be enough for you? Must you be confining and hedging me about at every turn, so that sometimes I feel that I cannot breathe?'

'Thea, my dear, you must understand — ' Michael began speaking, but Ashbourne interrupted him, holding up his hand.

'Thea is right, my son,' he said. 'She is old enough and sensible enough for us to trust her judgement. But,' he went on, turning to Theodora as she heaved a sigh of relief, 'we do have some right on our side as well. We are not giving you special treatment. Neither Jez, nor Evangeline, nor Gabriel's wife Eustacia would travel such a distance alone. It wouldn't be safe. However, would it suit your notions of independence, Miss Buckleigh, if you were to travel to London with myself and Jez? There I would make enquiries, not about the character of your friends the Wordsworths, whose reputation, I am sure, is exemplary, but amongst my acquaintanceS to see if anyone is intending to travel to Dorset and has a spare seat to offer?' When she hesitated, he went on. 'I promise that I will do just as I say. I shan't try to persuade you to stay for the season, which I suspect is what you fear.'

Theodora coloured at his perspicacity. 'I didn't think you would understand,' she said simply.

'Why?' Ashbourne asked. 'Because I enjoy the season? Must I therefore be unable to understand the feelings of someone who doesn't care for it?'

Theodora sighed with relief. 'Thank you. That plan would suit me very well.'

Later, after she had gone, Ashbourne said, 'You must let her spread her wings, Michael.'

'Yes, I know,' Michael responded. 'But it isn't easy. I'll wager you'll find it just as hard when Leonora is her age.' Lord and Lady Ashbourne's daughter Leonora had been born just the previous year.

Ashbourne grinned wryly. 'No doubt,' he agreed. 'Perhaps the years will lend me wisdom.'

★ ★ ★

'Well for my part, I cannot understand how you can bear to go to London and not have a Season,' said Amelia Lusty tossing her dark curls. Amelia was making a short stay with her parents, Sir Lyle and Lady Belton whilst her husband was visiting some of the local clergy on the bishop's behalf.

The original plan, made in spring the previous year, had been that Amelia and Theodora should share a London season. Since those plans had been made, however, The Rev'd Henry Lusty, the former vicar of Illingham, had inherited a large sum of money, and had become a very eligible *parti*. Lady Belton had snapped him up for her daughter, and Amelia had already been to London on her husband's arm, playing the part of a fashionable and flirtatious matron to the hilt during the little season the previous

54

autumn. Now, however, her activities were somewhat curtailed by pregnancy, but she was as lively in her manner as ever.

'I could not take part in most of the events,' Theodora pointed out, indicating her mourning attire. 'It would be quite improper.'

Amelia tucked her hand into Theodora's arm. When Theodora had first arrived in the district, Amelia had found it quite impossible to look directly at the other girl on account of her disability. Time and familiarity had helped. So, too, had the special shoes that Theodora wore nearly every day.

'I cannot believe that your father would have wanted you to miss all the fun,' said Amelia.

Theodora knew that Amelia would never understand the kind of man that The Rev'd Paul Buckleigh had been. He had never begrudged her anything that he considered to be good for her; but the idea of her wanting or expecting a season would have been utterly incomprehensible to him. He had had a very strict moral sense and no time for London manners, and he would have been horrified at the idea of loose behaviour of any kind.

With this in mind, she simply said, 'Possibly not; but you know how disapproving people can be.'

'I suppose so,' Amelia answered. 'Anyway,

you can always go another year. I could sponsor you myself. What fun that would be!'

Theodora did not try to make the other girl understand that she was more than happy to be missing the season. That, like the attitude of her late father, would have been quite beyond Amelia Lusty's comprehension.

That evening, Theodora wrote a letter to Dorothy Wordsworth.

You cannot imagine how much I am looking forward to seeing you again. London and its so-called season has no attraction for me. What does the word 'season' mean anyway? It is supposed to refer to a time of year, is it not? It sounds to me as if London is a place that is full of people who dress in the lightest of garments whether it is winter or summer, and who try to perpetuate their own youth, hoping that by a giddy round of pleasure-seeking they will be able to ignore the passage of time altogether! To be with you and William is what I long for, more than anything.

As she thought about what to write next, she doodled idly on the blotter. It came as no great surprise to her that in her abstraction she had written 'Theodora Wordsworth'.

'Foolish girl!' she muttered, scribbling the words out so that no casual observer would see them. 'To be still sighing over a man you have never met — and at your age!' But the tantalizing picture of setting up house with William and Dorothy on a permanent basis would not go away.

6

When Theodora heard Jessie scream, she hurried down the stairs of Lord Ashbourne's town house as fast as she could. They had been in London for just three days, but Theodora was already beginning to feel as if she had had as much of the London season as she could stand. Jessie had needed new clothes and had gone to the dressmaker for several fittings. Theodora had managed to avoid most of these outings, pleading her mourning state. Of course, Jessie had insisted on buying her a few new things, and Theodora had not objected. She might not have any fashionable aspirations, but neither did she want to appear shabby or ill-dressed.

She smiled at the kindness of Lord and Lady Ashbourne. No doubt they would be thinking that another year they would be able to give her a proper season. Perhaps, like Amelia, I shall be married by that time, she thought to herself, and allowed her mind to dwell upon Dorothy's unknown brother.

She knew that Lord Ashbourne had been making enquiries among his friends concerning her journey to Dorset, so far without success. She would not despair. After all, Lord Ashbourne would take her himself, if need be. One problem with that plan was that she could just imagine appearing at Dorothy and William's door in the Ashbourne carriage with the crest painted on it. The earl himself would escort her in, looking, as usual, as if his clothes had been painted onto him. It was not that she was ashamed of him, but he could at times be a little overpowering, with his astonishing good looks and faultless appearance.

The other problem with Ashbourne's escorting her was that in the three days since they had arrived, she had been able to see how much he enjoyed London. From their first day in the capital, he had made it his business to catch up with the gossip at his clubs. In addition, he had been keeping appointments with his tailor and boot-maker. The languor that was characteristic of him had increased, and his wit was in sparkling form. It hardly seemed fair to drag him away.

He was such a contrast to her own father, who had died just after Christmas. Theodora had not seen him since Michael's wedding. That occasion, being the first time that Michael's stepfather and natural father had met, had offered endless possibilities for embarrassment on every side. Michael, foreseeing this, had been determined not to have his wedding overshadowed by past history from twenty-eight years before. He had, therefore, introduced the two men and had left them alone to have a long conversation. No one ever discovered what was said, but thereafter the atmosphere between them had been courteous if distant.

Mr Buckleigh had performed the ceremony in Michael's own church, and had spoken words of blessing over Michael and his new wife as well as Theodora before returning to Oxford, where he had been living since his retirement from parish life. It had seemed to them both that he was looking thinner, although neither one had mentioned this to the other until later.

He had continued to write to both of them, almost invariably in Latin. His last letter to Theodora had been in English for the most part, and had been couched in a more affectionate tone than was normally the mark of his correspondence.

Your letters are always a source of pleasure to me, and I can say with perfect honesty that for me you have been nothing but joy. When I think about your future, Hoc est in votes (this is in my prayers), that you will continue in that good and virtuous way in which you have begun. Pride, as you know, is a sin; but it is one to which I must confess, for I have always been proud of you, and you have never done anything to make me regret that you are my daughter. Please believe that I write ex anima (from the heart). Ega me bene habea (with me all is well). May God's blessing rest upon you, my child, now and always.

She had wept over this letter at the time, never dreaming that the next piece of correspondence would be from the master of her father's college to Michael to inform him that Rev'd Paul Buckleigh had died in his sleep.

Lord Ashbourne had been present when she had heard the news, and it had been he who had taken her in his arms, and given her the fatherly comfort that she had needed. She owed them all so much. As she heard Lady Ashbourne scream, therefore, she hurried down without hesitation, to render whatever assistance might be necessary.

She looked through the open door of the drawing-room to find Jessie standing with her hands pressed to her cheeks and saying, 'I will never get used to it! Never!' Facing her was Lord Ashbourne, but it was Ashbourne as Theodora had never seen him before. Ever since she had known him, the earl had had long hair, tied back in a queue. Even confined with a ribbon, it reached partway down his back. Today, it was gone. He had not had it cut very short, but it now hung loose, barely touching his shoulders.

'But, my love, surely you would not have me look like some country squire, who is twenty years behind the times,' the earl complained.

'No, I suppose not. Who decides these fashions, anyway?' his countess grumbled crossly. 'I just wish that they would consult me.'

'I won't have it cut any shorter,' he assured her. He took a step or two closer to her. 'Not after you have told me on many occasions how much you like to run your fingers through it when . . . ' He paused, some sixth sense telling him that they were not alone. 'Theodora, my dear,' he said, glancing towards the door. 'Come in, and tell me how you like my new look.'

'I'm sorry, I did not mean to interrupt,' she said diffidently.

'You came in response to my screaming, no doubt,' Jessie suggested. 'Now you see the dreadful thing that so alarmed me.'

Theodora looked at Ashbourne, her head tilted to one side. 'Turn around,' she said. He did so, slowly, finishing with a flourishing bow in her direction. 'I like it,' she said eventually.

'Traitor!' Jessie declared, laughing. 'I was counting on your support.'

'But I think that you are right, Step-papa; it must not be cut any shorter.'

'I promise,' he replied, looking more at Jessie than at Theodora. 'By the way, Thea, I believe that I may have found a solution to your dilemma. I met a gentleman of Michael's acquaintance at my club yesterday evening, and it chances that he is committed to escorting his betrothed's aunt to Devon quite soon. I asked him whether he might be prepared to take you as well and he says that he will be happy to do so. It will be company for the other lady. Once he has delivered her safely to her home in Taunton, he will take you the rest of the way to your friends' house.'

'Oh, thank you,' said Theodora, beaming.

'So glad to leave us,' Jessie complained.

'Not glad to leave you, but looking forward to seeing Dorothy and meeting her brother,' Theodora assured her.

'I shall invite Mr Kydd to call,' said Ashbourne.

Later, after Theodora had gone upstairs to write to Dorothy with the glad tidings, Jessie

63

said to Ashbourne, 'Do you suppose that she has become a little infatuated with Mr Wordsworth?'

'A man she has never met? That would be unlikely, don't you think?'

'Perhaps. Even if I am right, I am not at all sure what we can do about it.'

'He's obviously a gentleman,' said Ashbourne. 'Should the interest be mutual, he will no doubt make his approach to Michael, in correct form. Then we will see for ourselves.'

★ ★ ★

It was arranged that Michael's acquaintance would wait upon Theodora before the journey took place. In the meantime, there were other things to be attended to. Theodora and Jessie had both ordered clothes, so they went together to the modiste so that they could try on the new garments to make sure that they fitted properly. Jessie's were suitable for town wear and appropriate to her station as a married lady, whereas Theodora's were for simple country living, and still in colours suitable for one in mourning. As Jessie looked at Theodora, she felt a stab of pity. Every other girl she had ever known had wanted a London season. What a shame that Theodora could not enter into such plans with any pleasure.

After it had been established that neither lady's garments needed very much alteration, Theodora asked if they might pay a visit to a new bookshop. 'Hatchard's has only just opened, and I would very much like to see if there is anything that I would like to read during the journey.'

Jessie readily agreed, but before they left the modiste's, she wanted to have a final word with the dressmaker. While this conversation was taking place, Theodora went over to the window to observe those who were passing in the street.

Soon she would be looking out on a very different scene. She had had a letter from Dorothy Wordsworth that very day.

I cannot tell you how much we are looking forward to your visit. Every day spent here reveals new delights. William and I took a walk of about five miles yesterday. We paused and watched a little family of rabbits at play. The young had fur a little lighter than the parents, with a paler sheen about it and one could almost feel the greater degree of softness just by looking at it. I fancied their eyes sparkled with the very joy of living. Do you think that foolish? How I long to show you all of this, my dear friend.

It was while she was thinking of these words, a smile still playing about her lips, that she became conscious of two ladies talking in low voices nearby. She might have missed their conversation completely, if it had not been for the fifth word uttered by the first speaker. It was a particularly emotive word for her, so it came over as clearly as if it had been shouted at the top of someone's voice.

'Who is the little crippled girl?' she said.

'I think she's being sponsored by Ashbourne,' replied the other, in the same low tone.

'The countess is here with her, I see. What's the girl's portion?'

'I've no idea.'

'It'll need to be large to enable any man to swallow that deformity.'

'Theodora! You must have been miles away. Are you ready to go to Hatchard's now?'

So caught up was Theodora with the unpleasant exchange that she had heard that Jessie had had to speak to her three times before she turned round. She looked about her, half anxious, half angry. There were several other ladies in the shop, so she could not be sure who had spoken.

She had been obliged to come out in lighter shoes so that she could try on her new clothes properly. Now, the limp which she had so successfully put to the back of her mind seemed intolerably clumsy and hideous as they crossed the street to go into Hatchard's. How could she ever have imagined that she could be happy staying with the Wordsworths? She could not go for a walk of five miles, however good her boots! Where would her immature little fantasy about Dorothy's brother William be then?

She felt almost sick with disillusionment as she accompanied Jessie across the road and into Hatchard's. For two pins she could have gone home, all her pleasure destroyed by the insensitivity of the two women whose conversation she had heard. The problem was that since she had been the one to suggest the visit to the bookshop only a matter of minutes ago, it would have sounded a little odd to say the least if she now declared that she did not want to go.

Although Hatchard's had opened very recently, it had already become quite the place to be seen. The shop was busy, crammed with both male and female customers. One or two looked round as they entered. Theodora imagined that they were all staring at her limp, and she raised her chin defiantly.

'Shall we meet here by the door in, say, half an hour?' Jessie suggested. 'There is a lady over there whom I have not seen for some time, and I do not think that our conversation would interest you, my dear.' Theodora agreed, and made her way rather listlessly towards the poetry section. She could never remain ill-tempered for long when there were books to be enjoyed, however, and she was soon searching for her favourite authors.

She had just taken down a volume of John Donne and was wondering whether this might appeal to her friend Dorothy, when she became aware of being stared at. She looked up and saw that she was the object of scrutiny by a gentleman who was standing just a few feet away from her, a book in his hand. He was looking towards her, his head not fully turned in her direction so that she could only see perhaps two thirds of his face. He had dark-brown hair, perhaps a little longer than the current fashion, and it hung straight, one lock flopping over his brow and the rest draping his shoulders. His complexion was olive, and his face and jaw were quite narrow. There was a careless grace about his stance, not the almost overpowering elegance of Ashbourne, nor the vigorous energy of Ilam; perhaps something in between.

Their gaze met and held for a moment,

68

until Theodora looked away, put the book back in its place, then took a step or two sideways to look at the next shelves. She glanced at him again; he tilted his head a little to the side, and looked as though he might speak. Then, before he did so, he appeared to glance down at her feet.

For Theodora, this apparent scrutiny came just too soon after the unkind remarks of the women in the shop. 'What are you staring at?' she asked him rudely. 'Have you never seen a cripple before?'

'Madam?' He seemed puzzled. His head was still tilted to one side, so that she could not see his full face.

'Pray do not pretend that you were not looking,' Theodora went on, her voice trembling a little. 'It would not be so bad if you were not too deceitful and too cowardly to admit it.'

He drew his brows together in a slight frown. 'Madam, I assure you — ' he began.

'You can assure me as much as you like,' she replied, her voice trembling a little. 'A *true* gentleman would at least have the courtesy to look straight at me.' She turned awkwardly and limped away.

Soon afterwards, she rejoined Jessie and they left the shop and went home. Theodora said nothing to anyone else about this unfortunate encounter. Looking back, she wondered whether perhaps she had mis-judged the man. She suspected not. It always seemed strange to her that people in London's 'polite society' could be so rude in the way they stared and commented upon others. It was high time that one of their number got a taste of his own medicine!

★ ★ ★

An officer of dragoons stepped out of the shadows in the bookshop, from where he had observed the incident unseen. 'A pretty little thing,' he remarked. 'Not afraid of speaking her mind, either.'

'Ah, well, that may be because she has a first-class brain to inform her speech,' replied the other.

'You know her?' said the officer. 'That was not my impression.'

'I don't know her,' answered Theodora's observer as he put his book back. 'I believe from the evidence of that unusual hair colour that she is Michael Buckleigh's sister.'

'Good lord!' exclaimed the officer, laugh-ing. 'The young lady you're escorting to the West Country? That wasn't a very good start, was it?'

The two men made their way out of the

bookshop and into the sunlit busy street. 'A better start than having her run screaming from my presence,' Theodora's escort replied, turning his full face towards his companion. It could now be seen that the left-hand side of his face was marred by a deep scar.

'I think you do her an injustice,' the officer replied. 'If she's as intelligent as you say, then she will have the wit to see beneath the surface. Besides, what does it matter what she thinks? Once you've delivered her safely to her friends, you won't have to see her again.'

'Very true,' the other man agreed, after a short pause. 'Shall we go to White's? They've rather a good claret I think you should try.'

7

'It isn't that I'm not pleased to see you, my boy. It's simply that Titchfield isn't here. He's gone to join friends in Kent, I think.' The Duke of Portland poured a glass of wine for his visitor.

The young man did not look noticeably disappointed; but that did not surprise his grace. Alexander Kydd had always been quite adept at hiding his feelings, an ability which had only increased following the injury that had spoiled his looks. 'I'm sorry to hear that, sir,' Kydd replied, taking the glass of claret handed to him by the tall, handsome aristocrat.

He had known the Duke of Portland since his school days. He was exactly the same age as the duke's heir, the Marquess of Titchfield. The two boys had attended Westminster school together, and young Alexander had often received invitations to spend the holidays here at Bulstrode House. It had been with a sense of pleasurable anticipation that he had ridden over from London, hoping to spend the day with the marquess before his own journey to Devon. His sense of disappointment was keen but, as the duke surmised, he did not allow his feelings to show.

'He'll be sorry too,' remarked the duke. 'You've only just missed him. I'm aware that I'm a very inferior substitute, but may I serve you in any way while you're here?'

Alex smiled, the scar on his cheek giving this expression a slightly crooked appearance. He had known the duke for a little under twenty years, but their families had been loosely acquainted for longer, for the duchess and Alex's mother were friends. Through work that he had done more recently for the government, some of it quite secret, he had come to know the man before him, now Home Secretary, in another capacity.

'In no way in particular,' Alex replied, 'unless you feel inclined to let me know the name of your wine merchant. This is excellent.'

Portland smiled. 'Naturally I shall oblige you. I might even let you have a case. I understand that congratulations are due.'

'You are referring to my engagement, I collect,' answered Alex, after taking another sip of his wine.

'Your betrothed is Miss Markham, is she not?' The duke indicated a chair, then took one himself opposite his guest.

'That is so,' Alex agreed. He had become engaged to Vivienne Markham the previous Christmas. He had known her all his life, and his mother favoured her as a daughter-in-law. Although he had no title, his name was an old one. He had no brothers and he had always known that it was his duty to marry. He had a fondness for Vivienne and could not think of anyone else whom he cared to marry.

The idea of love he discounted. Perhaps, ten years ago, when he had been something like handsome, there might have been a chance of it. Now, however . . . He ran his finger down the scar on his cheek, made by an enemy sabre in the Netherlands shortly after France had declared war upon England and Holland. That had been four years ago, in 1793. He had been twenty-six and engaged then as well, but not to Vivienne. He could never forget the look of revulsion on the face of his betrothed when she had seen his disfigurement for the first time.

'Miss Markham's a sensible young woman,' said Portland. 'She'll make you a good wife, I should think.'

'And so do I think it,' responded Alex with a smile. He could not bear to see his face at such times. He would have been astonished to learn how many ladies found his crooked smile rather appealing, and he would probably not have believed it if he were told.

'You must bring her to visit us here when you are wed,' said the duke.

'I shall be delighted to do so.'

The two men chatted idly for a little longer, until Alex remarked that he ought to be leaving. 'Since Titchfield isn't here, I mustn't keep you from your duties, sir.'

'Don't go so soon,' the other man replied. 'The duchess is from home, and I will be eating a solitary nuncheon if you don't join me.' As Alex had nothing pressing to be doing, he allowed himself to be persuaded, and soon they were sitting down together in a comfortable parlour, enjoying bread and cheese, ham, some fruit and an apricot tart.

For a short time, they ate in silence, until Portland laid down his knife. 'Do I recall you saying that you were going to Devon?' he asked.

'Yes, that is so,' Alex replied. 'I'm escorting Vivienne's aunt to her home, and then taking a young lady to visit friends in Dorset.'

'I see.' Portland resumed his meal, leaving Alex with the distinct impression that he had weighed up in his mind whether to say anything, and decided against it for the time being. Knowing better than to pry, Alex continued with his own meal, sure that if the duke wanted to confide in him, he would find an opportunity.

Sure enough, after they had retired once more to the drawing-room, Portland said, 'Before you go, there's a matter about which I would like to ask your opinion.' Alex made a gesture to indicate his assent. 'What do you know about the Corresponding societies?'

'That they have been suspected of being hotbeds of traitorous activity,' Alex responded in a neutral tone. 'Surely though, they have had their day?'

The societies, formed largely at the beginning of the 1790s, had been a means to instruct ordinary working people about their democratic rights, as well as to encourage parliamentary reform. Whilst Britain was at peace with France, the British Government had tolerated their existence, seeing no harm in them, but with the war had come a different, more suspicious attitude, and with it heavy-handed legislation to stop such groups from meeting. Alex was one of many people who thought that parliamentary reform was badly needed. He wished that the government could have found some means of using the corresponding societies to educate people about what was being done by their leaders, instead of repressing what was undoubtedly harmless in the vast majority of cases.

'By and large,' agreed the duke. 'However,

in these uncertain times, the network that they have provided could easily be used by someone anxious to render our country unstable through the sowing of dissent.'

'Reform must come,' said Alex slowly, looking down into his wine.

'Reform — but not revolution,' answered the duke. 'The French revolution may have begun nobly enough. God knows, something needed to be done, with Louis and his court so out of touch with the people. But the nobility of the enterprise seems to have been swallowed up in greed and violence.'

Alex nodded. 'Agreed; but then most Englishmen who espoused the French cause have been repelled by the aftermath.'

'Most, but not all. There are some who see the violent results of the French Revolution as a necessary price that may have to be paid in order to achieve a change. Others believe that for England to be defeated by France would bring about a better order here.'

'I don't doubt the existence of such views,' Alex answered. 'I fail to see how this affects me, however.'

'Some of the most vocal and eloquent supporters of the French Revolution have been active in the part of the world that you'll be visiting shortly. Bristol in particular has been a hotbed of intrigue. I've had it in mind to send one of our agents to look into the matter, but before I take such a step, I would prefer to have your thoughts on what is occurring. Some of these agents, though keen, are unable to discern fine distinctions. You would be able to detect whether any individuals concerned are simply intellectuals philosophizing, or people with evil intent towards our country, who ought to be watched.'

'Do you have any names to give me?'

The duke went over to a table in the window, bent down, dipped a pen into some ink and wrote briefly on a piece of paper. Then he handed it to his guest.

Alex pointed to one of the names written thereon. 'I know of this man. He's clever.'

'Let us hope that he is not dangerous as well.'

8

Mr Kydd called at Ashbourne's town house the following morning at about eleven o'clock. The ladies were sitting together in the pleasant south-facing drawing-room. Theodora was sewing. She was making some cushion covers to give to Dorothy on her arrival at Racedown. She had been working on them for some time. Now, the visit that had been anticipated for so long was looming nearer, and it gave her task an added urgency.

Jessie was also sewing. She and Theodora were chatting idly off and on. From time to time Jessie referred gently to some of the functions which she and Ashbourne were to attend over the next few days, glancing discreetly at Theodora to see how she would react. The younger woman had consistently maintained that she did not feel badly done by, not being in London for the season. Certainly she seemed contented enough, smiling as she worked. Was she infatuated with William Wordsworth? If so, then Jessie feared that heartache might be in store, whatever the outcome.

She had an acquaintance who was married

to a poet, and her existence was anything but romantic. Her husband would disappear to write at odd hours of the day and night, sometimes leaving roomfuls of guests, or failing to attend the dinner table. Home and family would be neglected, and the income that was needed to feed his wife and two children seemed to be very precarious. He appeared to drift about, quite untouched by the concerns of the real world, whilst his wife looked increasingly careworn and disillusioned. It was not a fate that Jessie would wish upon Theodora. She deserved to be loved and cherished.

Every woman deserved that, she decided, smiling as her thoughts inevitably turned to Lord Ashbourne. Then, as if they had actually conjured him up, he entered at that very moment, accompanied by a young man whom Jessie had not seen before.

All her attention was given to her husband and the newcomer. Consequently, she did not witness the look of surprise followed by consternation that crossed Theodora's face, for the visitor was none other than the man who had stared at her in Hatchard's. She was sitting at an angle from the doorway, and so she chanced to see exactly the same portion of his face as she had done in the bookshop. At once, she was conscious of a surge of hostility. Bad enough that she should be stared at in public. Heaven forbid that she should have to put up with it in her own home!

The ladies rose to curtsy, and the gentlemen both bowed — Lord Ashbourne only ever being neglectful of this courtesy in the most intimate of family gatherings.

'Jez, my dear,' said his lordship, 'you must permit me to introduce Mr Kydd to you. Mr Kydd — my wife, Lady Ashbourne and my stepdaughter by adoption, Miss Buckleigh, who is to travel with you to Dorset.'

Theodora curtsied but her face was stormy. This rude young man, then, was the one who was to accompany her on her journey. Splendid!

'Mr Kydd, you are very welcome. Please sit down while Raff rings for refreshments,' said Jessie indicating a chair quite close to Theodora's whilst Ashbourne rang the bell before taking a chair next to his wife.

As Kydd turned, Theodora saw him full face for the first time. Until now, she had not realized that he was scarred. Hardly knowing what to think, she coloured and turned away. He had certainly stared at her in the shop. How could he have been so insensitive when he himself must be daily subject to similar scrutiny? From being angry, she found herself feeling confused.

Kydd also recognized the young lady from Hatchard's. He had been staring at her for reasons of his own, but keeping the scarred side of his face in shadow whenever possible was now a habit with him. He had become used to female revulsion at his disfigurement. Noting Theodora's embarrassment, he smiled cynically, thinking that he knew its cause.

'Are you making a long stay in Devon, Mr Kydd?' Jessie asked him, glancing briefly at Theodora, who had picked up her sewing. She was always inclined to be shy, but her behaviour today was bordering on rudeness.

'My plans are uncertain,' Alex replied. 'I am escorting Mrs Trowbridge, my betrothed's aunt, to her home in Taunton. My betrothed is visiting in the area, and I also have friends to see, so I may linger for a while.' He turned to Theodora. 'Is it your first visit to the West Country, Miss Buckleigh?' he asked, taking her by surprise.

'Oh. Oh, yes,' she answered breathlessly.

'And you are visiting friends?'

'Yes; Miss Wordsworth and her brother.'

'I believe that you are acquainted with my husband's son, The Rev'd Michael Buckleigh,' Jessie said to their visitor whilst Ashbourne was pouring the wine that had been brought in on a tray by the butler.

'Yes, that is so, Lady Ashbourne,' he

replied. Theodora had picked up her sewing again, but Alex could tell by her posture that she was listening to the conversation.

'How did you meet?' Jessie asked. 'Were you at school together?'

Alex shook his head. 'We met at Oxford,' he said. 'Michael gave me some coaching in Greek. In return, I gave him some fencing lessons.'

Theodora smiled to herself. Her half-brother had never had anything by way of personal income until he had inherited some valuable antique pottery from an old acquaintance. At university, therefore, he had improved his lot by offering coaching in academic subjects in exchange for lessons in boxing and fencing. This young man's need for coaching argued that he was one of those aristocrats who had only gone to Oxford because it was the thing to do, rather than for any academic reason.

'You did not become a clergyman like him, though,' said Jessie.

'No indeed, I do not have that calling,' he responded. 'After Oxford I went into the army.'

'Cavalry?' Ashbourne asked as he brought a glass of lemonade for Theodora and wine for his wife.

'Indeed,' Alex agreed, his fingers going to

his scar. He glanced briefly at Theodora, remembering how she had shied away from looking at it. 'After I was wounded, I returned home to recuperate. It was then that I realized how much my mother was struggling with the estate. I concluded that my duty was to remain in England.'

Theodora found herself feeling rather annoyed. Of course, he had to stroke his scar just to draw attention to how valiant he had been! Then he looked at her, probably just to make sure that she was watching him. Her own disability was nothing to be proud of — she had only been born with it. Nevertheless, he need not think that she was going to be impressed by him. Plenty of other men had come home wounded, some far more grievously than he. No doubt he had received his wound because he had been showing off.

Mr Kydd stayed for a little over half an hour, during which time arrangements were made for Theodora's departure. 'Mrs Trowbridge wants to leave London on Monday,' he said. 'Then we will easily reach our destination without having to worry about whether or not to travel on a Sunday, which I know would not be agreeable to you, Miss Buckleigh.'

Theodora put up her chin. The daughter

and also the sister of a clergyman, she would no more have dreamed of travelling on a Sunday than of flying to the moon. Doubtless the former soldier thought her scruples ridiculous. 'I shall be ready,' she assured him.

He bowed and left, but the memory of the fragile-looking slender, dignified figure clad in black stayed with him after he had gone, and haunted his dreams a little.

★ ★ ★

The next few days passed in a flurry of activity, as Jessie rushed to make sure that Theodora had everything that she needed. 'Such a pity that you must still be in black for your papa,' she said, with kindly sympathy. 'Dark colours always seem sadder in the country.'

'I know,' Theodora answered. She mourned her papa sincerely, and did not want to be backward in any duty; but to appear before Mr Wordsworth for the first time in unrelieved black seemed very unfair.

'Of course, you have very nearly reached six months of mourning,' Jessie said carefully. 'I see no reason why we should not purchase some ribbons and trimmings in white, or grey, or even in mauve.'

'Do you really think so?' Theodora asked anxiously.

'Certainly,' Jessie answered positively. 'You can show respect for your father's memory whilst still adding a touch of colour. And a straw bonnet is a straw bonnet, you know.'

So it was that when Mr Kydd arrived at Lord Ashbourne's house the following Monday morning, Theodora was waiting, dressed in a black travelling gown with pale mauve trimming, and a straw bonnet with ribbons of the same colour.

'How delightful to find you ready, Miss Buckleigh,' said Kydd with a polite bow.

'Contrary to general opinion, there are many ladies who are capable of punctuality,' she replied, sounding frostier than she had intended.

It proved to be much harder to say goodbye to Jessie and Lord Ashbourne than she had expected, and she clung to both of them, but particularly the earl, before saying goodbye with tears in her eyes.

Kydd observed her with a narrowed gaze. He remembered that although Lord Ashbourne was the natural father of his friend Michael Buckleigh, he was not related to Theodora in any way.

Alex had met Ashbourne for the first time at his club a few days before. He had heard that the earl was something of a ladies' man, elegant, suave and handsome. The reality had, if anything, cast the rumour into the shade. Would it be at all surprising if Theodora were smitten with the handsome earl? True, he was married and over twice her age, but when had that stopped a woman falling for an attractive man? The girl to whom he had been betrothed before his injury was now married to a man considerably older than herself.

Alex helped Theodora into the carriage, his lips set into a thin line. He had already assisted Mrs. Trowbridge to take her place. Theodora noticed his expression and wondered what she had done to annoy him. She had hoped to find out in conversation, and was somewhat put out when she discovered that he intended to go on horseback. It was a lowering reflection to conclude that he preferred to ride alongside his groom rather than engage her in conversation.

'Well that is a mercy,' said Mrs Trowbridge placidly. She had stepped down politely to go into the house and exchange compliments with Lord and Lady Ashbourne before entering the chaise. 'We ladies can always share secrets more comfortably when the gentlemen are out of the way, can we not?'

Theodora was quite a reserved person, and

this suggestion that she might divulge her most intimate concerns to a lady she had only just met sounded very worrying. She soon discovered, however, that Mrs Trowbridge was so fond of talking herself that she only needed to interpose the occasional comment such as 'Is that so?' or 'How interesting!' and Mrs Trowbridge did the rest.

Theodora found out during the course of the journey that her companion was a widow in her mid forties, with no children of her own, but a deep affection for her niece Vivienne Markham. Indeed, the younger woman soon felt that she knew as much about Mr Kydd's fiancée as Mr Kydd himself.

'They have known one another all their lives,' said Mrs Trowbridge. 'No unpleasant surprises for either of them! You may not have heard that he was engaged to another young lady before his injury. He was very handsome until then. Needless to say, it was a nasty shock to her when he came home with his face so disfigured, and I am afraid that she threw him over. Vivienne, bless her, did not let it make any difference to the way in which she treated him. I think that that may have been why they decided to marry. I don't suppose that he could have found anyone else who would take him, and Vivienne is no beauty herself, although she has a sweet nature.'

It did not seem to Theodora that this was a particularly propitious start to the match — the two being driven together because no one else would want to take either of them. Fortunately, because of Mrs Trowbridge's garrulousness, she was not obliged to make any response.

When they made their first stop, in order to change the horses and take some refreshment, Mrs Trowbridge thanked Mr Kydd who came over to help them down after he had dismounted. 'How glad we shall be of some sustenance, and something to drink in particular,' said the older lady, as she stepped down and Kydd moved forward to perform the same service for Theodora. 'I do not know how it may be, but when we ladies get together we cannot stop chatting.' Theodora glanced involuntarily at Kydd, and he cast her a lopsided grin that was full of fellow feeling. It was the first time that they had exchanged a sympathetic glance in this way.

Mercifully, after they had refreshed themselves and the ladies had resumed their places, Mrs Trowbridge closed her eyes, and fell into a deep sleep, untroubled by the movement of the coach. This left Theodora free to look out of the window and to think her own thoughts. It was the first time that she had travelled without a member of her family for over a year, when she had gone to live with Michael in the cottage provided for him by Lord Ilam.

This journey was very different. For one thing, she was not travelling on the common stage, so she was physically much more comfortable. She changed her position slightly, turning to give her weaker hip some support. She had not been able to do *that* on the stage! What was more, this carriage, belonging, she supposed, to Mrs Trowbridge, was exceedingly well sprung, so much so that Theodora almost felt like following her companion's example.

Hastily, she pinched herself to make sure that she would stay awake. To drop off now would be to waste these precious moments of quiet. Far better to wait until Mrs Trowbridge looked to be stirring, and then close her eyes!

She opened a small bag that she was carrying with her and took out a copy of Mary Wollstonecraft's book, *A Vindication of the Rights of Woman*. This book had an interesting history. First belonging to Lady Ilam before her marriage, it had passed into Jessie's hands. Jessie had given it to Evangeline after her marriage to Lord Ashbourne, and Evangeline, in her turn, once

90

she was Mrs Michael Buckleigh, had said that Theodora might have it. The latter had already read the book, but she had decided to bring it with her, believing that it merited further study. She opened it at a page where some lines were written concerning the lot of some women in society.

Proud of their weakness, however, they must always be protected, guarded from care, and all the rough toils that dignify the mind.

For a moment or two she thought of her own situation, for she, too, was protected and guarded. But she was certainly not proud of her weakness. On the contrary, at this moment, she was proud of her courage. She was having an adventure, and her dear protectors, much though she loved them, were far away!

She took out the notebook into which she had copied all of her correspondence from Dorothy Wordsworth, and opened it at random. Dorothy was commenting upon how, unable to sleep one night, she and William had walked together, then found a quiet place where they lay on their backs and looked up at the stars. Perhaps soon she, too, would be accompanying them on such expeditions. Smiling, she closed her eyes. The next thing she knew, the carriage was drawing to a halt outside the Red Lion in Salisbury, and they were getting down in order to spend the night.

Theodora accepted Kydd's hand as before, then after she had moved a little away from the carriage, he leaned inside with an exclamation. He picked up Theodora's notebook, which was lying open on the floor of the carriage, whence it had fallen after it had slipped from her hand while she slept. 'Is this yours, ma'am?' he asked, smiling politely.

'Yes. Thank you,' she said a little sharply. She had remembered how she had written down some of her speculations about William Wordsworth, and she was anxious that he should not read any of them. Quickly, she snapped it shut, almost under his nose. 'It is very private,' she said, staring at him anxiously.

He obviously read mistrust in her eyes, for his smile disappeared. 'I am not in the habit of reading other people's diaries, I assure you,' he said coldly whilst Mrs Trowbridge was fussing over the folds of her gown. Unable to think of a reply, Theodora simply turned away.

The two ladies were walking towards the

inn door, when a group of rather noisy young bucks came out, looking as if they might be inclined to be boisterous. Both ladies halted, a little unsure of the wisdom of proceeding. Before they could be subjected to any kind of annoyance — if that had indeed been part of the young men's intention — Mr Kydd stepped forward.

'By your leave, gentlemen,' he said. His tone was neither raised nor threatening, but it contained an unmistakable air of authority. As if by magic, the rowdy young men suddenly became sober citizens, who moved courteously to one side to allow the ladies to pass. Whatever her feelings about him might be, Theodora was obliged to acknowledge that he was certainly a useful man to have around.

9

Their plans to travel on the following morning met with a setback when Mrs Trowbridge failed to appear for breakfast. Theodora knocked on the door of her room in order to find out what had detained her, and found the older lady still in bed, her complexion pasty, her eyes heavy.

'My dear Mrs Trowbridge, what can be the matter?' Theodora asked at once, her voice full of concern.

'A migraine,' Mrs Trowbridge replied in a thread of a voice. 'I'm afraid that I will be quite unable to move today. We will have to stay here for twenty-four hours.'

'I *am* sorry,' Theodora answered, with ready sympathy. 'Of course we must stay here until you are better. Is there anything that I may procure for you, or ask the landlady to get?'

'No, nothing,' answered the sufferer. 'I have some water, and that is all that I can stomach. Later on, when I am a little better, I will send for some tea.'

'Would you like me to stay with you?'

Mrs Trowbridge remembered just in time

not to shake her head. 'No, thank you,' she replied. 'Some peace and quiet is all that I require.'

Theodora went downstairs and reported the situation to Alex. 'There's nothing to be done,' he told her. 'I am aware that Mrs Trowbridge seldom has these migraines, but when she does, they lay her out completely for several hours. You do not have a pressing reason for arriving on a particular day, I trust?'

Theodora shook her head. 'They are expecting me, but not on a specific date,' she answered.

'There is no need to worry, then. Since we cannot travel on, I suggest that we explore Salisbury a little. I don't know about you, but it is not a town that I know very well. I have passed through on several occasions, but have never done more than simply spend the night and then move on.'

'I have never been here before,' Theodora admitted.

'Then we will explore together.'

Theodora was rather doubtful as to how enjoyable this might be. Their acquaintance had not got off to a very good start. What was more, she had given the impression that she had thought that he was prying into the contents of her notebook, an imputation which any of the menfolk of her own family would have deeply resented. What if he had deliberately chosen to avoid her by riding on horseback because he did not like her attitude? Given these circumstances, she could not imagine what they would find to say to one another.

After breakfast which, since Theodora was unchaperoned, they took very properly in the public dining-room, Alex said, 'I thought that you might like to take a look at the cathedral. It is said to be very fine. Or do your clerical connections mean that you feel tempted to say *not another church*?'

She laughed. 'No, indeed. I was fascinated to catch a glimpse of the spire this morning, and would love to see more.'

'Are you happy that we should walk?' he asked her.

'Perfectly happy,' she responded, with a hint of challenge in her voice. She was wearing a pair of her specially made boots, and knew that a walk to the cathedral — which could not be more than two or three streets away — would be well within her compass.

'Then shall we meet downstairs in, say, half an hour?'

The walk to the cathedral was as short as Theodora had supposed, and in no time they were staring up at the highest spire in England.

'One has to admire the skill involved in constructing something like that,' said Kydd. 'I suppose you have seen a good many cathedrals.'

'No, I have not,' she admitted. 'I have travelled very little, and St Paul's in London was the first that I had ever looked inside. My stepfather took me.'

'Ah yes, Lord Ashbourne,' murmured Alex, recalling the suspicions that he had entertained with regard to Theodora's feelings for the earl.

'Of course, he is not really my stepfather,' she went on, quite unaware of the nature of his thoughts. 'It is all rather complicated, and would, I am sure, be very dull to someone not acquainted with the people involved.'

'I do not think I would find it dull,' Alex replied, not wanting to appear as if he were trying to force a confidence. 'My family life is dull, if you like. I am an only child. My father is dead. My mother resides at the house I inherited from him.'

'Where is your estate?' Theodora asked him.

'In Buckinghamshire,' he replied.

'Mrs Trowbridge said that you had known your betrothed for many years. Does she live near to your estate?'

'Yes, Vivienne's family and mine are neighbours. Our lands march together, and our parents were friends. Vivienne's brother Peter and I were contemporaries. We grew up getting into mischief together and sharing all the kinds of outdoor exploits dear to the hearts of boys brought up in the country.'

'Damming streams, climbing trees and stealing apples,' Theodora suggested.

Alex laughed. 'Exactly so. There were no girls of Vivienne's age in the vicinity, so it was natural for her to want to be with us. She was not the kind of child who whined or told tales, so we deigned to include her.'

'Very gracious of you.'

'We thought so. As we were so inseparable, our parents decided to send us to the same school.'

'How I envy you,' said Theodora with a sigh. 'I always wanted to go to school.'

'Foolish child,' replied Alex. 'You have no knowledge of the degree of torture involved in a school education. Anyway, we survived, and so did the school.'

'Then you went to university where you met Michael,' put in Theodora.

'Indeed,' Alex agreed. 'Peter and I drifted apart a little after that, although we did join the cavalry together and saw action in the

Netherlands.' He paused, then added gravely. 'I came back. He did not.'

'Oh, poor Miss Markham,' exclaimed Theodora. 'Was he her only brother?'

He nodded. 'It has been very hard for her parents, who now show a quite understandable tendency to cling to her.'

'Yes of course. I can imagine how dreadful that must be. The thought of anything happening to Michael makes me feel quite sick.'

They were silent for a short time. Then, because he had been so open, Theodora dared to say, 'Mrs Trowbridge told me that you had gained your scar when you were in the cavalry. I did not observe it the first time that I saw you in Hatchard's.'

'No, I took good care that you did not,' he replied. 'Your expression gave you away when you saw me in your stepfather's drawing-room. You must not worry, Miss Buckleigh. I have long since become used to the revulsion that your sex tends to feel concerning my scar.'

'I was not revolted,' she protested. 'How could you even think such a thing, when I . . . ?' She broke off. 'I do not like being stared at myself, you see.'

'Did I stare?' he asked. She thought that he flushed a little.

'You did. You stared at my . . . my limp.'

'Was that why you were so — '

'Rude?' she suggested blushing.

'I was going to say forthright,' he answered. 'I hadn't even noticed your limp. Would you think me insensitive if I said that it really isn't that noticeable? I knew that I was escorting Michael's sister to Dorset, and I was wondering whether you might be she. You have the same hair colour, you see. It is quite distinctive.'

'Oh,' she responded. 'That had not occurred to me, I confess.' There was another silence.

'I know that both your parents are dead,' Alex said eventually. 'Is it very long since your mother passed away?'

She nodded. 'My mother died when I was born, so I never knew her. My father died earlier on this year, as you know.'

'Were you very close?'

'No, not really. I think that he liked books better than he liked people. He married my mother later in life, and never expected to be a father, you see. In lots of ways, Michael filled the place of a father for me.'

She glanced up at him, hesitated, then said, 'Michael only met his own father, Lord Ashbourne, last year. Then he discovered that he had a half-brother as well, because Lord

Ashbourne has a legitimate son. Although none of Michael's relations is linked to me by blood, they have all welcomed me as if I were really a member of the family. That's why I call Lord Ashbourne Step-papa. He is just like a father to me, and I love him very much.' Her face softened as she spoke.

'In that case, I wonder that you were anxious to leave,' he said. His tone was rather hard, but she was too preoccupied with thinking about what he had said to notice.

She hesitated for a moment. She had confided more than she had intended, but she did not want to say anything about her menfolk being too protective. It might sound critical and even disloyal. 'A change is always good,' she said. 'It makes one appreciate home all the more.'

After they had looked round the cathedral, they found a little shop where they could enjoy a cup of tea and a cake. Then, refreshed, they made their way back to the Red Lion. Their expedition had been spent in friendly conversation, but there had also been comfortable silences and they had corrected a misunderstanding or two. Perhaps, Theodora reflected, Alex could be a friend after all.

On their return, Theodora went straight up to Mrs Trowbridge's room and found her sitting up in bed. 'I have sent for tea,' the older lady explained. 'I am feeling a good deal better, and am hopeful of dining with you this evening.'

Her prediction proved to be correct. Indeed, so recovered was she that Theodora and Alex found themselves exchanging rueful glances as Mrs Trowbridge chattered merrily throughout the meal, barely allowing either of them to get a word in.

Their journey the next day was equally as comfortable as the first. Theodora had wondered whether Mr Kydd might spend some of the journey inside the carriage, now that the two of them had made up their differences. Instead, he continued on horse-back seeing them only when they broke the journey. 'He is always happiest in the saddle,' said Mrs Trowbridge.

'Was his groom with him in the army?' Theodora asked. She had noticed that the two men usually rode together, exchanging the occasional remark.

'Yes, I believe so,' the other woman replied.

As the day's travelling neared its end, they entered the town of Taunton, which was where Mrs Trowbridge lived. It had been decided that Theodora would stay at her house for one night. On the following day, Mr Kydd would escort her the remaining thirty odd miles to Racedown Lodge, which was where the Wordsworths were living.

'You would be very welcome to stay with me for much longer than just one night,' the older lady assured Theodora, as they went inside followed by Kydd. 'I am sure that we have been very companionable on this journey. Why, Alex, you would hardly believe it, I am sure, but we scarcely drew breath for the whole journey!' Theodora exchanged glances with Alex, and they both smiled.

Mrs Trowbridge's house was a handsome, brick built property in the centre of the town. Taunton itself looked to be a very ancient place. Theodora decided that she might like to explore it some day, and said so.

'I would be most happy to have you stay with me at any time,' said her hostess. 'In fact, if your friends are not expecting you for any specific function or event, you might stay on now for a few days.'

'The castle is well worth a visit,' Alex put in, 'and the assembly rooms are very fine.' Theodora might have weakened, for the thought of meeting Mr Wordsworth for the first time suddenly made her feel rather shy. It was the mention of the assembly rooms that made up her mind. In her experience, such places invariably meant dancing, and all the humiliation that went with not being able to move gracefully like other girls.

'Thank you, but I believe I must not keep my friends waiting,' she said.

They were about to go upstairs when a lady in a dove grey gown appeared from one of the rooms off the hall. She was not a very young lady, probably being nearer thirty than twenty, but she was attractive enough, with dark hair and even, if rather sharp, features.

'I hope I am not intruding,' she said, 'but I thought that I would come over and greet you. How was the journey?'

'Vivienne, my dear,' exclaimed Mrs Trowbridge, hurrying forward to embrace her. 'How delightful! Have you come to stay with me?'

'For a few days only,' Vivienne replied. 'I have been in Bristol with friends, and have promised to visit Cousin Kathryn in Bridgwater, but I could not resist being here when you arrived.'

Theodora had guessed that this must be Mr Kydd's fiancée. Her surmise was confirmed when he approached the lady in grey and took her hand. 'Vivienne; how kind of you to come and welcome us,' he said, smiling. He turned to face Theodora. 'You must allow me to present to you Miss Buckleigh, who has been your aunt's companion throughout the journey. Miss Buckleigh, this is Miss Markham, my betrothed.'

The two ladies murmured polite gratification at meeting one another. 'I hope that you do not think that I am presuming, Aunt,' said Miss Markham, 'but I gave instructions for tea to be served as soon as you arrived. Someone should be bringing it to the drawing-room at any moment.'

'You have not presumed at all,' Mrs Trowbridge replied warmly. 'It will be just the thing to refresh us before we change for dinner. Such a pleasant journey as we have had,' she continued as they walked towards the drawing-room. 'Mind you, I did have a vexatious migraine on the day after we arrived in Salisbury.' Theodora had to smile, as Miss Markham only just managed to fit in an exclamation of dismay before her aunt began to speak again.

★ ★ ★

Theodora did not want to delay the meal, so she made haste to dress and come downstairs. As she reached the top of the flight, she saw Miss Markham just arriving at the bottom. She hurried down, and approached the door through which the other lady had just gone, assuming that this would be the place where everyone would be gathering for dinner. She pushed the door open, at the same time hearing voices from within. Suddenly, she realized too late how maladroit she was being. Miss Markham and Mr Kydd were engaged to be married. They had been apart for some little time. Now here she was, interrupting their first chance of a tête-à-tête. They might even be embracing.

To her surprise, however, the betrothed couple did not look particularly self-conscious. Indeed, they were not even close together, for Mr Kydd was looking out of the window and Miss Markham was standing near the fireplace.

'Do come in, Miss Buckleigh,' Miss Markham said, smiling as she gestured to Theodora to approach her so that they could sit down together. 'Alex has told me how heroic you have been.'

'Heroic?' Theodora echoed, puzzled.

'Why, yes,' Vivienne answered, twinkling. 'You sat with my aunt for the entire journey, I believe. To listen to her for that length of time requires true heroism.'

Theodora laughed. 'She does talk a great deal,' she admitted. 'But she is very kind.'

'She is not very kind to one's ears,' Alex murmured.

'I do not know how you would know that, when I daresay you did not spend more than half the time in the carriage,' Vivienne remarked.

'He did not spend any time in the carriage at all,' Theodora replied. 'He went on horseback for the entire journey.'

'Oh, really?' Vivienne said curiously.

'I did not want to cramp the ladies,' Alex said, colouring slightly. 'Besides, Miss Buckleigh needs the space to stretch her . . . ah . . . limbs.'

Theodora looked at him in surprise. She had not thought that he had noticed her need to adjust her position from time to time. Mrs Trowbridge came in soon afterwards, and they all went into dinner, Alex giving his hostess his arm, whilst Miss Markham and Theodora walked behind.

Dinner was a cheerful occasion, with interesting conversation and some laughter; for with a greater number present, Mrs Trowbridge was unable to dominate every conversation. The meal was well cooked and presented, and Theodora reflected with some relief that it was very agreeable to be able to enjoy it without the thought of another long journey the next day. True, she would be travelling to Racedown, but that would be a journey of a mere thirty miles or so, nothing to what they had covered over the past days. After that, her travelling would be over for the time being.

Later, however, Theodora found herself remembering the evening with a feeling of disquiet. As she lay in bed, she tried to work out what it was that might be disturbing her. At last it came to her and the recollection caused her to wake up completely.

She remembered how on one occasion Lord Ashbourne had been obliged to go to London over a matter of business that he had been conducting for his old friend, Lady Gilchrist. Jessie had not made herself look foolish by running to the window every time a carriage was heard, but there had been no doubt that she was missing him very much. He had finally arrived without warning, when Jessie and Theodora were standing in the hall of Ashbourne Abbey. His carriage had met with a slight accident, and he had ridden the last part of the journey on horseback.

'Raff! What a wonderful surprise!' Jessie had exclaimed, casting herself into his arms.

'Jez, my darling,' he had answered, returning her embrace and pressing a brief but firm kiss upon her lips before turning to greet Theodora.

No doubt married couples became used to one another, Theodora reflected, but there had been a delight in the way in which Ashbourne and his wife had greeted each other that had been quite absent from the reunion between Kydd and his intended. Of course, Alex and Vivienne had been acquainted for many years; but so, too, had Lord and Lady Ashbourne, having met briefly for the first time when Jessie was only twelve. Had the earl and his countess been the couple in the drawing-room before dinner, Theodora would almost certainly have found them locked in one another's arms. Kydd and Miss Markham could hardly have been further apart had they taken measurements. Obviously they knew what suited them. Theodora only hoped that when she found a husband, there might be more between them than that rather bloodless affection. Her thoughts automatically turned towards Dorothy's poetical brother. When at last she fell asleep, she was smiling.

★   ★   ★

The following morning, as Theodora came down to the hall and prepared to say goodbye to her hostess — who, although garrulous, had been extremely kind — Alex Kydd came in by the front door. 'I've just been having the team put to,' he explained. 'Do you know the precise location of your friend's home? The coachman knows more or less where to go, but would appreciate

109

some specific directions.'

'I have written it down,' said Theodora. Dorothy had sent instructions in a letter and Theodora had copied it down into her book. After she had dropped her book earlier on in the journey, and had feared that Alex might read it, she had written the instructions down again on another piece of paper, which she now handed to him with a blush, for fear that he might somehow guess what she had done.

'My thanks,' he said, before taking them to the coachman.

While he was doing this, Mrs Trowbridge came into the hall to bid them farewell. 'Pray do come to visit me, and bring your friends,' she said, as she embraced Theodora fondly.

This day's travelling was the least comfortable of all as they were now journeying on less frequented and less well-maintained roads. Fortunately the day was fine, and Theodora was too excited to worry about any minor discomfort caused by the jolting to her person, which though bad, was not as unpleasant as she had feared. As on every previous day, Alex chose to go on horseback.

As they travelled, he glanced at her through the carriage window from time to time. She was not to know that he had given the coachman strict instructions to make the journey as smooth as possible for her sake.

Eventually Racedown Lodge came in sight. It was a fine, three-storeyed house, less than 300 years old, with a handsome porch, the frontage approached by a curving drive.

Hardly had Theodora set one foot upon the ground, than a diminutive dark-haired figure hurried out of the front door, wiping her hands on her apron. 'Theodora, my dear, how wonderful to see you,' exclaimed Dorothy Wordsworth, her expressive eyes full of affection as she hugged her friend. 'I have been counting the hours.'

'And I,' Theodora agreed. 'Such an age it has seemed.' Remembering her escort, she added, 'But you must allow me to present to you Mr Kydd, who has been kind enough to bring me here safely. Mr Kydd, my friend Miss Wordsworth.'

'Your servant, ma'am,' said Kydd, bowing politely. Theodora noticed that he had a healthy colour after his ride.

'Will you not come in for some refreshment before you return, sir?' Dorothy asked him.

Kydd shook his head. 'I am expected back in Taunton to dine, and must allow myself time to change,' he replied. He turned to Theodora. 'I will do myself the honour of calling upon you on another occasion, if I may.'

'Yes, of course. Thank you,' answered Theodora a little shyly. She was thinking about what a happy day they had enjoyed together in Salisbury and how companionable they had been. When they had first met, she had been less than courteous. She was very conscious that she owed this man a considerable obligation, and now he was about to leave. Suddenly, he felt like her last link with home. She wanted to say something more, she hardly knew what. 'Pray — ' she began, then broke off, completely at a loss as to how to finish her sentence.

'Yes, madam?' He turned to face her, his hat in his hand.

'Pray . . . ride carefully,' she concluded lamely, her face on fire, and feeling stupid because he had been a cavalryman.

'You may be sure that I shall do so — as always,' he answered, his expression turning to one of quizzical amusement.

She was still very unsure as to what she felt about him, so she was rather annoyed with herself for experiencing a twinge of disappointment when he rode away in front of the carriage, his groom at his side.

'What an unfortunate disfigurement that young man has,' said Dorothy as they stood watching the retreating carriage. 'Does it pain him at all?'

'What?' said Theodora. She had become so used to Alex's appearance that she had completely forgotten the scar. 'No; no, I don't think so.'

'Come in, come in!' cried Dorothy after a brief pause, catching hold of her arm and breaking her mood of abstraction. 'You must view our little kingdom for yourself. Everything here is of the most desirable. But turn around for a moment, dear Theodora, for you can see the sea from our front door!'

Theodora turned and gasped with delight. Her visits to the sea had not been very frequent. 'Oh, Dorothy, I know I am going to love it here!' she exclaimed, as they embraced.

'We have two parlours,' Dorothy told her as they went into the house, their arms around each other's waists. 'One is rather grander than the other.'

'May I hazard a guess that you prefer the smaller one?' Theodora asked.

'How well you have come to know my tastes,' Dorothy smiled. 'The smaller one is the prettiest little room that can be, and we use it nearly all the time. But come, you will see for yourself. Mary is there with little Basil.'

'You have other guests,' Theodora murmured, not wanting to intrude.

'Just my dear friend Mary Hutchinson,' Dorothy replied. 'You will recall that I have written to you about her before. And of course, little Basil is staying with us all the time, as you know.' Theodora nodded. She recalled Dorothy telling her in a letter that she and her brother William had been entrusted with the upbringing of a small boy called Basil Montagu.

They entered the parlour and a lady who had been sitting on the floor with a boy of about three, got to her feet. She was tall and graceful, not pretty and with a slight squint; but there was a gentleness about her smile as Dorothy introduced them that was very engaging. 'I am so pleased to have met you before I leave,' she said. 'Dorothy has told me so much about you.'

'Oh, are you to leave soon?' Theodora asked her.

'Tomorrow, I am afraid,' Miss Hutchinson replied. 'But I have had a good long stay, and am quite ready to return.'

Shortly after this, a servant girl whom Dorothy addressed as Peggy came in with a tray of tea. 'I thought that you might like tea first, before you go to your room,' Dorothy said to Theodora, who nodded. The ladies were soon engaged upon an animated conversation, which only ceased when a sound at the door told them that another person had arrived. Dorothy sprang to her feet, her eyes shining. 'Theodora, my dear, may I have the great honour of presenting to you my dearest brother, William?'

PART TWO

Infatuation

10

The meeting with William Wordsworth had not been anything like her imagining, Theodora acknowledged to herself, as she and her hosts busied themselves in the garden a couple of days later. It was not that he had been unkind in any way. On the contrary, he had been everything that was courteous and welcoming. In his person, he was tall, but then she was used to associating with tall men in her own family. He was slim, gaunt even, with a solemn face and deep furrows cutting through both cheeks. His lips were full, and his fine hair was slightly receding from his broad brow. Although not a handsome man, his looks were striking enough. She had spent some considerable time thinking that he might be the man for her, and with even a little encouragement, she could easily have fallen in love with him.

One thing that Mr Wordsworth had not been was encouraging, however. Mary Hutchinson had left the day before, as agreed. While she had still been there, Theodora could not help seeing that there was a tenderness between her and William.

'They have known one another since they were children,' Dorothy had confided. Theodora had smiled with understanding, but she could not help wishing that Dorothy, enthusiastic correspondent as she was, had dropped a hint as to her brother's inclinations. It would have saved her, Theodora, a good deal of trouble and wasted daydreaming. Her hopes had been dashed; and whilst it would have been very foolish of her to have accused anyone of having raised them, she could not help mourning their loss that night as she lay in bed. She closed her eyes and tried to recall the picture that she had built up in her mind: the flowing locks, the flashing eyes, the sparkling conversation. Her dream had been an appealing picture, but nothing like the reality.

Nevertheless, she told herself firmly, despite any imagined disappointment, she was still on holiday, and with a most congenial and sympathetic friend. No doubt William would be a good friend too, if he could be nothing more. Determinedly, she turned her attention to the patch of green vegetables, over which she was attempting to secure a fine net so that they were protected from butterflies.

As she stood up to look at her work, Wordsworth called out to them across the garden. 'Look,' he said, pointing. Dorothy and Theodora both followed the line of his finger, their hands raised to shade their eyes from the early evening sun.

The house had a cornfield at the back with a lane which skirted around the edge of it. Diagonally across from where they were working was a gate, and standing behind the gate was the figure of a man. He waved vigorously to them. 'It's Coleridge,' said Wordsworth, sounding pleased.

'I'll go round to the front of the house to welcome him,' said Dorothy. Then, before she could do so and as they watched, the man vaulted over the gate, and came bounding towards them through the corn, his coat flying, his long, untidy dark curls dancing about his face. Theodora gasped. As an entrance, it was quite unforgettable.

'It is William's friend,' said Dorothy, catching hold of Theodora's hand.

'Wordsworth!' exclaimed Coleridge, a little out of breath as he reached them, and the two men clasped hands joyfully. It was the most animated that Theodora had ever seen her host, for he tended to be rather serious. After Wordsworth had greeted his visitor, he turned to introduce him to his sister and her friend.

Theodora was used to the classical, chiselled beauty of her brother and Lord

Ashbourne. Mr Samuel Taylor Coleridge was certainly not handsome in a conventional style. He was a big man, and, as Theodora soon discovered, almost always as untidy as he appeared at their first meeting. He had a wide mouth with thick lips, an unremarkable nose, and a broad brow with heavy eyebrows; but any deficiencies in his appearance were at once forgotten when he fixed his large, brilliant grey-blue eyes upon her. 'Dorothea and Theodora!' he exclaimed, his voice melodious with a light Devon accent. 'Great heavens! Light and dark; sunlight and moonlight; no, say rather, moonlight and starlight! Are you two different people, or simply two sides of the same coin?'

Dorothy made some laughing rejoinder, but Theodora could only stare at him, her heart beating rather fast. If William had been a disappointment to her, this man was surely the embodiment of all her dreams. She also judged him to be a little younger than Dorothy's brother — possibly no more than twenty-five or so.

'Never say you have walked the whole forty miles today, Coleridge,' said Wordsworth, catching hold of his friend's arm in order to lead him inside.

'No, I set off after preaching at Bridgwater yesterday morning,' the other man replied, his eyes sparkling. 'I love a solitary walk — do not you?' he said in general to the rest of the company. 'I find that the effect of nature is very soothing — it fills me with affection.'

'Oh that is a very bad omen,' Dorothy replied. 'You will certainly not want to walk with us, then.'

'You misunderstand me,' he declared. 'A walk with like-minded people will be a taste of heaven indeed. It is the company of those whose differences jar unspeakably that is hard to bear.'

'You must be thirsty, Coleridge,' said Wordsworth. 'Let's go in and take some refreshment.'

Theodora hung back, suddenly conscious of feeling a little out of place, which, since there were four of them altogether, ought not to have been the case. Coleridge turned his grey blue eyes upon her. 'Miss Theodora,' he said kindly. 'Come, take my arm. You have been overdoing things, I think.'

'No, sir, I am lame,' she responded, surprising herself with the matter-of-fact nature of her tone. 'I have been so since birth.'

'Really?' Coleridge said in an interested tone. 'One would not know it unless one was looking very carefully.'

'I wear special shoes,' Theodora told him, a

little shyly. 'My stepfather procured them for me. One is a little higher than the other.'

'Ingenious,' he remarked. 'I would like to examine them later, if you would permit it.'

This was a revelation to Theodora. She had always thought her disability very tiresome. Her usual experience of other people's reactions was that they tended to be embarrassed if anything. Others were careful not to take any notice at all. Nobody ever wanted to talk about it. Yet here was a man who found it interesting.

'You said that you were preaching yesterday,' she ventured. 'Are you then a clergyman, sir?'

'No,' he replied. 'That honourable calling is not mine, although I have considered it.'

'My brother is a clergyman,' she told him.

'Indeed.' He turned his blue eyes upon her again. 'I would be very interested to know how he balances the needs of his parishioners with his need to feed his own spirit.'

Theodora soon found that this was typical of the man. He seemed to be interested in everything, and there were very few subjects about which he knew nothing. On the contrary, his contributions tended to be informed and imaginative and Theodora felt that she could sit listening to him all day. The most remarkable revelation for her, was the difference in Wordsworth. With the arrival of his friend, he had become lively, his mood seemed lighter and his laughter rang out more. Yet Coleridge was a good listener too and only a very short time after his arrival, they were all gathered around Wordsworth as he recited a new poem.

After tea, it was Coleridge's turn, reading for them two and a half acts of his tragedy, *Osorio*. Theodora felt very privileged to be there with her sewing on her lap whilst Coleridge's powerful tones echoed around the parlour in which they sat. The evening was a fine one and the moon was full, but when the reading was finished, no mention was made of Mr Coleridge's departure. Eventually, Wordsworth said, 'You'll stay of course.'

'By your leave,' the other man answered smiling. 'We've barely touched on all the things I want to discuss with you, and I'm not expected back.'

Eventually, Theodora was obliged to take to her bed, her head nodding. The others wished her a polite 'good night', but it was plain that the conversation would continue for a good deal longer. Indeed, she had not been in bed for very long when she heard the back door open and, tiptoeing over to the window, she saw three figures stroll out into the garden, still talking animatedly.

She lay in bed for some time thinking before dropping off to sleep. Now, her thoughts were not of Wordsworth, but of his charismatic friend. How much more was he as she had imagined Dorothy's poet brother! Before she could spend any time weaving fantasies around him though, she told herself to be cautious. She had wasted enough time dreaming about William Wordsworth, and to no avail. For all she knew, Mr Coleridge might already have an attachment.

Instead of thinking about his compelling blue eyes and dark curls, therefore, she tried to think about her family members and decide what to give each one for their next birthday. It was while she was puzzling over whether to get Michael a book or a pin for his cravat that she fell asleep; but when she awoke, it was with the memory of Coleridge's expressive voice ringing in her ears.

★ ★ ★

Unsurprisingly, Theodora was the first to rise the next morning, and she entertained herself by playing with little Basil, who had been given his breakfast by the maid. Dorothy did not emerge until eleven o'clock. She did not offer an apology, simply saying, 'We talked

126

and walked half the night. William and Coleridge are just stirring, I think.'

Coleridge was the first of the men to come down, entering the room just as the maid was taking Basil away to have his napkin changed. 'A delightful child,' he remarked with a smile. 'He reminds me — ' He broke off as he caught sight of Theodora's copy of *A Vindication of the Rights of Woman*, which lay on the table next to where she had been sitting. She had brought it down with her so that she would have something to read if she was obliged to wait for the others. 'This is yours, Miss Buckleigh?'

'Yes, it is mine,' she answered a little tentatively. In her experience, people's responses to Mary Wollstonecraft's writings could sometimes be quite hostile.

'And what do you think of it?' he asked her.

His frank interest gave her courage. 'I find that she has very sensible things to say,' she said, her head held high. 'Women are capable of far more than being merely ornaments. They should not be treated like dolls.'

'You are very right,' Coleridge agreed. 'I cannot argue with the sense of what she says, but I find her writing disorganized. Did you meet her in London?'

Theodora shook her head. 'I did not have that honour,' she replied. 'Is she not married

127

now to Mr Godwin?'

'That is so. I know Godwin well, and have enjoyed many a lively argument with him. He professes himself to be an atheist, but I have no doubt that wiser counsels will sway him in the end.'

After both men had consumed a simple breakfast, Wordsworth read his play *The Borderers*, while the rest of them sat and listened, Coleridge on the edge of his seat, his eyes sparkling. 'Wonderful,' he declared, the reading over. 'Absolutely wonderful! There is a profundity of feeling in your work which is not often found, except in Shakespeare.'

Another day passed and yet another and still Coleridge did not leave. Indeed, he seemed to have no idea of doing so, and clearly neither Wordsworth nor Dorothy expected it of him. Every day, there would be a walk of some kind. Theodora knew from Dorothy's letters that she and her brother liked to walk for miles, and Coleridge's accomplishment of the thirty-six-mile walk from his cottage in Nether Stowey in two days gave an indication that his tastes were similar. Knowing that she would never be able to keep up, she made no attempt to do so, and instead would walk a short distance with them, with Basil's hand in hers, before turning back again.

It was Coleridge who, after this had happened the first time, took her hand and asked her earnestly whether she had felt left out. 'For,' he went on, 'I would not have you do so for the world.'

'Oh no,' she replied honestly, her heart fluttering at the sensation of her small hand resting in his large one. 'I am very used to my own company. It was kind of you to think of it, Mr Coleridge. If you tell me everything that you see when you come back, then I will feel included.'

'I will certainly do so, you may be sure,' he answered. He was as good as his word, throwing himself down on the grass next to her at the end of their excursion. 'We have walked about ten miles,' he told her. 'The sea is very blue today. The sea amazes me; does it not you?'

'I do not know the sea well,' Theodora answered. 'I have spent most of my life living far from it. It does intrigue me, I must confess.'

'Then we must take you!' he exclaimed. He thought for a moment. 'A donkey,' he declared. 'Dorothea, we must procure a donkey for Miss Buckleigh!' He turned to Theodora. 'What do you say, Miss Buckleigh; may I call you Theodora, and will you call me Coleridge?'

'Yes, of course,' Theodora answered, smiling. 'But please do not procure me a donkey! What a figure I should look! Instead, please carry on with what you were saying before. You were telling me about the sea, I think.'

'So I was.' He took a small leather-bound book out of his pocket. 'I carry a notebook with me always. I write in it anything that occurs to my mind. Such a variety of colour and shape,' he continued. 'And the movement so changeable, depending upon the proximity to the shore, the quantity of seaweed, or the presence of a vessel. There was a little boat far out, tossing about and creating little splashes of white.' He spoke for a little longer, describing the sea with such eloquence that Theodora had to put her sewing down and listen. His account was almost like a poem in itself.

That evening, the meal which was, as always, a simple repast, dragged on whilst the company around the table talked about all kinds of subjects, ranging from the political situation in France to the nesting habits of skylarks.

This proved to be the pattern over the days that followed. Often she and Dorothy simply sat at the table, their chins resting on their hands, as they listened to the lively discourse tossed to and fro between the two men.

On one occasion, they were talking about one of the later Roman emperors. This was a topic that Theodora had discussed with her father, and she joined in the conversation with enthusiasm. It was only when the topic was exhausted that she realized she had been speaking in Latin. Coleridge looked at her admiringly, and Wordsworth made some comment about her ready grasp of ancient Roman affairs. It was the first time since adulthood that she had been thankful for the rather odd education that she had received, and the first time that she had been commended for it. Most other young ladies thought her knowledgeability very odd, and scorned her because she did not speak Italian or paint in watercolours.

Theodora continued to find Coleridge fascinating and, as time went by, she began to acknowledge to herself, at first timidly than with increasing confidence, that she was falling in love with him. As to his feelings for her, she could not make a judgement. He was always very kind to her, but then he was kind to everyone, from herself and little Basil and Peggy the maid, to any chance met acquaintance. While this general benevolence stirred her admiration for him, it made her cautious about taking that last step and giving her heart completely. After all, he was no kinder to her than he was to Dorothy, with whom he was able to share many more interests and activities. Nevertheless she could not help hoping that he might be staying partly because of her.

She was not alone in her admiration of him. 'He is a wonderful man,' Dorothy told her. 'So good-tempered and cheerful, and so interested in everything.'

'I never tire of listening to him,' Theodora agreed. She was reminded of Mrs Trowbridge, whose conversation had sometimes had the effect of making her want to jump out of the coach and run screaming down the road. She shared this thought with her friend.

Dorothy laughed at this description. 'Coleridge's conversation is never like that,' she responded. 'He may talk a lot, but what he says is always full of interest and spirit.'

Theodora continued to write faithfully to Michael. For the first time, however, she was conscious of holding something back. She did not want to write so much about Coleridge as to make her brother suspicious about her preference for him, but she did mention her new friend's strong Christian faith, as she knew that this would be pleasing to the recipient.

Michael wrote back entertainingly, his

letters full of incidents from parish life, and news of the family. There was often a paragraph or two on the end from Evangeline. She also received letters from Jessie and Eustacia, and the occasional note from Ashbourne. The earl's communications were always franked, and she tried to conceal them from Coleridge and Wordsworth, who, as far as she could tell, seemed to have republican sympathies.

The letters that she received did not exactly have the effect of making her homesick, but she did think about her family a good deal. Playing with Basil brought back memories of Clare, Gabriel and Eustacia's daughter who would be of a similar age. It was after a game with the little boy, and while he was lying down for his nap, that Peggy came in to tell Theodora that some visitors had arrived. She laid aside the letter that she was writing to Michael and stood to receive them, wondering who they might be, for Dorothy and Wordsworth did not really mix with local people. Mr Kydd had promised to call but she had not really expected it, so she was surprised when he walked in with Miss Markham on his arm.

She was immediately struck by the contrast between Kydd's appearance and that of Coleridge and Wordsworth. Coleridge was inclined to be careless, even slovenly about his attire, whereas Wordsworth often looked neater although rather threadbare. Kydd, on the other hand, was impeccably presented for morning visiting in glossy boots, tan breeches and a dark-green coat.

Miss Markham was neatly if unimaginatively turned out in a walking gown of fawn with light brown embroidery around the hem. 'My dear Miss Buckleigh, I do hope that you will forgive the intrusion,' she said, smiling. 'The fact is that Alex is escorting me to visit some acquaintances in the area, and when he reminded me that you were staying here, I insisted that he make a slight detour.'

'I am very glad that he did,' Theodora replied, smiling in return. 'Do sit down and I will ask Peggy to bring us some tea. Have you been staying with your aunt all this time?'

Miss Markham nodded. 'She pressed me to do so,' she answered. 'I sometimes wonder whether she talks so much because she is lonely.'

'A strange irony if that were so, for when she does have company she does not give them a chance to get a word in,' Alex retorted.

'And have you been staying with Mrs Trowbridge as well?' Theodora asked, as Peggy came in answer to the bell. 'Tea, Peggy, please.'

'No,' he answered. 'I have been dealing with some business in Bristol. I'm now staying at the Bridgwater Arms. I generally make it my headquarters when I'm in the West Country.'

'And *I* always get reprimanded by my cousin in Bridgwater when you do not stay with her family,' Vivienne put in, with a smile.

'You know that I often have a number of visits to make and I do not want to be accused of making use of her,' replied Alex. 'I'm also hoping to take a little sea air before going back to London.'

'Some sea air; that sounds lovely,' said Theodora, causing Alex to look at her curiously. They were only a few miles away. How did it come about that her friends had not yet taken her to the coast?

They talked idly for a little longer, until Peggy came in with the tea. There were just three cups on the tray.

Alex frowned. 'Are you alone?' he asked, after the tea had been set down and Peggy had left the room.

'Yes,' replied Theodora as she poured. 'My friends are fond of long walks, but I am not able to walk so far, and I generally stay behind.'

'Indeed?' Kydd's voice was carefully neutral. 'Does this happen frequently?'

'Oh yes,' Theodora answered cheerfully. 'Sometimes they walk as much as fifteen miles in a day. That would be far too much for me.'

'In that case, I would have thought that it would have behoved them to take a shorter walk,' he said.

'Alex,' said Vivienne warningly.

'I do not see why,' said Theodora defensively.

'When a guest is invited to stay, it seems to me to be quite odd, to say the least, to disappear for a day's ramble, leaving her quite alone.'

'But I am not really alone,' Theodora objected. 'There is little Basil. He is only three, and I look after him while they are out.'

'I see. So you are not just neglected, you're being treated as a nursemaid as well.'

'Alex,' said Vivienne, this time in an exasperated tone. 'Really, it is none of your business. If Miss Buckleigh is quite happy, I do not know why you should have anything to say in the matter.'

'I do not wish to be rude,' said Theodora carefully, 'but we do not all need to have people dancing attendance upon us every minute of the day. I like my own company. I was well aware before I came that my hosts enjoyed long walks. Besides, I am not Mr and

136

Miss Wordsworth's only guest, and they have a duty to him as well as to me.'

'Very true,' Vivienne replied. 'Shall we change the subject? How are you enjoying the West Country?'

Apart from snorting 'What bit she's seen of it' as a muttered response to his fiancée's second question, Alex bore very little part in the next part of the conversation, instead strolling to the window and looking out at the garden in which Theodora worked with William and Dorothy, and played with Basil.

After a short time, however, he came and sat down with them, eventually saying when there was a lull in the conversation, 'You mentioned that there was another guest staying here, Miss Buckleigh.'

'Yes; the little boy called Basil,' put in Miss Markham. 'Were you not listening, Alex?'

It would have been so easy for Theodora to say nothing and allow Alex to think that there was no one else staying, but pride would not allow her to do so. 'Mr Wordsworth's friend Mr Coleridge is staying as well,' she said, putting up her chin. She could feel herself colouring a little, but it gave her a foolish feeling of pleasure just speaking his name.

'Coleridge!' exclaimed Alex, for once unable to hide his astonishment.

'You have heard of him,' said Theodora, surprised.

'Yes, I've heard of him,' replied Alex. 'I've read some articles that he has written.' His tone sounded a little grim. He got up again, walked over to the window once more, and stared across the garden, quite oblivious to the scene in front of his eyes. Coleridge's name had been one of those on the paper that the duke had given him. In fact, Coleridge was the one to whom he had referred as being clever. He had made a few enquiries in Bristol already. He would go back to see if he could discover anything more as soon as he had delivered Vivienne safely to her destination.

'I've heard of Mr Coleridge too,' put in Miss Markham. 'I am a little acquainted with his wife's family. They are from Bristol.'

'His wife's family?' faltered Theodora, unable to conceal her shock. Coleridge had not said anything about being married, and nor had the Wordsworths. Surely Miss Markham must be mistaken. The visitor's next words put paid to that hope.

'Yes, we have known the Fricker family for ever,' she said. 'I know Mrs Coleridge's sister Edith better, as she is nearer my age. She is married to Mr Southey, the poet. You seem surprised, Miss Buckleigh.'

138

'Yes,' she replied, desperate to recover herself. She glanced quickly towards the window, relieved to see that Alex appeared to be preoccupied. 'It . . . it is always surprising to me how small the world is. That you should know Mrs Coleridge is . . . is indeed extraordinary.'

It was not long after this that the visitors took their leave, and Theodora was free to go upstairs to her room. She had come to Dorset dreaming of William Wordsworth. Finding him to be quite different from her imaginings, she had turned from him, only to fall in love with Coleridge. Then one little phrase had been sufficient to cut up all her hopes.

If she closed her eyes, she could still hear Vivienne Markham's voice saying, 'His wife's family live in Bristol.' His wife's family. She thought about her feelings before and after that fatal moment. Before, she had been happy, in love, and full of hope. If only those words had not been said! But even if they had not been, it would not have altered the facts.

She sat on her bed, slow tears running down her cheeks. She thought of his kindness, his exuberance; the essentially lovable nature of the man. How easily she had responded to that! Now she discovered that it was not her privilege to do so, for he belonged to another. She had deliberately turned her thoughts away from Wordsworth when she had found out that he was not as unattached as she had supposed. Then Coleridge had appeared, utterly beyond her reach, and she had not discovered it until her affections were engaged. It really wasn't fair.

By the time the three others had returned from their walk she had had time to dry her tears, splash her face with cold water, and recover her complexion. True, she could feel her colour heightening at sight of Coleridge, but she was able to hide the reason for this by dropping something hastily, then picking it up again.

'Shall I tell you about our walk?' he asked her, his large eyes filled with warmth.

'Please do,' she answered. Her tone was less welcoming than before; she could not help it. He looked at her keenly, but made no reference to her changed manner, and gave her his description as usual.

As he turned from her to talk to Wordsworth and Dorothy, she wondered, not for the first time since Alex's visit, whether this man had deliberately deceived her. She could not believe it of him, but she wanted to subject him to a little test. When there was a lull in the conversation, she said, 'Does Mrs Coleridge not miss you? Will she not be anxious?'

He smiled, without the slightest hint of consciousness or guilt in his expression. 'Mrs Coleridge is used to my long walks,' he replied. 'Besides, she knew from the very first how much Wordsworth impressed me. She will not be surprised that I have chosen to spend more of my time with him. I told her that I might well do so.'

'She is surrounded by friends and acquaintances, is she not?' Dorothy put in. 'She would be quite dull here, I am sure.' Then, suddenly becoming aware of what she had said, she turned to Theodora. 'That is not to say that your company is dull of course, my dear Theodora. But we are a little isolated here. Coleridge lives in the heart of a village, do you not?'

Coleridge smiled reminiscently. 'Dear Stowey,' he replied. 'Sara has company there, which she sorely needs, having been brought up in the city. Her friend, Mrs Cruikshank has a little girl of about the same age as Hartley, our own son, so they have much to talk about.'

Theodora glanced surreptitiously at Dorothy and her brother. Neither of them seemed surprised by these disclosures. She could only conclude that they had been so well acquainted with the fact that Coleridge was a married man with a son that they had simply not bothered to mention it. Doubtless there may have been some talk about Mrs Coleridge and baby Hartley whilst the three of them were rambling in the hills.

Later, as she thought about the matter after she retired, she decided that she could acquit Coleridge of deliberate deceit. But how she wished that someone had told her! Had she known that he was a married man, she would never have allowed herself to dream about him. Now, she would have to put him out of her mind, and out of her heart; but that would be very difficult, when he was with them all the time. She turned her face into her pillow and, like many a lovelorn damsel before her, cried herself to sleep.

11

From wondering whether she could dare to show Coleridge how she felt about him, even in a modest way, Theodora was now desperate that he should not discover it. Previously, she had tried to find excuses to linger in his company. Now, she began to avoid him whenever possible. In some ways this was not difficult, for he, Wordsworth and Dorothy continued to enjoy their long rambles together. In others, it could be very hard indeed, for he was just as kind and communicative towards her as before. He was, moreover, a man who noticed a good deal. Sometimes she caught him looking at her a little curiously, and wondered whether he had guessed her secret. If he had, he never said anything to indicate that such was the case.

One bright sunny day, when the three of them had set off with fond good wishes and promises to bring her tokens of their walk, Peggy came out to the garden to tell Theodora that a gentleman had called.

'A gentleman? Did he give his name?'

'It's the same gentleman as came before

with the lady,' said Peggy. 'Him with the scar on his face.'

Theodora's thoughts had been a little melancholy that morning. From thinking about Coleridge and how he could never be hers, she had been remembering her loved ones at home, and missing them. The arrival of one who in some senses provided a link to Michael, Ashbourne and the others, could not help but be welcome. 'Alex!' she exclaimed, delighted, as he walked to her across the grass. Then she coloured as he reached her side. 'I beg your pardon,' she said in embarrassed tones. 'I should have said Mr Kydd, of course.'

'Not at all,' he answered, grinning. 'Together we have endured the extraordinary experience of Mrs Trowbridge's conversation. That ought to entitle us to use first names, surely.'

'But you did not endure it — at least, not as much as I did,' Theodora answered. 'You were riding.' She eyed him suspiciously. 'Was that why you offered to escort me — so that you would have an excuse to keep in the saddle the whole time?'

'You cannot expect me to answer that, surely,' he replied blandly. 'But talking of riding, I remember someone telling me that that is something you enjoy. I have taken the liberty of procuring a mount for you. I thought you might like to ride to the coast today. It cannot be much more than six miles if we take the back roads. I hope that that will not be too much for you.'

Theodora's eyes lit up. Coleridge's suggestion of a ride on a donkey had not been repeated and besides, she had not cared for the idea. Apart from the thought of being so conspicuous amongst a group of walkers, she had a recollection of having ridden a donkey once before and had found it very uncomfortable. A horse ride was a very different proposition, however. 'I should love it!' she declared. 'Is Miss Markham coming too?'

Alex shook his head. 'She is not a rider, so I knew that she would not care for it. But my groom is with me to play propriety.'

'Give me a quarter of an hour to change,' said Theodora, hurrying from the room.

If her pleasure had been keen at Alex's invitation, it was greatly increased when she saw the dainty grey mare who was to carry her on the expedition. 'She's beautiful,' she declared. 'Where did you get her?'

'I rode over from Bridgwater and paid a call on a squire living near Beaminster. Vivienne is acquainted with his family and I learned from her that his wife is expecting a child so cannot use her mare. He was glad to

145

lend the horse as she is short of exercise at present. Her name is Snowflake. May I help you into the saddle?'

The mare was as good-natured as she looked, and they were soon setting off towards the coast, with Alex's groom riding behind. 'Where are we going?' Theodora asked, after she had spent a little time savouring the pleasure of being in the saddle.

'I thought you might like to visit Lyme Regis,' said Alex. 'It's a pretty place, and is becoming popular for people to visit for their health. We could walk by the sea, and perhaps have something to eat in one of the inns by the quay. Then, if your courage and the weather hold out, I might have a surprise for you.' She smiled. 'You don't ask me what it is,' he added after a brief pause.

'You forget that I have a brother,' Theodora replied. 'I know the rules. You tell me that there is a surprise to come. I pester you to tell me what it is. You refuse to say and take delight in baiting me about it. I refuse to play the game.'

'Spoilsport!' he retorted, but he was grinning.

Theodora had spoken the truth when she had told her friends that she was perfectly content to be at home. Over long years, she had taught herself to be contented whatever her circumstances. Nevertheless, this did not mean that she could not enjoy unexpected treats, and she determined to relish this one to the full. She looked round at the countryside, not wanting to miss a thing. Coleridge tells me all about his walks, she thought to herself. I must tell him about my outing in return. Then suddenly she felt sad because she remembered that she ought to try not to enjoy his company so much. Instead, she would write it all down in a letter for Michael.

Alex, watching her, wondered what it was that had caused a shadow to cross her face. Then moments later, she was turning to him with a comment about the passing scenery and he wondered whether he had imagined it.

Lyme was a bustling town, its steep main street leading down to the sea which lay before them, blue and inviting. Alex watched Theodora carefully, unsure as to how she would manage her mount now that they were surrounded by noise and activity. She proved herself to be just as capable a horsewoman in a town as in the country however, and he soon relaxed again as they made their way to an inn on the waterfront. Graves stabled the horses for them, and Alex escorted Theodora onto the famous Cobb so that she could admire the sea at close quarters.

'It is wonderful,' she declared, her eyes shining. 'Truly beautiful. Mr Coleridge is right. One could never tire of looking at it.'

Alex glanced at her as she said Coleridge's name, and thought that she blushed. 'Very true,' he answered. 'It must be an anxious business to live here at the water's edge during a storm, though.'

'I had not thought of that,' she replied. 'Yes, you are right. But what a magnificent sight it must be. Have you ever been in a storm at sea?'

'Yes I have, and a very worrying affair it was too,' Alex replied. 'Our horses were tethered below and they were terrified.'

'They must have been,' Theodora responded, 'Poor beasts. I doubt they would ever want to go to sea again.'

'My own mount took some persuading,' Alex agreed ruefully.

After they had walked about a little, they returned to the inn, where they sat down to a delicious meal of freshly caught fish. Alex told Theodora something about his estate in Buckinghamshire, and in her turn, she told him about life at the vicarage with Michael and Evangeline. When eventually they put down their knives and forks, Alex said, 'And now for your surprise. Are you brave enough?'

'I cannot tell. Is it very daunting?'

'Come,' he said, getting up and putting out his hand.

She allowed him to lead her outside and down to the sea again, where a small boat was waiting. 'Alex?' she said, questioning.

'Get in,' he replied. 'It's all right. The boat is clean. I insisted upon it. You won't end up smelling of fish.' She did as she was bid with his assistance, and while she sat down on a cushion, and a fisherman held the boat steady, Alex took off his coat and his cravat. 'This will be warm work,' he said, as he got in, sat down and took up the oars.

The fisherman helped them to cast off, then stepped back with a farewell wave, and they were floating on the sea. It was a sensation quite unlike anything that Theodora had experienced before, and she sat thoughtfully, a little tense until she decided that she liked it.

'You're not going to be sick, are you?' Alex asked her, plying the oars as he got into his stride. 'If so, I'd be obliged if you'd do it over the side.'

'Sick? Oh no, no,' she answered, smiling as she began to relax. 'It's wonderful — beyond anything.' She put her hand down outside the boat in order to trail it in the water. 'It's cold,' she said.

He grinned. 'What did you expect?'

The sun was bright, almost dazzling as it sparkled on the water, and Theodora lifted her hand to shade her from the glare. As she did so, it brought the figure of Alex into sharp focus. He handled the oars like one who knew what he was doing. His movements were long and easy, achieving their steady passage through the water with an admirable economy of effort. The breeze tugged at his hair, ruffled the opening of his shirt around his throat, and moulded the sleeves to his arms, so that the contours of his muscles could be clearly seen. He must be very strong, she decided, then remembered that he was, for he had lifted her off her horse with the greatest of ease. Suddenly, she felt embarrassed at staring at him, and looked away hurriedly.

'Where are we going?' she asked him.

'I thought perhaps across to France?' he said. Then, as she looked back at him in surprise, he laughed, laying down the oars for a moment. 'Only teasing,' he said. 'We're just taking a little trip across the bay. It's quite safe. The wind and the tide are in our favour. The fisherman whose boat we're using is keeping an eye upon us from the shore. Do you like it out here, Theodora?'

'I love it,' she replied. 'It's so peaceful. It's

like being rocked in a great cradle.'

'Well don't fall asleep,' he warned her. 'Otherwise all my efforts will be in vain.'

'I shouldn't dream of doing so,' she replied. 'I don't want to miss a single minute. Where did you learn to row?'

'On the lake at Brambles,' he replied.

'Brambles?'

'My country estate. Vivienne's brother Peter and I used to row out together. Sometimes we persuaded Cook to pack us a picnic and we would row to the island and play at being pirates.'

'What, both of you? Theodora asked. 'Was not one of you a loyal member of the Royal Navy?'

'I'm afraid not,' he answered with mock regret. 'One of us was Red Beard and the other Black Beard. It was Vivienne who always had the unenviable task of representing law and order.'

'Unenviable? Surely not! Good must have triumphed in the end.'

He shook his head. 'Evil triumphed every time. I'm afraid that on one occasion, Red Beard even tied the Royal Navy to a tree on the island and left her there. It meant that Black Beard was obliged to row over to the rescue.'

'Oh no! How shocking!' Theodora exclaimed,

laughing. 'But I'm glad that your conscience awoke in the end.'

There was a short silence, during which Alex carefully avoided her gaze. 'Rowing on the sea is more testing than on the lake, I find,' he said eventually.

Theodora looked shocked. 'Alex, you didn't!'

'I must confess that I did,' he said ruefully. 'Peter was a good brother. I was a little horror, I'm afraid.'

She looked around. 'There aren't any islands around here, are there?'

He roared with laughter and picked up the oars. 'Nary a one — I promise.'

'Poor Miss Markham,' said Theodora. 'You are very fortunate that she forgave you sufficiently to consent to marry you.'

There was a short pause before he spoke. 'Fortunate indeed,' he agreed.

After he had rowed in silence for a time, Theodora said, 'Do you miss him?'

He looked at her sharply. She was the first person to ask him that question. 'Peter? Yes, very much.'

The only time when he and Peter had been less than inseparable had been after university when they had both become enamoured of the same young lady, and for a time were good-natured rivals for her hand. When she accepted Alex's proposal, Peter had offered his congratulations with a good grace. Nevertheless, it was perhaps not surprising that he had put a little distance between himself and the happy couple. Even so, when Peter had told Alex of his wish to join the army, it was only to discover that Alex had already made the same decision.

They had fought side by side until one day when an enemy bullet had picked Peter off as the two of them were returning from a reconnaissance mission. After that, although Alex had continued to do his duty, he had no longer relished the occupation. The wound he had sustained, together with his father's death and the need to look to his estate, had provided him with a reason for leaving; but in truth, he was glad to be done with soldiering.

Squire and Mrs Markham, deprived of their only son, had clung to Alex, as did Vivienne herself. Together, the two of them had explored the haunts of their childhood as he was recuperating. Alex's fiancée, repelled by his injury, had found an excuse to end the engagement. It was Vivienne whose friendship had sustained him through that difficult experience. They had relived times spent with Peter, laughed at memories, and comforted each other. Inevitably, it had seemed only sensible to take the next step of getting engaged. It was a decision that had delighted Vivienne's parents and Alex's mother too. The rest of the family had appeared to be similarly pleased with the arrangement. Sometimes Alex wondered — severely chastising himself the while — whether he was the least delighted of all.

All this was going through his mind as he rowed for shore in silence. To his surprise, he discovered that they were almost back where they had started without his being aware of the journey. He looked at Theodora, who had simply sat in the boat, allowing him to have his own thoughts. It occurred to him that she was a very restful person.

'Was my surprise worth waiting for?' he asked her, after they had returned the boat to its owner, and Alex had put his coat back on.

'Beyond anything,' she replied, turning a glowing face towards him. 'What a lot I shall have to tell my friends this evening. Usually, they are the ones with all the news, and I have very little to say.'

'Indeed,' Alex responded. Then, because he felt that he had been a little uncommunicative he added, 'Is Mr Coleridge staying for long?'

'I . . . ' It was on the tip of Theodora's tongue to say that she hoped so. Then realizing that this would be an improper expression, she said 'I do not know. He and

William have much to discuss.' Suddenly, her eye was caught by some large sea birds swooping and diving. 'Oh Alex, look,' she said, pointing.

He allowed his attention to be diverted, but there was a slightly grim set about his mouth as they returned to the inn. She seemed to him to be showing a greater interest in a married man than he really liked; but he was not sure that he could do anything about it.

12

'Theodora, Coleridge has had the most splendid plan,' Dorothy told her one morning, a short time later. 'He is to return to Nether Stowey, but he and William do not want to be apart, so we are all to go and stay with him in his cottage in Lime Street. Will not that be delightful?'

'Will there be space?' Theodora asked doubtfully. 'How will Mrs Coleridge manage? They have a baby too, remember.'

'Oh, there will be space enough,' Dorothy answered optimistically. 'You and I can share, after all.'

On receiving this news, Theodora decided, a responsible guest would say that she would leave straight away. A sensible girl who wanted to cure herself from an infatuation would do the same. She could only conclude that she was neither responsible nor sensible, for she wanted to stay. After all, she told herself, a strong dose of reality would be good for her. To see Mrs Coleridge in company with her husband might be the means of affecting a cure from her malady.

Coleridge himself was in a state of high

156

excitement amounting almost to exhilaration at the thought of welcoming his friends into his home. Theodora ventured to suggest to him that his quarters might be a little cramped, especially in view of the fact that he had invited two other gentlemen to join them, but was only sure of the acceptance of one.

'Cramped? Say cosy, rather,' he replied, his large blue eyes alight with the infectious enthusiasm that was characteristic of him. They were sitting outside in the garden, where he had been reading some of his poems to Theodora and Dorothy. Dorothy had just stepped inside as she had heard someone arriving at the front of the house. Coleridge looked about him. 'Anyway, it is the summer and we will be spending the best part of every day out of doors. Besides, I really could not endure to part from my newest friends for one moment longer than necessary.'

Theodora knew that he meant William and Dorothy in particular, but she could not help her heart giving a guilty little skip of pleasure. 'You are very kind,' she answered.

'Merely truthful,' he responded, grinning. Then he added more seriously, 'Wordsworth is the greatest man I know.'

'Even including yourself?' she asked, half-teasing him, half surprised. By now, she knew that Coleridge was well known as a poet and a journalist, whereas Wordsworth had barely begun to make his mark.

'He makes me feel small,' he said simply.

The sound of footsteps made Theodora look round, to see Alex Kydd approaching them across the grass. There looked to be a slight frown on his face, but that might just have been the effect of the sun slanting through the branches, for when he drew closer, Theodora could see that he was smiling.

'Mr Coleridge,' said Kydd, greeting the other man after Theodora had introduced them. 'I have read some of your work and am intrigued to meet the man in person.'

'You are very good,' Coleridge replied. 'I would be interested to hear what you have read.'

Kydd bent and picked up the book that Coleridge had laid down on the grass. 'Your *Poems Upon Various Subjects* I found very pleasing, for the most part. I have come back to some of them again on more than one occasion.' He paused. 'Your political views I find less congenial, I confess.'

'In what respect, sir?' Coleridge asked him, obviously intrigued and not noticeably annoyed.

'I agree that war is undesirable; but war

158

with France, I fear, is, and always has been, unavoidable. Your criticism of Pitt is very harsh; he is our best chance.'

'Our best chance of what, sir?' Coleridge asked, his eye kindling. 'Of seeing the poor suffer more than they do already?'

'The suffering would be far greater, surely, if we turned away from the blood-bath that France has become, and allowed ourselves to be sucked into it through failure to act.'

'It's an odd line of reasoning that seeks to avoid one blood-bath by plunging the country into another,' Coleridge remarked.

'Oh please, don't argue,' Theodora implored. Both men looked at her with surprised expressions on their faces.

At this point, Dorothy reappeared with a tray with glasses and wine. Kydd turned back to Coleridge. 'I have only just met you, sir. I come in peace, and I have no intention of quarrelling with you in another man's garden.'

Coleridge grinned. 'I relish honest debate, and would enjoy talking with you more on this subject; but our vigour is alarming the lady, I think.'

'I do find confrontation alarming, I confess,' she admitted.

'I suspect that we were both brought up on school and university debating societies,' said Kydd.

'Indeed,' the other man agreed.

'You are fortunate to find us still here,' said Dorothy cheerfully, as she poured the wine. 'We will shortly be removing to Nether Stowey to stay with Coleridge.'

'Then I come in a good hour,' replied Kydd, taking a glass to Theodora before receiving one himself. 'I am due to return to London shortly. I will be able to escort Miss Theodora back to her family.'

'But she must not leave us so soon,' Dorothy protested. 'She has been with us for a bare three weeks — no time at all.'

'Indeed, we should be very sorry to see her go,' Coleridge agreed. He smiled at Theodora. 'Dorothea's other half,' he added.

'But her family will be glad to see her again,' Kydd pointed out. 'How soon can you be ready to go, ma'am?'

Theodora looked at him incredulously. The day when they had gone to Lyme and enjoyed such camaraderie might as well never have happened. It seemed as if he had already decided that she should leave, without even asking her how she felt about the matter. Really, it could not be borne! He would be marching her up to her room to supervise her packing in a moment. She opened her mouth to object, but before she could say anything, William Wordsworth approached them across the grass, smiling his rare smile.

'Forgive me,' he said, when he had been introduced to Alex. 'My mode of composition sometimes requires solitude.'

The conversation became general, and the possibility of Theodora's leaving was not referred to again, but she was itching to speak to Kydd and give him a piece of her mind. How dare he make such assumptions? He knew Michael, it was true, and he had escorted her here. He had shown her a good deal of kindness on more than one occasion. The day when he had brought Snowflake for her to ride, and taken her to the sea was a case in point. But just because he had put himself out for her, he must not think that he could lord it over her. She was so vexed that she could barely keep up with the conversation.

As for Kydd, had he been asked, he would have been at a loss to explain his feelings at this moment. On one level, his decision to return to Racedown had been a calculated political act. From the moment when he had realized that Samuel Taylor Coleridge was a guest there, he had determined to find out more about his activities.

He had certainly read some of Coleridge's poetry, but he had also heard of his political involvement. Like many, Coleridge had initially been a supporter of the French Revolution. That was not in itself alarming: Alex could have given a list of a dozen others of his own acquaintance who had felt the same. True, there was no indication that Coleridge still actively supported it now that it had become a blood-bath, but he had certainly been very active in radical circles in Bristol. Not only that, but he had the kind of silver-tongued eloquence that could easily sway others. He did appear to have largely withdrawn from public life, but his work was widely read and his influence large. A second reading of one of the issues of *The Watchman*, a publication for which Coleridge had been responsible had confirmed Alex's fears.

If that had been all, it would have been bad enough, but there was more. Wordsworth, too, had been involved in similar activities and was regarded locally with some suspicion. Alex had also discovered, after some enquiries, that Coleridge and Wordsworth had met in Bristol, that cauldron of political debate. The Duke of Portland would certainly want to know whether either of these two highly intelligent young men was still connected with the corresponding societies in Bristol.

Satisfying the curiosity of the Duke of

Portland was not the only reason for his concern. He was also anxious about Theodora. He doubted very much whether Michael would want his sister associated with a radical group. She could so easily become embroiled in all kinds of turmoil, and, whilst remaining wholly innocent, have her reputation irredeemably blackened.

He had told himself that it had been partly to make sure of her innocence that he had invited her to go out with him for the day. If he were honest, however, he would have been obliged to admit that only a very small part of his mind had ever considered that she might be anything other than innocent. The truth was that it had troubled him to discover that her host and hostess were going out regularly and leaving her behind. She had not appeared to object to it, but that was beside the point. Her friends should not be so negligent. Then when he had escorted her to Lyme and taken her out in the boat, it had warmed his heart to see her face alight with laughter. That particular joyful look would be one that her friends would surely never see if they were so prone to leaving her behind.

He had smiled as he had arrived at Racedown, remembering that glowing look on her face. The first thing that he had seen as he had entered the garden had been

Theodora in intimate conversation with Coleridge, her happy face turned up to his. One look at her expression told Alex that she fancied herself in love with the charismatic young poet. He, Alex, had taken her all the way to Lyme to make her happy. All Coleridge had to do was look into her eyes.

As he had approached them across the grass, his mood had been one of fury, together with surprise that Theodora should be so besotted. The man was not classically handsome after all. What was more, a woman accustomed to the company of the immaculately presented Lord Ashbourne could not help but find Coleridge careless to say the least, although it could not be denied that the latter had a certain earthy sensuality.

By the time they had all sat together and shared in conversation, Alex was both more fearful for Theodora, and more understanding of her feelings. Coleridge was a fascinating man, humorous, quick-witted, and wide-ranging in his interests. Even Alex could see that. What was more, unlike some clever men, he did not give the impression of simply waiting for someone else to finish their sentence so that he could make his own contribution. On the contrary, he listened to whoever was speaking, fixing his large blue eyes upon them, weighing their views and amending his response according to what had been said.

There could not be any doubt about it. A good friend of Theodora Buckleigh would get her out of this heady company as soon as possible. Alex might not be a friend of very long standing, but he hoped that he had her best interests at heart. What was more, his acquaintance with Michael put him under some sort of obligation. He had no doubt concerning what Michael would wish him to do; hence his suggestion that she should leave.

There was a slight lull in the conversation. Alex saw Coleridge's perceptive gaze upon him. The younger man said, getting to his feet, 'I've a sudden fancy to go and look at the sea. Would anyone like to come with me?' Almost inevitably, Dorothy and her brother both agreed to go, and before long, Theodora was alone with Alex.

He opened his mouth to tell her that she ought to return to London, but before he could say anything, she spoke first. 'I have been meaning to thank you again for taking me to Lyme,' she said, spiking his guns. 'On occasions such as today, when my friends walk to the sea, I can picture in my mind where they may be going. That is thanks to you.'

'It was a pleasure,' he replied honestly. Then, because he considered the matter to be so important, he said, 'Are you quite sure that I cannot persuade you to come to London with me?'

'No, thank you,' Theodora replied politely, taking up her sewing. She was sorely tempted to pick up Coleridge's volume of poetry, which he had left on the grass, but she decided that that would be too provocative.

Alex was determined not to lose his temper with her. 'There would be certain advantages in such a course of action,' he pointed out carefully. 'It would mean that you would be able to join Lord and Lady Ashbourne, and spend some of the summer with them.'

'I am in regular contact with my step-papa, and am aware of the advantages,' she replied.

There was a short silence. 'But despite those advantages, you will not come with me?' he questioned.

'I have already said that I will not,' she answered.

He paused, yet again weighing his words. 'Theodora, you have not thought carefully enough about this,' he said, perhaps not wisely. 'Have you any idea how small Mr Coleridge's cottage is?'

She coloured a little at Coleridge's name.

'If he does not care, then I do not see why you should,' she retorted.

'He may not care, but what of his wife?' he said swiftly.

'What are you implying, sir?' she asked him, drawing her brows together.

'Nothing; I am implying nothing,' he said, running his hand through his hair. This interview was not going as he had either planned or hoped. 'It is simply that there will be much work cast upon her by extra visitors.'

'Then the visitors will have to help, will they not? Besides, I have accepted Coleridge's invitation now. It would be rude to go back on my word.'

His brow darkened. 'I see that you use his name without any title in front,' he remarked coldly.

'He has asked me to do so,' Theodora answered. 'He is my friend.'

'Am I not your friend too?'

She hesitated. 'I don't know,' she said at last, looking at him suspiciously. 'I thought that you were. If you were truly my friend, though, would you challenge all my motives and question my decisions?'

'Sometimes those are things that only a true friend can do,' he replied. There were other things that he would have liked to say to her; things about Coleridge's political involvement, and warnings about becoming too fond of a married man, but he held his tongue. He had a feeling that anything that he might say on that score would only arouse her antagonism. Better by far to let things be for now. If they parted on good terms, it would be easier for him to visit her later, and see how she was getting on. Already, he was thinking in terms of putting off his return to London. A brief note to the Duke of Portland for the time being would let him know how things stood.

He smiled ruefully. 'Enough of that for now. I can see that you do not intend to return to London just yet. In that case, may I wish you a pleasant stay at Nether Stowey? The countryside around there is very lovely, and should please you, I think.'

Theodora had braced herself for further opposition, and his sudden acceptance of her decision both pleased and disturbed her. 'Thank you,' she said cautiously. Then she added in a suspicious tone, 'You are not going to write and tell Step-papa or Michael to bring me home, are you?'

'I wouldn't dream of doing anything so presumptuous,' he said with a laugh. 'But if I may presume in another way, may I write to you and let you know my plans?'

'If you are sure that Miss Markham will not mind,' she said.

'No — no, of course she will not,' he replied. For the space of that conversation he had forgotten Vivienne completely.

★ ★ ★

He rode to Taunton in a very unsettled frame of mind. He could not remember when he had been so worried about anyone before. No, perhaps worried was the wrong word: call it concerned. He did not have a sister of his own, and he supposed that this feeling must be because she was Michael's sister. In his absence he felt a certain brotherly responsibility for her.

Yet if she had been his sister, he could have insisted on her compliance. As it was, his hands were tied. He could not imagine that she would cast her reputation to the winds and settle for an irregular arrangement with Coleridge, even if the man were to offer such a thing, which seemed unlikely. Nevertheless, he could see only heartbreak ahead of her, and there was nothing that he could do to prevent it. He found that it grieved him to think of her suffering in that way.

He was still thinking deeply about the matter when he arrived at Mrs Trowbridge's house in Taunton, where he was engaged to dine. To his surprise, both the ladies were out. 'Do you know where your mistress has gone?' he asked the butler.

'I believe the ladies have gone on a party of pleasure with Lady Martyn,' the butler replied.

Alex struck his forehead. 'God Almighty! I should have been there too! I meant to be back but, well, events overtook me. Were they very angry, Jones?'

'The ladies were a little perturbed, sir,' the butler admitted.

Alex grinned reluctantly. 'I'll bet they were. No idea where they've gone, I suppose? No, don't tell me,' he went on quickly. 'Tell them' — he took out some coins and pressed them into the butler's hand — 'I got back when it was too late to join them. It probably is now, I should think.'

'Almost certainly, sir,' replied the butler. 'Shall I get you a glass of sherry?'

The ladies returned from their outing shortly before it was time to get changed for dinner. To his surprise, of the two, Mrs Trowbridge appeared to be the more annoyed. 'Really, it is too bad of you, Alex,' she said irritably. 'You put dear Vivienne in an exceedingly awkward position. We had no idea where you were or what had detained you. It was very difficult to make your excuses.'

'I am sorry,' he responded. 'I had another call to make earlier on, and some business arose which had to be dealt with immediately.'

'What business?' Mrs Trowbridge asked.

Before he could speak, Vivienne said tranquilly, 'Alex does not have to account for his movements, Aunt. I am sure that he must have had very good reasons for his absence.'

Perversely, now that he had been excused from explaining himself, Alex felt a strong urge to do so. 'I had a conversation with a member of the government before leaving London,' he said. 'He had some concerns about the safety of the realm. My business was connected with those concerns.'

'Safety of the realm! Good heavens! Never say that there is a threat of invasion!' Mrs Trowbridge cried, her hand at her throat.

'Not to my knowledge,' Alex answered, smiling faintly.

'Well I am glad that that is settled,' answered Vivienne. 'You are forgiven, Alex. But if you have to attend to any more vital business that clashes with an engagement, do you think that you might contrive to inform me beforehand?'

'I will endeavour to do so,' he answered, feeling that he had got away with his misdemeanour very lightly, but at the same time unaccountably annoyed with her for accepting his excuses so placidly.

13

Although the inhabitants of Racedown were only supposed to be going to stay with Coleridge on a temporary basis, Theodora gained the distinct impression that Dorothy was not expecting to return. 'William wants to be closer to Coleridge, so we may well look round for a property that is nearer to Nether Stowey,' she explained. The two women were sitting on a rug on the grass playing with Basil.

'It will be hard to find another property upon such advantageous terms,' Theodora suggested.

Dorothy nodded. The house at Racedown had been loaned to them rent free by a family named Pinney. 'I know,' she said. 'But William must be able to consult Coleridge at this time.'

'They seem to work well together,' Theodora agreed. The two women looked towards the spot under the trees where until very recently, there had been a table set out with a chair at either end. On the table would have been pens, ink, and papers spilling onto the ground. There, the two men had worked.

At times, the scratching of pens would be heard, then a little conversation, and occasionally, a burst of laughter, generally begun by Coleridge, in which Wordsworth, in his quieter way, would eventually join.

Dorothy smiled at this memory. 'I do not know anyone who is able to make William laugh as Coleridge does,' she said. 'I think that they are good for each other. That benefit is surely more important than any financial consideration.'

After Coleridge had gone back to Nether Stowey, taking William with him, the house seemed very quiet. Dorothy still went walking, but not to the same extent, and it was therefore pleasant to spend a little more time with her, to talk about all kinds of subjects, and to enjoy afresh Dorothy's ability to notice the detail in what was happening around her. Theodora decided that it was good for her to have this reminder that it had been her correspondence with Dorothy that had drawn her here in the first place. She still loved Coleridge, although she was trying to teach herself to think of him in a different way; but she must not be so obsessed by him that she neglected this first valuable friendship.

Two days after the men had gone to Nether Stowey, Dorothy went out early and came back with the post, including two items of correspondence for Theodora. As she handed them over, Dorothy glanced at one of them and said, 'It's from Coleridge.'

'Coleridge?' exclaimed Theodora, colouring. 'But why should he write to me?'

'He has written to both of us,' Dorothy replied, showing her own letter, which was clearly in the same hand.

Had anyone consulted Theodora's wishes, she would have said that she would much prefer to read her letters in private. She knew Dorothy and William's habits, however, and was used to the way in which they shared information from their correspondence. She was not surprised, therefore, when Dorothy opened one of her own letters then and there and began to read.

Following her example, she put the one from Coleridge to one side, and opened the other first. She did not recognize the handwriting and was a little surprised when on looking at the signature she discovered that it was from Alex Kydd. It was true that he had promised to write, but she had not been sure that he would do so. Her mind immediately went back to their last conversation, when he had attempted to persuade her to leave Racedown. Would this letter be more of the same?

To her relief, it was nothing of the sort. It was simply a friendly communication, giving an entertaining account of a chance encounter upon the road, followed by a prank that he and Michael had got up to at university. To her surprise, he seemed to be writing from Bristol, whereas he had definitely said that he would be going to London. Why had he changed his mind? For one, nasty unworthy moment, she wondered whether he was planning to spy on her, then report to Michael, but she dismissed this idea almost immediately. Surely he would never stoop to such grubby tricks. Besides, she was in regular correspondence with Michael, and told him all her news.

There was a little more information about some of his own social activities before Alex closed with good wishes for her continued happiness, signing with his Christian name. It was a kind and interesting letter. She thought about the information that he had disclosed on their journey down here, about his having no family, apart from his mother. Of course he would soon have Miss Markham as part of his family, together with her relations. She found this a curiously depressing thought, and concluded that this must be because it seemed to be such an unromantic match. He deserved better, and so did Miss Markham, of course.

She reflected upon her own situation. Had Michael not found his father, and thus bestowed upon her a substantial number of relatives, she would now be alone in the world, save for him. How fortunate she was! She felt a little ashamed now of being so irritated at the protectiveness of her male relatives. How quickly she had begun to take them all for granted!

To her surprise, Theodora found that a tear was running down her cheek. Suddenly, she was missing Michael too. She wondered suspiciously whether Alex had mentioned her brother to remind her of the home that was so far away. She refused to be sorry about her decision to remain in the West Country. This adventure had opened up her world and brought her new friendships that she would not have missed for anything.

With this thought in her mind, she picked up the letter from Coleridge. As she turned it over in her hands, she could feel her heartbeat quickening. He had touched this very piece of paper. He had written her a personal note, and however brief it might be, it was from him to her. He must like her if he had written to her so quickly!

Sternly, she quenched this idea. How dare she think of him in this kind of way? He was a married man, and not for her. Perhaps, to avoid temptation, she ought to tear his letter in pieces? But Dorothy would be sure to ask why she had done something so inexplicable and peculiar.

In the event, there was nothing in his letter that might not be read by anyone else. He had copied out one of his poems, *To an Infant*, which she had particularly admired and, perhaps because of the subject matter, had made some comments upon a scene of children at play that he had witnessed on one of his walks. He also gave her the news that his brother-in-law, Robert Southey, had had some poems published. She put the letter down. Now that she thought about the matter, she remembered that he had mentioned Southey early on in their acquaintance. He might even have referred to him as his relative by marriage. All the signs that Coleridge was a married man had been there. She simply had not wanted to see them.

As anticipated, Dorothy was eager to share her correspondence. In his letter to her, Coleridge had written of his hopes that they would soon be able to settle permanently near to where he was living. 'He is keeping his eyes open for somewhere suitable,' she disclosed.

After a short pause, Theodora said,

'Dorothy, are you sure that you want me to stay? I have been thinking about what Mr Kydd said, and I am wondering whether perhaps I will be a nuisance when you go to Stowey.'

'Good heavens, no,' Dorothy responded without hesitation, leaning forward to clasp her hand. 'How can you even think it? I love having you with me, Theodora. But I think that you might be well advised to pack all your things as I don't believe that we will be coming back here.'

★ ★ ★

By the second of July, they were all settled in Coleridge's cottage. Coleridge himself had collected Dorothy and Theodora in a gig, which took them over forty miles of very bumpy and uncomfortable roads. Peggy and Basil were to join them later, when the Wordsworths had found somewhere suitable to settle near Stowey.

The journey was agony to Theodora, despite the bittersweet pleasure of being so close to Coleridge, who appeared to be a competent whip. She nobly resisted saying anything about her sufferings, as her two companions were in such high spirits at the prospect of being together again under one roof. She could not help remembering how much more comfortable a similarly rough road had been when Alex had had the responsibility for the ordering of her journey. Of course the chaise had been much better sprung than the gig.

Coleridge's cottage was on the outskirts of the village of Nether Stowey, facing a cider house. From the outside, after the spaciousness of Racedown, it looked to be very cramped.

As they arrived at the door a pretty young woman of about Coleridge's own age, with an excellent figure and a head of plentiful dark hair, appeared in the doorway. She looked pleased to see them but, Theodora thought, a little harassed.

'Samuel,' she said, as Coleridge got down and turned to help his passengers alight. 'Your friend Mr Wordsworth went out earlier, but he is now here.'

'Splendid,' Coleridge answered, as he set Dorothy on her feet. He then turned to help Theodora down, but, as he set her on the ground, her hip gave way and she cried out. 'Theodora, my dear,' he exclaimed, catching hold of her waist. He turned to his wife. 'My love,' he said, leaning over to kiss her briefly on the cheek, whilst still holding on to Theodora.

'One of these ladies must be Miss Wordsworth I suppose,' said Mrs Coleridge, smiling at her two visitors with something less than complete delight.

'I'm Dorothy Wordsworth,' answered that lady, her eyes sparkling. 'This is my friend, Theodora Buckleigh.'

'Miss Buckleigh,' said Mrs Coleridge.

Suddenly, it occurred to Theodora that Coleridge might not have told his wife about herself. She coloured, and stepped away from his supporting arm. 'Pray forgive me, Mrs Coleridge,' she said in her soft voice. 'I don't think that you were expecting me. I do not want to be an imposition upon you.'

'Nonsense!' Coleridge exclaimed. 'None of our friends is or can be an imposition. Just an extra blessing — eh, my love?' He put his arm around his wife's waist and gave her a little squeeze.

The lady grinned reluctantly in response. 'Your other blessing is in the garden,' she said. He hurried away around the side of the house, whilst the lad who had run out from the back garden took charge of the gig.

Sara Coleridge turned to Dorothy and Theodora. 'You will want to see your room, I expect,' she said. 'I'll have to put you in together, I'm afraid. We have only three bedrooms, you see.' She looked momentarily anxious. 'You don't have servants expecting a bed, do you?'

Dorothy laughed. 'Do we look as if we can afford servants?' she asked. 'I think I'll go straight round into the garden and see my brother, if you don't mind.'

'Please, do treat my house as your own,' Mrs Coleridge responded. The words and tone were cordial, but the expression, as Dorothy left them, less so.

Anxious to make some kind of amends by showing an interest in the arrangements that had been made, Theodora said, 'I would very much like to see the room that you have prepared.'

'Do come this way, then, Miss Buckleigh.' Theodora took a few steps, and immediately Mrs Coleridge noted her halting gait. 'Have you injured yourself during the journey — a touch of cramp, perhaps?'

'No, I have had a limp from childhood. Journeys over rough roads such as today's take their toll, I'm afraid.'

'Oh, I see,' responded Sara, her manner imperceptibly more cordial. Theodora wondered whether Mrs Coleridge had suspected her of flirting with her husband and was at once very glad that she could have no idea of her guest's fondness for him.

Stepping indoors did nothing to alter

Theodora's first impression of the cottage. They walked through the front door into a narrow passage, with doors to right and left. Mrs Coleridge opened the door on the right to reveal a parlour, with a window which looked out onto a yard at the back. 'If Samuel takes it into his head to invite anyone else, they'll have to sleep in here,' she remarked. Fortunately, since Theodora could not think of anything to say in response to this, she did not seem to expect an answer. Sara then opened the door on the other side of the passage, and invited Theodora to go in. 'We dine here,' she said. 'This is also the way upstairs. I dare say you are used to much more spacious accommodation, Miss Buckleigh.'

Deciding that it would not be tactful to mention Ashbourne Abbey, or the earl's town house, she said, 'My brother's vicarage is certainly larger, but the cottage where I lived with him for a time when he was a curate was smaller than this.'

'Samuel is a man of so many gifts,' said his wife, as she led Theodora through the small parlour and up the stairs at the other side of it. 'He could easily occupy a position in the church, I think. But he cannot seem to settle to anything definite.' There were three doors at the top of the stairs, and Mrs Coleridge opened one of them. 'You and Miss Wordsworth can sleep in here,' she said. 'I hope you don't mind sharing a bed. Fortunately it's a large one.'

'I'm not sure what has happened to my things,' Theodora ventured.

'I'll ask Samuel to bring them up.'

Theodora was about to thank Mrs Coleridge again, when a little cry was heard, proceeding from one of the other rooms. Sara's expression softened. 'That'll be Hartley waking up,' she said. 'His father will be glad to see him, no doubt.' She opened the door to the bedroom, and walked over to a small crib. 'So you are awake now, my precious,' she said, picking up the baby. 'Come to Mama, then.'

'How old is he?' Theodora asked.

'Just over nine months,' Sara answered. 'Is he not beautiful?'

'Yes indeed,' Theodora responded readily. She thought that the baby might have a little look of his father, but she could not be sure.

'I'll go down with the baby,' said Sara. 'Come when you're ready.'

Theodora went back into the room that had been assigned to herself and Dorothy. There was very little other furniture in the room apart from the bed, which was, Theodora decided, just as well, as the room was rather small. It was certainly a good thing that they did not have to find room for a bed for Basil as well. One modest chest of drawers was provided for their clothes. Fortunately, neither of them had a great deal to put in it. She wondered fleetingly how her sister-in-law Evangeline would have managed in these circumstances, with her profusion of fashionable clothes, and was obliged to smile.

★   ★   ★

Three days later, they had settled into some sort of a routine. Every day, there was a long walk, sometimes including Sara, but always involving Dorothy, Wordsworth and Coleridge. There would be meetings and conversations with their neighbour and friend, Thomas Poole, whose book-room often provided a refuge for the two men. There would be noisy conversations over the table, and busy writing sessions. Frequently, Dorothy and Coleridge would be found poring over a draft of a poem, or some notes that she had taken. And in the midst of it, Sara would be working hard to keep the household together and ensure that everyone was fed.

As Theodora walked back from the village after undertaking a small errand, she thought about the day when Coleridge had arrived at Racedown to bring them to Stowey. She remembered how her heartbeat had quickened as he had come bounding in, his face full of delight. She had done her best to quell this feeling, but it was very hard when she found him so engaging.

She thought about her hostess. She was clearly a practical woman, with a lot to do. Even though there was a girl who came in to help, extra guests, particularly those who were not expected, inevitably cast a good deal upon her. Of course, the house was Coleridge's too, and he was surely entitled to invite his friends. Nevertheless, looking at Mrs Coleridge and how his activities caused more work for her, Theodora could not help thinking, with a twinge of guilt at her disloyalty, that at times he must be a very exasperating husband.

She entered the cottage and made her way down the passage. She could hear voices coming from the kitchen, which was at the end of the corridor, so she walked towards the open door.

The room had two occupants, namely Coleridge and his wife. Mrs Coleridge appeared to be busy at the fireplace, and her husband was sitting nearby. They seemed to be engaged in animated conversation.

'I beg your pardon,' said Theodora diffidently. Sara turned, a pan in her hand, Coleridge stood courteously and somehow the two collided. Then he let out a great shout as the boiling hot contents of the pan cascaded onto his foot.

14

'This is deucedly tiresome,' said Coleridge fretfully, not for the first time. Theodora was sitting with him in the back garden of his cottage; or, more accurately, the portion of the back garden which adjoined that of his friend and neighbour, Thomas Poole. Coleridge sat with his bandaged foot resting on a stool. A low table at his elbow, with paper, pen and ink, together with his current notebook, bore witness to his attempts to write. Theodora occupied a chair nearby, a pile of mending next to her. She had offered to help Mrs Coleridge with the household sewing and that lady had willingly collected a number of items to be mended. The day was almost over, and Theodora was wondering how much more sewing she would be able to do in the light that remained.

The milk from Sara's pan had badly scalded Coleridge's foot. Active man though he was, he was obliged to sit and rest it whilst day after day his friend Mr Charles Lamb, recently arrived from London, together with Dorothy and Wordsworth explored the countryside. Sara did not always go with them, but she had accompanied them on this occasion. Naturally Theodora was unable to participate in their prolonged outings, but as she had not expected to do so, she did not repine. Furthermore, she had the bitter-sweet pleasure of Coleridge's company. Not that he was particularly cheerful or stimulating at present.

'I wonder what they are doing at this moment,' he mused. 'Where do you think they are, Theodora?'

'No doubt they will have walked quite a distance,' she replied. 'I have never known people who walk as much as you do; not for pleasure, anyway.'

'What of your brothers?' he asked her.

'Michael walks a good deal, but that is so that he will be able to stop easily and speak to his parishioners,' she answered. 'Gabriel walks as well.' She paused, not wanting to be deceitful; yet, being aware of Coleridge's dislike of aristocratic pretensions, she was reluctant to say that Gabriel's reason for walking was to get a good understanding of the lands that he owned and administered.

Seeming not to notice her hesitation, Coleridge spoke again. 'Perhaps they have walked as far as the dell.'

'The one you spoke of?' asked Theodora. 'The deep, narrow one that is only ever speckled by the midday sun?'

'Yes,' he replied, nodding slowly. 'And the waterfall.' He looked around him. 'Yet here I am in . . . in prison.'

Theodora looked up at the trees that shaded them, dappled with the evening sunshine. She laughed. 'It isn't a prison,' she answered. 'It's more like a . . . a bower.'

'A lime tree bower,' he answered. 'No doubt some would say that it's good for me to be left behind for once. It's probably good for my soul.' An arrested look crossed his face, he took up his pen, then for some little time afterwards he wrote with great concentration.

★ ★ ★

'We walked to Holford as you suggested, and think we have found the very place,' said Dorothy in excited tones.

'It's a fair walk for a city fellow like me,' said Charles Lamb, easing his aching limbs as he sat down in one of the chairs in the parlour. Coleridge was already sitting there, his foot up on the same stool that Theodora had brought in from the garden. His wife had returned just in time to assist him back into the cottage. Watching them as they walked, Coleridge's arm about his wife's shoulders, Theodora was conscious of a twinge of heartache. She told herself firmly that this closeness between husband and wife was a very good thing.

'Poor Charles,' Coleridge said, half teasingly. Then he turned to Dorothy. 'The very place? You really think so?'

'I believe it would suit us very well,' said Wordsworth, coming in behind his sister, who had not even bothered to take off her bonnet before giving the good news.

'Poole will look into it for you,' said Coleridge, smiling with pleasure. 'We shall be able to see one another every day.'

'Yes indeed,' agreed Mrs Coleridge. Theodora thought that she looked pleased. She was probably relishing the idea of having the house just occupied by her own family for a change.

Less than a week later, the agreement was signed, and the Wordsworths, together with Basil, Peggy the maid and Theodora, moved in.

★   ★   ★

Alfoxden was a beautiful, south-facing mansion less than a hundred years old, and Theodora liked it immediately. The sea view entranced her, and the presence of deer in the park reminded her a little of some of the vistas to be seen at Ashbourne Abbey. It provided much more spacious accommodation than Coleridge's cottage, and Theodora almost felt ashamed at the relief of having a room to herself once more.

Needless to say, Coleridge, his foot now mended, was over to see them almost from the moment that they had moved in. 'You must have a party,' he declared, 'to celebrate your arrival.'

'What a splendid idea,' Dorothy replied. 'Whom shall we invite?'

'Leave it to me,' said Coleridge. 'I'll speak to Poole about a quarter of lamb.'

Later that day, Coleridge arrived back at his front door at almost the same time as Alex Kydd appeared on horseback, accompanied by Graves, his groom.

'A fine evening,' said Alex. He had returned from Bristol to the Bridgwater Arms the day before, and had also called upon Vivienne, who was now staying with her cousin in the same town. That cousin had invited him for the evening, but he had pleaded another engagement. Telling his groom that he wanted to gauge local opinion, he had set off for Nether Stowey, and arrived, most fortuitously, at the same time as the man in whom he had the most interest.

'It is, is it not?' the other man agreed, in response to Alex's remark 'I have just walked back from Alfoxden Park where our friends the Wordsworths are settled. The setting sun was truly spectacular this evening.'

'They are no longer here, then.' That meant that Theodora was not at the cottage either. Alex was conscious of a much greater disappointment than ought to have been felt by an engaged man at the absence of a young woman who was not his fiancée.

'I feel their loss; but the walk to see them is a fraction of what it was when they were at Racedown. Come and share a glass of wine with me.'

Alex wanted to dislike this young man who had cast such a spell over Theodora, but, looking down at the upturned, cheerful face, he found it quite impossible to do so. Young Coleridge was rather like a very engaging puppy, albeit one with a soaring intellect and a very active social conscience. Reminding himself of Portland's concerns, he decided to spend a little more time with Coleridge. It would be good to understand something of how his mind worked. 'Thank you,' he answered, getting down from his horse, and handing the reins to his groom.

He glanced up at the cottage. He had never visited Ashbourne Abbey, but he knew how extensive it was. He also knew that the vicarage inhabited by Theodora's brother

193

Michael was a handsome property with a fine garden. How had Theodora felt about living here in such cramped conditions?

To Alex's surprise, Coleridge did not lead them into the cottage. 'Best not disturb my wife and the baby,' the young man said. 'Poole will be glad to welcome us. Tell your man to take your horse round to his stables. He won't mind.'

After indicating the way that Dawes should go, he led his guest through the garden and the orchard into the gardens of a handsome, brick-built house, which must, Alex surmised, have a frontage onto one of the other streets in the village.

* * *

If Alex had any doubts about the welcome that they might receive as two unexpected visitors, Poole soon dispelled them. He was a stout, plain young man, whose broad smile reassured them that he was delighted to have some evening company and conversation. A less discerning person would have judged him by his appearance and his West Country accent, to be limited in both his interests and his understanding. A short time in his company was sufficient to convince Alex that he was neither.

As they all spoke about the current political situation, the French war and the needs of those who depended upon the land for their bread, Alex recalled the names on the piece of the paper that the Duke of Portland had handed to him. Coleridge was one; Poole was another. 'In '94 he was reckoned to be one of the most dangerous men in all England,' his grace had confided. 'I should like to know what the fellow is up to, I must confess.'

And so Alex accepted the glass of excellent claret that he was offered, smiled, talked a little and listened more. By the time he was ready to take his leave and go in search of a night's lodging at one of the local inns, he had come to the conclusion that Poole and Coleridge, though radical in their views, were neither unpatriotic nor a danger to the realm. Indeed, Poole's work in assisting the poor of the area probably did more to quell unrest than arouse it.

'I shall be walking over to Alfoxden in the morning,' Coleridge said after offering Alex a bed, which he refused. 'Would you care to accompany me? Or do you need four legs to manage any distance?'

'I shall be able to keep step with you, you may be sure,' replied Alex, grinning at the challenge.

He did not stay late, but allowed Poole to

point him to The Globe Inn, whilst Coleridge went home to his wife. 'I feel a very bad host,' Poole complained. 'You will not allow me to give you a bed for the night.'

'Coleridge will want to be up betimes,' Alex answered politely. 'I should be much happier if I felt that I was not disturbing you.'

'You'll at least allow me to house your horses and groom though,' said Poole good-humouredly.

'I'm much obliged to you,' Alex replied. 'I'll have a word with him first.'

Graves had been on more than one mission with Alex, and was well aware of the errand with which the duke had entrusted him. He had already assisted in making enquiries in Bristol. 'See what you can discover amongst the servants here,' Alex told him in an undertone, when he was sure of not being overheard. 'I'm walking to Alfoxden in the morning.'

'What, walking, when you've a good horse to ride?' Graves exclaimed, looking at his master as if he must be deranged.

Alex laughed. 'I'm going with Coleridge,' he replied. 'Bring the horses to meet me there later. You can tell me then what you've discovered, if anything.'

Having bade Graves farewell, he went to the inn. There were still some locals gathered in the tap room at the Globe, so instead of going straight up to the room which he was assured was available, he wandered in to join in the conversation.

His advent was greeted with suspicion at first. His willingness to buy everyone present another drink did much to allay this. As he had family connections in the West Country, and, being a passable mimic, was able to adopt a very softened form of the local burr, he was soon accepted as a reasonable fellow with whom to share an evening's conversation.

'Spending long here, sir?' the landlord asked him.

'Just passing through, really,' he replied easily. 'My future wife has friends and relatives in the area. It's a pretty place.'

'Ah, not so pretty when you're up at dawn to be about your work,' remarked one of them.

'That'll be the day when I see you getting up at dawn, Thomas Riggs,' another man retorted.

'T'will indeed, for you'd have to get yourself up out of bed to see me,' said the first. There was a roar of laughter.

'Many people pass through here, do they?' Alex asked casually.

'Odd times they do,' said a wiry looking

man of indeterminate age. 'Nothing much to see here, though.'

Alex, thinking of Coleridge's love for the hills and the countryside, had to hide a smile. He completely forgot this train of thought, however, when an elderly man who had been sitting quietly in one corner spoke for the first time. 'We have had Frenchies around here, though.'

'Frenchies?' Alex echoed, remembering his conversation with the Duke of Portland. 'When?'

'Now steady on, Ned, we don't know as they was Frenchies.'

'Well, what else could they be?' the old man asked. 'They didn't talk like us, or like any Englishman as I've ever met; and what about the look of them?'

'The look of them?' Alex prompted, intrigued.

'On the swarthy side,' the old man explained. 'And wandering round at all hours of the night. Up to no good, I reckon. Too secretive by half.'

The landlord came forward at Alex's signal, and offered to refill everyone's glass, a gesture which was welcomed most appreciatively. 'Now Ned, you've got to remember that they were staying with Mr Coleridge — up at Gilbard's.'

'Ah, and there's another funny one,' Ned put in. It seemed as if having once begun to talk, he could not make himself stop.

'He is funny, I grant you,' one of the other men agreed. 'But he's a proper Englishman, and as civil and pleasant as you please.'

'Then what's he doing having those Frenchies to stay?' Ned asked.

'I expect he was worried that you might not have enough to talk about, Ned,' said the landlord, beaming at the burst of mirth that he had caused before he went off for another jug of ale.

Soon afterwards, Alex went off to his bed upstairs, conscious of a feeling of disquiet. The house where he had been born had been close to a village, and he well remembered the kind of gossip that might take place at the local inn of an evening. He and Peter had sometimes dropped in to hear the kind of wild speculations that might be going on there. Usually, they had been entertaining and amusing; something to be laughed over then forgotten.

On one occasion, the group in the tap room had been discussing the absence of a local farmer, who had given no reason for going away. All that was known was that he had taken some items of property to sell. Ideas had ranged from the suggestion that he might be smuggling, to the speculation that he was off to try to make up money that he had lost gambling. Fortunately, before the poor man's reputation was torn to shreds, the rector, who had entered unseen, had roundly condemned them all for such dangerous gossip. He had revealed that he was privy to the farmer's reasons, which were honest and innocent, and with that the conversation had fizzled out. Eventually, it had turned out that the farmer's daughter, living in another part of the country, had lost her husband and needed some extra money to make ends meet. Who knew to what unkind looks and comments the farmer might have been subject had the rector not stepped in.

Gossip could be a dangerous thing. Now, plainly, the subjects of the gossip were Coleridge's visitors. To people who had lived here all their lives, in this village nestling in the lee of the Quantocks, a Cumbrian accent, such as could be heard on the lips of Wordsworth and his sister, must have sounded strange indeed. Their colouring, too, was certainly on the olive side; and their habit of nocturnal wandering must seem eccentric in the extreme to those who, by reason of their occupations, were obliged to rise with the sun and retire when it got dark. What was more, their preoccupation with literary matters, quite alien to most of the locals, made them appear secretive. It would be funny if it were not so concerning.

To his relief, no one had mentioned Theodora. But then, she did not go out with them at night. Did she? Suddenly, he had a picture in his mind's eye of Theodora wandering in the moonlight with Coleridge, the moon turning the ash blond of her hair to silver. Putting down the sick sensation that he was feeling to too much ale, he settled down to sleep, reminding himself that he would need to be up betimes to accompany Coleridge in the morning.

★ ★ ★

'We have visitors,' said Dorothy, coming into the drawing-room of Alfoxden Park, where Theodora was making a gown for Basil who appeared to be growing out of his clothes with alarming rapidity. The younger girl laid aside her work, and got up to greet the newcomers. The advent of Coleridge was not surprising, for she had come to expect him every day. She greeted his arrival with a delighted smile; a fact which Alex, following slightly behind, noted with a feeling of irritation.

The appearance of Alex was quite unexpected. He had not said anything about returning from Bristol in his last letter, and she knew that he had had plans to go to London. She was surprised at how pleased she felt at seeing him, but his scowling expression seemed to indicate that the feeling was not mutual. Nevertheless she greeted him in a friendly manner, and was rewarded with a smile. 'You have had an agreeable morning for your walk,' she remarked, looking at the sunshine outside.

'Yes, it has been delightful,' Alex answered. 'I have benefited extremely from Coleridge's knowledge of the area.'

'I am up in the hills nearly every day,' the other man replied. 'They give me room and freedom.'

'No doubt you have benefited from Coleridge's conversation as well,' said Words-worth, entering shortly afterwards and greeting both men. 'I doubt it ever flagged.'

'You are quite right in that surmise,' Alex answered with a twinkle. 'However, you may be sure that I bore my part as well.'

'We did allow a short pause to listen to the sounds of nature,' Coleridge assured them.

'The stream and the waterfall,' Dorothy suggested.

Coleridge nodded. 'They are the same every day, but always different.'

He was clearly anxious to share some of his

ideas with William and Dorothy, which left Alex free to speak with Theodora. 'I see that you have moved house yet again,' he said with a smile. 'Do you know whether you are on your head or your heels?'

Theodora laughed. 'It has been a little hectic, but I truly believe that we are settled here now.'

'And for how long are you to stay with the Wordsworths?'

Theodora looked at him a little suspiciously, fearing that he might be attempting to organize her life yet again. Seeing nothing in his face but friendly interest however, she said 'I am not certain. My stepfather writes about perhaps taking Jessie to Lyme Regis to get some sea air when they leave London. They will collect me then, I think.'

'We had a happy day there, did we not?'

'It was lovely,' she agreed wholeheartedly.

After they had all had some refreshment, Alex asked Theodora to show him the gardens.

'I have not finished exploring them myself,' she admitted, as they left the house by the front door and looked up towards the hills from which Alex and Coleridge had come that morning. 'You did not argue with Coleridge, did you?' she asked anxiously, saying the first thing that had come into her head after they got outside.

Alex, suspicious about this obvious continued interest in Coleridge but determined not to reveal his feelings, said merely, 'Did we look as though we had been arguing?'

'No,' she agreed. 'No, you did not. Would you like to see the sea? There is a fine view from the back of the house.'

'I would like it of all things,' Alex agreed. He and Coleridge had not argued at all. In fact, had he not been so concerned about Theodora and her attachment to this group of rather radical intellectuals, he would have sought him out as a friend, for Coleridge was a most engaging companion. His conversation was not heavy and portentous, but neither was it trite and meaningless, and through his observations, Alex had found himself looking at the world around him with new eyes. Certainly, as Wordsworth had so acutely speculated, conversation had not flagged.

As they walked around the house and looked out at the sea, Alex reflected with some thankfulness that he was glad that they were away from Nether Stowey and the gawping locals. Doubtless now that they were out in the countryside, the Wordsworths' liking for walking at unsociable times would be less noticeable. Observing Theodora's exquisite little face alight with pleasure as she looked across at the glistening sea, Alex resolved to say nothing to her about the gossip concerning her friends. It would only make her think that he was trying to cause trouble, and would, moreover, bring a frown to those sparkling eyes. Alex suddenly realized that he did not want to do that.

'Do you not think we have made a good choice, Mr Kydd?' said Dorothy on their return to the house.

'A charming situation indeed,' Alex agreed. 'I have never lived in a house with a sea view.'

'We are enchanted by it,' Dorothy agreed. 'And to celebrate, we are to have a party. It is all Coleridge's idea.'

Coleridge had been sitting with Wordsworth and studying some papers which they were passing one to the other. Now he sprang to his feet. 'It will be on the twenty-third of July. Would you like to come, Kydd? And your betrothed, of course. Miss Markham, is it not?' He and Alex had dispensed with formality during the course of their walk.

Alex glanced at Theodora. On her face was a look of hopeful expectation. He was glad that he had not spoken of his conversation in the Globe. 'I'm obliged to you,' he answered. 'I cannot answer for Miss Markham, but as for myself, I should be delighted.'

'Dinner at Alfoxden on the twenty-third? Oh no, I fear that will not be possible for me,' said Vivienne when Alex informed her of the invitation. 'I have already promised to dine with the Garnetts. Indeed, I had half promised that you would be there as well.'

He was conscious of a feeling of irritation. After all, *he* had made no such assumption with regard to *her* availability. 'I wish you had not,' he replied. 'I have given my answer, and cannot withdraw in all courtesy.'

'Let me be frank with you,' she said. They were standing in a parlour in her cousin's house in Bridgwater. 'I am sure that you find much to interest you in this group of people, but from what I could see of them when I visited them with you, they seemed to be a rather harum-scarum party. I cannot imagine that it would make any difference to them whether you were there or not.'

'Perhaps not,' Alex agreed. 'All the more reason why I should show them a good example of courtesy.'

'I suppose so,' Vivienne agreed with a sigh. 'Well if I cannot break my engagement and you cannot break yours, we had better go to different events.'

He eyed her curiously for a moment.

'Vivienne, are you not disappointed that we cannot be together on that evening?'

'Naturally I am,' she answered in an even tone. 'But I am quite pleased that I am not obliged to mingle with a group of poets. I am far too matter-of-fact, I'm afraid.'

15

On a rainy morning when they expected no one except, perhaps, Coleridge, who came nearly every day, whatever the weather, Theodora was very surprised when a carriage bearing Lord and Lady Ashbourne called at the door of Alfoxden House. She had said very little about her illustrious connections, and was afraid that Dorothy might be angry with her, but such was not the case. 'It had not escaped my notice, Thea, how at ease you seem to be in a house of this size,' she said. 'And Lord Ashbourne's letters to you are franked, you know.'

Lord and Lady Ashbourne were dressed for the country, but even so, their attire cast that of Wordsworth and his sister in the shade. Theodora herself, accustomed to Dorothy's more haphazard approach to clothing, was conscious that she had not dressed quite as carefully as she would have done when in London or even in Derbyshire. Her instinctive reaction, on the entrance of the noble couple, was to tuck a stray curl behind her ear, and to try to recall how clean her shoes were without looking down.

Jessie hurried across the room and enfolded her in a warm embrace. 'How we have missed you!' she exclaimed.

'Where is Leonora?' Theodora asked when she had embraced them both. 'Have you not brought her?'

'She has recently developed an aversion to long carriage rides, so we decided not to subject her to this one,' Jessie answered.

'Sea air agrees with you, my dear Thea,' said Ashbourne. Her hand went to her hair again. ''A sweet disorder in the dress,' my dear,' he protested, catching hold of her hand and giving it a gentle squeeze.

''Kindles in clothes a wantonness',' Wordsworth added, completing the quotation from Robert Herrick. 'Your servant, sir.'

'My wife and I are staying at Lyme Regis for our health,' the earl explained, when Theodora had performed all the necessary introductions. 'The day not being conducive to strolling by the sea, we decided to come and see my stepdaughter. I trust that we do not intrude.'

'By no means,' Wordsworth answered. 'You are very welcome.'

Ashbourne turned to Dorothy. 'Not wishing to place an added burden upon your household, madam, we have taken the liberty of bringing some provisions, trusting that our gesture will not be misconstrued.'

'You are very thoughtful, my lord,' Dorothy replied, going to see about refreshments.

'I can tell by your voice, sir, that you are not from these parts,' said Ashbourne, courteously, turning again to Wordsworth. 'May I ask what is your native county?'

'I am from Cumberland,' Wordsworth replied. 'I was born in Cockermouth.'

'An interesting part of the world,' Ashbourne answered. 'My own lands are in Derbyshire.'

Wordsworth smiled one of his rare smiles. 'Only a man who has lived among the hills appreciates what it is to be deprived of them.'

'Very true,' Ashbourne agreed. 'An unhappy situation that is not yours at present. Are the Quantocks to your liking?'

While they were speaking, there was the sound of the front door opening and the murmur of voices in the hall to be followed, almost inevitably, by the entrance of Coleridge.

No contrast between two people could have been more marked. Theodora had never seen Lord Ashbourne looking anything other than immaculate. Today, he was in a coat of rich brown cloth with breeches of a lighter shade. His waistcoat toned nicely with his breeches, and had on it an intricate pattern that matched his coat, set off with a fine gold thread. His boots, in which he had walked from the carriage into the house, appeared to be as glossy as on the day of their purchase. Altogether, he looked as though he had stepped straight from the ministrations of his valet.

Coleridge, on the other hand, had walked across the hills, through the bracken, and had jumped the stream on several occasions, once from necessity and several times out of sheer exuberance. Mercifully, he had left his outdoor coat in the hall, and had removed his boots, replacing them with a pair of William's shoes. Nevertheless he looked wet, untidy, and none too clean, but his face was rosy and beaming with delight to be among them. 'Lord, what a wet day,' he exclaimed. 'At times like these, I do so envy dogs that amazing way that they have of shaking themselves from nose to tail tip. What an advantage that must be!'

'And if you could do it, no doubt you would shake drops of water all over everything, and I should be obliged to put you out by the scruff of your neck,' said Dorothy cheerfully, as she came back in with a tray bearing a bottle of claret — which Ashbourne had brought — and some glasses.

In common with many people, Theodora

always had a desire that those she loved should appreciate one another. Today, however, as she introduced the earl and his countess to the newcomer, she had the distressing feeling that Coleridge and Ashbourne disliked one another on sight. Hardly had the conversation progressed beyond half-a-dozen sentences, than Coleridge's views, often tending to be rather unfavourable towards the aristocracy, began to turn positively hostile, whilst Ashbourne, always suave and polished, became haughty as well. Theodora desperately wanted to mend matters, but she had no idea of how to do so. Glancing from one to the other she discovered, to her great distress, that it was Ashbourne of whom she felt ashamed, and she hated herself for feeling that way. He was just too perfect, too suave, too assured.

Given that they were all shut in for the present because of the weather, it would have been unfortunate in the extreme had this state of affairs continued. Fortunately, one small incident did much to improve the atmosphere. Jessie had wandered over to the window and was allowing Mr Wordsworth to explain to her how they had come to rent the house. Having looked her fill, she began to make her way to a chair by the fireplace. As she did so, she caught her foot on the corner of a rug, and was briefly in serious danger of falling. It was Coleridge who sprang forward and caught hold of her, steadying her and thus saving her from injury.

'Thank you, Mr Coleridge,' she said, looking up at him gratefully. 'I fear I am a little clumsy at present.'

'Then you must take extra care,' he said gently, his eyes full of understanding as he helped her to sit down.

'Jez, my dear,' said Ashbourne, breaking off his conversation with Theodora and coming swiftly towards his wife, all his languor gone in an instant.

'It's all right, Raff,' replied Jessie, reassuringly. 'Mr Coleridge has been gallantry itself and I am quite safe as you can see.'

'Then I am much obliged to him,' said Ashbourne inclining his head in Coleridge's direction, which courtesy the other man returned.

Jessie smiled. 'I am expecting our second child, you see. The condition makes me unsteady at times, and Raff becomes very protective.'

'As is natural for a husband and father,' Coleridge replied.

Thereafter, the day proceeded in a more cordial manner. Even so, everyone was glad when after nuncheon — a delicious meal, for which Lord Ashbourne had provided a ham, a large cheese and a selection of cakes — the weather cleared up and a walk in the grounds became possible.

'Are you having an agreeable stay, dearest?' Jessie asked Theodora as they walked arm in arm on the grass. The sea, which had had rather a grey aspect earlier, was now blue and inviting.

'Yes, very agreeable,' Theodora answered. 'My hosts are so kind. I feel as if I have known them for ever.'

'Does Mr Coleridge come over frequently?' the countess ventured. She had not missed the look of concern on Theodora's face when Ashbourne and Coleridge had been at their most hostile.

'Nearly every day,' Theodora answered honestly. 'He and William often write together. They are both poets, you see.'

'That must be a precarious living,' Jessie observed.

'I think that it is,' Theodora agreed. 'Coleridge is also a journalist, but even so, I know that Mrs Coleridge worries about how her husband will provide for her and their baby.'

'I am sure that she must,' Jessie agreed. 'What age is the child?'

∗ ∗ ∗

The Ashbournes did not stay late, and as they left, promised to return to collect Theodora on their way back to London, and thence, to Derbyshire. 'There is no rush,' Dorothy assured them as they got into the coach. 'We love having her, and will feel badly done by if we are not allowed to keep her for another fortnight at least.'

'What do you think?' Ashbourne asked his wife as they drove away. 'Is she in love with him?'

'Which one?' Jessie asked.

'Dear God, you don't suppose she could be in love with that over-grown puppy dog with the radical ideas, do you?'

Jessie laughed. 'Coleridge?' she said. 'Nothing could be more certain, my dear.'

'What can she possibly see in the fellow?' he asked her. 'No looks, no style, no . . . '

'Hairbrush?' Jessie suggested. 'Perhaps not, but he does write some very pretty poetry.' She held up a slim volume.

'Where did you get that?' he asked her.

'Mr Coleridge gave it to me,' she replied demurely.

'Don't tell me that he is attempting to ingratiate himself with my wife as well as my stepdaughter.'

Jessie laughed again. 'I do not believe that he ever intends to ingratiate himself with anyone,' she answered. 'Besides, he is a married man. Knowing Thea, she will have given herself a stern talking to. Perhaps even now, she is coming to realize what a difficult husband he would be.'

'I was worried about her taking a fancy to Wordsworth. Having met him, I think that he would be a better match,' the earl observed. 'However, I did not detect any spark between them.'

'Not so much as a glimmer,' Jessie agreed.

'You need a spark,' Ashbourne drawled, lifting his wife's hand and raising it to his lips, fixing her eyes with his the while.

'Enough of your rake's tricks,' she said spiritedly. 'They have no effect upon me whatsoever.'

'Indeed?' he said in the same drawl, pulling her into his arms this time. 'Then I will have to try harder, will I not?'

16

Mr and Mrs Creed, Vivienne's cousin and her husband, lived in a house on the outskirts of Bridgwater. Kathryn Creed, who bore a slight resemblance to Vivienne, welcomed Alex warmly. 'It must be twelve months at least since I have seen you,' she said, smiling. She had not been at home when Alex had last visited Vivienne to tell her about the party at Alfoxden.

'I cannot believe that it is so long,' he replied.

'And yet our daughter Imogen is nine months old and she was not born when you were last here.'

'I'm told that it is only old people who say that time flies, so I shan't make such an observation,' he said with a rueful grin.

'Would you care for some refreshment, or do you want to go and find Vivi? She's walking in the garden.'

'I'll look for her first, by your leave.'

'I'll send for refreshments then we can all enjoy them on the terrace,' she replied. 'The gardens are not at their best at this time of year, I'm afraid, but you should find some flowers out.'

He left the house by the French doors as his hostess had indicated, and ran lightly down the terrace steps onto the grass. Something about the arrangement of the lawns and paths reminded him of his own gardens in Buckinghamshire.

He thought guiltily that he should have returned there before now. It was true that his mother was very capable and had an excellent adviser in Vivienne's father, so he did not need to hurry back on her account. Nevertheless, had it not been for his concern for Theodora he would have done so. But with all her male relatives so far away, he felt that he owed it to Michael to keep a brotherly eye upon her.

He paused, frowning. There was something wrong with that thought. Before he could determine what it might be, however, he heard voices, and recognizing one as Vivienne's, made his way in the direction from which they were proceeding.

He saw his betrothed and her companion before they saw him. Vivienne was accompanied by a man of about Alex's own age, and they seemed to be engaged upon an earnest conversation. Alex paused, then hurried forward, his hand held out, a smile on his face. 'Laurence Ormsby, by all that's holy! From where did you spring?'

'Alex!' the other man responded, smiling, but also looking a little self-conscious. He held out his left hand to grasp Alex's right; his empty right sleeve was pinned to his coat.

'It's devilish good to see you,' said Alex. Then, belatedly remembering his manners, he added, 'Vivienne, my dear,' and raised her hand to his lips. 'What brings you to these parts?' he enquired of Ormsby, falling in beside them. After a moment's hesitation, Vivienne tucked her hand into Alex's arm.

'Oh, family business,' Ormsby replied. 'I've an uncle in these parts — or rather, I had an uncle who passed away recently.'

'I remember,' Alex replied. 'Wasn't he in the military himself?'

'Rose to the rank of colonel, then bought himself out,' the other man responded. 'He's left me his estate in Wiltshire, so I came down this way to have a look at what needs doing. As I was in the area, I decided to come and see Vivienne.' Her cleared his throat. 'Just taking her for a walk, old chap. Nothing improper, I promise you.'

'Lord, no,' Alex answered easily. 'I wouldn't have thought it for a moment. Are you staying for dinner?'

'Are you by any chance inviting your friend to dine at my cousin's house?' Vivienne asked playfully.

'Good heavens, so I am,' he answered guiltily.

'It's all right,' she assured him. 'Laurence has already accepted an invitation to dine, and you're more than welcome.'

'Good,' he said. 'There's something I'd like to ask you about.'

'Which one of us?' Vivienne asked.

'Both of you, come to think of it.'

'I must say this is very agreeable,' said Alex, as he stretched his legs out in front of him, a glass in his hand. Mr and Mrs Creed had always been hospitable, and Alex and Laurence had both joined them for dinner, before repairing to the Bridgwater Inn, where Laurence had also booked accommodation.

'Surprised you're not staying with the Creeds, old chap,' said Laurence Ormsby.

'I tend not to, although I know I'd be welcome. I have many other calls upon my time, and I don't want to look as though I'm making use of them. Didn't they ask *you* to stay?'

Laurence's rather thin, pale face flushed. 'Well yes, but I . . . to tell you the truth, I didn't quite like to.'

'Why ever not?'

'Vivienne, my dear fellow. I'm not the one who's engaged to her. It wouldn't have been proper.'

'Nonsense,' Alex responded. 'If I don't care about such things, why should anyone else?'

He frowned. Truth to tell, he was not feeling particularly pleased with Vivienne. He had hurried to dress, hoping to have a few words with her before dinner. The question of Theodora and her infatuation for Coleridge was uppermost in his mind. He desperately needed to talk to someone and, as his oldest friend, Vivienne was the obvious choice. He had managed to catch her alone, but her response to his concerns about Theodora had been most unsatisfactory. She had not appeared to be particularly worried that the younger girl was infatuated with an unsuitable man, and had had no advice to offer him concerning her removal.

'Really, if her own family is not concerned over the matter, I do not see what you have to say about it,' she had said. 'You would do much better to return to Buckinghamshire and tend your estate. You cannot possibly stop her from getting her heart broken. It will probably do her good in the end.'

It had been a blessing that there had been another family sitting down to dinner that night, as Alex had not felt in a particularly amiable mood with his betrothed and might even have got into an argument with her.

'Why the stern look?' Laurence asked,

breaking into his reverie.

'What? Oh, nothing.' He paused, whilst Laurence waited. 'Did you ever meet Michael Buckleigh?'

Laurence shook his head. 'Not that I recall. The name's familiar. Stay, though. Didn't you escort a female of that name when you brought Vivienne's aunt home?'

'Theodora Buckleigh. That's right. Michael Buckleigh's a friend of mine and her brother. He's a long way away in Derbyshire, so I feel a degree of responsibility for her.'

'Understandably — but that's not what's brought the frown to your face.'

'I'm concerned about the set she's running with,' answered Alex, getting up to pour them both another glass of brandy.

'Rakish? Licentious?'

Alex grinned wryly. 'Rather political — and poetical.'

'Political in what way?'

'Some of those she's staying with have had connections with the corresponding societies in Bristol.'

'Anyone I might have heard of?'

'Coleridge is one,' Alex replied, looking down into his glass.

He had not thought that he had pronounced the man's name with any particular feeling. Laurence must have noticed something, however, for he ventured, 'You don't sound as if you like him much.'

Alex looked up in surprise. 'Not like him? On the contrary, I've met him on more than one occasion. He's very engaging.'

'I've not met him, but I've heard of him and in a way that might surprise you. Did you know that he had been in the army for a short space of time?'

'No, I wasn't aware of that. I can't imagine it, myself.'

'It wasn't for long, and he enlisted under an assumed name. I had it of Makepiece, who was also in the Light Dragoons. By all accounts he made a pretty appalling cavalry-man. In fact, he was so bad that he was set to nursing a sick trooper. The only thing was, the trooper turned out to have smallpox.'

'Good God!' Alex exclaimed. 'What did Coleridge do?'

'Nursed the man back to health. Didn't shirk his duty, either.'

'Oh, I've no doubt he has all the virtues,' said Alex, the bitterness in his voice making Laurence look at him rather curiously. 'I'd better not tell Theodora that story, or she'll be even more besotted with him than she is now.' Conscious that he might have said too much on that score he added, 'It's the radical ideas that she might pick up that really concern me, though.'

'That won't do her any harm, surely,' said Laurence, taking his glass with a word of thanks. 'She'll come away with a few daft notions, but she'll soon shake those off when she gets back home to Derbyshire, to the farmer or squire that I expect her brother's got lined up for her.'

Alex looked at him in surprise. 'Do you think so?' he asked.

'Not a doubt of it,' Laurence replied. 'One of my sisters went to a lecture where some crackpot was saying that it was possible to teach animals to talk. She spent hours and hours mouthing words at our old dog Rufus. The whole thing only stopped when neighbours of ours had guests with sons of her age to stay; then at last Rufus got some peace. He never did talk, incidentally.'

Alex laughed at this, and allowed Laurence to change the subject. The only trouble was, thinking about it later, after he had gone to bed, he realized that he didn't actually feel reassured by what his friend had said. Eventually, he came to the uncomfortable conclusion that the most unsettling thing about the whole conversation had not been the odd ideas that Theodora might have picked up, as Laurence had supposed. It had been the thought that she might be married off to a squire or a farmer. She seemed to him to deserve better.

He sat up, caught hold of his pillow, gave it a good punching, and then replaced it. What on earth had got hold of him? He had been giving far too much thought to Theodora and her situation. Laurence was right. She would grow out of her foolishness soon enough. The best thing that he could do would be to spend some time with Vivienne and then return to his Buckinghamshire estates to prepare for his marriage.

The following morning, Alex noticed a curious phenomenon. He had heard it said that the night brought counsel. He had always understood this to mean that foolish ideas which had occupied the mind during the night gave way to common sense in the cold light of day. With him, it seemed to be quite otherwise. The very sensible course of visiting Vivienne then going home seemed flat, insensitive and almost cowardly when compared with the urgent need to make sure that Theodora was in no danger. With this plan in mind, therefore, he breakfasted with Laurence, then walked with him to the Creeds'.

'I have some commitments which I must not break,' he said to his betrothed, 'so I will leave Laurence to entertain you. I will wait upon you later.' He did not note the glance that they exchanged with one another as he left.

On his arrival at Alfoxden, he was told by Peggy Marsh that Miss Theodora was in the garden. 'She went out with Mr Coleridge only a few minutes ago,' she disclosed. 'Mr Wordsworth and Miss Dorothy are attending to Master Basil.'

'I'll go into the garden and find them,' he answered. He left by the back door and, looking around, he was just in time to see Theodora standing, with Coleridge on one knee at her feet. With lips tightly set, he strode off across the garden. If the man was philandering with her, then he, Alex, would knock his teeth down his throat. Let him try to write a poem about that!

★ ★ ★

'Did you ever see such clouds? The formation of them is quite extraordinary! I have been observing them all the way from Stowey.' Coleridge's face was ruddy from his walk and his blue eyes were sparkling.

'It's to be supposed you kept at least part of one eye on the path,' Wordsworth remarked, his lips twitching. 'Otherwise you would by now be reposing in a ditch.'

'Where is Dorothea?' Coleridge asked. 'We must all go and look at these clouds at once, for as they pass, so will our opportunity.'

'Dorothy is seeing to Basil,' Wordsworth replied. 'I'll tell her you're here.'

Theodora was sitting in the parlour with some sewing on her knee. Coleridge snatched it from her and threw it down on a nearby table. 'Now, Theodora. You must come at once.'

Laughing, she allowed him to pull her from her chair. He caught hold of her hand, and led her from the room, then out of the back door and down the slope to where there was some longer grass. 'Now!' he said. 'Lie on your back!'

'I beg your pardon?' she said, colouring. The intimate-sounding nature of his suggestion took her by surprise.

'It's the only way to look at the sky,' he explained, clearly quite unaware of the nature of her scruples. He went down on one knee. 'Lie down,' he urged her. Not wanting to draw further attention to her anxieties, she allowed him to assist her. Soon, they were lying side by side, looking up at the sky.

'Now, is that not better?' said Coleridge, when they were both lying on their backs. 'Just look at all the shapes. Would you not say that this looks like a kingdom in the sky?'

Diverted from her embarrassment, Theodora looked up at the sky that was causing him to be so fascinated. 'There is a palace,' she said, pointing.

'So there is,' he agreed. 'It could be a palace made of ice, could it not; with terraces and turrets and secret caverns?'

'With a river running in between — look,' said Theodora, pointing to where two clouds, close together, were separated by a narrow channel of blue.

'Yes indeed,' Coleridge agreed. He turned his bright blue orbs upon her. 'Have you never done this before?'

'Not for very many years,' she confessed. 'Adulthood tends to drive such activities out of one's life.'

'Mistakenly, in my view,' Coleridge answered. 'One can learn so much from children, if they themselves are permitted to learn in the right environment. I try to encourage Hartley to learn as much from nature as possible. But look again, Theodora. Can you not see a horse up there?'

'I can,' she answered. 'A heavenly horse, with wings.'

'Like Pegasus,' he agreed.

'I trust I am not interrupting anything,' said another voice coldly. Looking up, Theodora saw Alex's face, and even though it was upside down, she could tell that he was exceedingly annoyed. She sat up quickly. Coleridge sprang to his feet, and greeted Alex

228

with unaffected pleasure. It was quite apparent that he saw nothing untoward in his actions.

Alex acknowledged his greeting courteously enough, but then said, 'What is happening here?'

Suddenly, Theodora saw the incident through his eyes and blushed. 'We were only looking at the clouds,' she said. She turned to Coleridge. 'Were we not?'

At that moment, Wordsworth and his sister approached them. 'Have you been looking at the clouds?' Dorothy asked. 'Are they as spectacular as Coleridge has been saying?' She turned to Alex. 'He almost fell into a ditch on the way here, so eager was he to keep his eyes on the heavens,' she added.

Theodora could have kissed Dorothy's hands and feet for confirming her story. Nevertheless, she could see that Alex, although smiling for politeness' sake, was still angry. She was not altogether surprised when, as Coleridge, Dorothy and William decided to walk to the coast to see whether the sea was reflecting the sky in an interesting manner, Alex asked for the favour of a private word with her.

Theodora could not think of a good reason for refusing him, even though she was nervous of what he might say. 'Do you want to go inside, or stay here?' she asked him.

'We will stay outside, I think,' he said. 'We will then be much less likely to be overheard.' He paused briefly. 'Theodora, how could you?' he asked her, his anger too great for discretion. 'Do you know what I saw when I came out of the house?'

'The garden?' she suggested, nervousness making her flippant.

'I saw Coleridge kneeling before you,' he said. 'Can you imagine what any other person would have made of that, had they witnessed it?'

'I have no idea,' she responded, turning away from him.

'Well I have,' he replied. 'He is a married man, in case you had forgotten. No doubt your infatuation makes you careless of appearances, but I assure you that the opinion of any onlooker would have been very unflattering to you.'

'Then let me tell you that I have no interest in the opinion of such a judgemental and ill-informed onlooker,' she flashed. 'Coleridge had offered to show me the clouds. He was simply helping me so that I might lie down and observe them properly. Our activity was wholly innocent.'

'Your activity might have been innocent, but you are being naive in the extreme if you think that that is how it looked.'

'I do not care how it looked,' she retorted passionately. 'We were doing nothing wrong. It was beautiful and exciting, and there was nothing immoral in it until you came, with your commonplace opinions and your — ' She was going to say your evil mind, but she stopped herself in time.

'Was there not?' he asked her. 'Can you honestly say to me that you lay down on the ground next to him without a single qualm?'

Theodora blushed. She knew perfectly well that she had been shocked at Coleridge's suggestion, but she would have died rather than admit it. 'Why should I have a qualm?' she asked, her head held high. 'William and Dorothy often lie down to look at the stars. I have heard them say so. You will not suggest that they are immoral, I hope.'

'They are brother and sister,' Alex reminded her.

'What of that?' she asked him.

'It makes the case utterly different,' he said. Theodora knew this as well as he did. Had he said no more on this score, he might have persuaded her to acknowledge the justice of his opinion. Unfortunately, however, his next words were unforgivably provocative. 'You will not try to tell me, I hope, that you regard Coleridge as a brother.'

She looked up into his eyes, her own full of hurt, and a suspicion of unshed tears. Then with a little inarticulate cry, she half ran, half stumbled back to the house, whilst Alex, inwardly cursing himself, watched her go.

17

'What a mercy it's fine,' Dorothy said as she and Theodora went upstairs to change. Theodora nodded in agreement. The party at Alfoxden had begun at eleven o'clock with a reading of William's tragedy under the trees. A wet day would have driven everyone indoors. Theodora was a little sorry to be missing the play reading, but she had heard the tragedy before, and the absence of the guests from the house meant that the final preparations for the dinner could be made.

She could not help contrasting this affair with dinners that she had attended at Ashbourne Abbey. There, Jessie would take a personal interest in all the preparations, often going down to the kitchens to offer a word of encouragement to the staff. She would certainly not expect to stay in there to cook the dinner, however, as Dorothy had been doing earlier with Peggy's assistance. Nor would she have to run the flat iron over the table linen, or polish the silver, as Theodora had done the previous day. At least they had had plenty of help. Peggy did not mind being pressed into service once Basil was resting. In addition, an old woman had come from the village, and Mrs Coleridge had sent the girl who worked for them to lend a hand. A local man had also been engaged as a waiter.

'What with one thing and another, I've never had so many servants at my disposal in my life before,' said Dorothy cheerfully.

After the reading of the tragedy, the party of fourteen would gather in the parlour before sitting down to dinner in the fine dining-room where they would be able to enjoy excellent views of the sea.

As Theodora changed, she wondered what Alex was making of Wordsworth's tragedy. She knew that he enjoyed poetry and drama, for he had said as much when he had been visiting before. Her room overlooked where the company was sitting, and she lifted a corner of the curtain to peep out and see what was happening.

As she was watching, a shaft of sunlight shot down and caught Alex's hair, turning the brown to something like chestnut. How glossy it is, she thought to herself, then dropped the curtain hastily, suddenly remembering what had happened the previous day. On that occasion, she had run back to the house, then up to her room, where she had sat on her bed, the tears running down her face. For a short time she had forgotten

Coleridge's married status, and had simply responded to his warmth and enthusiasm. She had behaved in a bold and daring manner with a married man who was not related to her. In this poetic, unconventional circle her behaviour had seemed strange, but innocent. Looking at it through Alex's eyes, it had seemed outrageous. His words had made her feel grubby and cheap, and she had wept for very shame. What would Michael have thought? Or Jessie, for that matter? Or, worst of all, Papa had he been alive? She could not imagine how she could ever face Alex again.

Theodora was not the only one to recall their last meeting with regret. Alex had thought about it several times, cursing himself for his brutality. Even now, whilst William Wordsworth's compelling voice rang out and the rest of the company sat rapt, he could not stop thinking about Theodora, and the way in which he had spoken to her.

He had known almost immediately that her and Coleridge's actions had been entirely innocent. Yet he had suddenly felt so enraged that he had spoken without restraint. He had nearly turned back several times after leaving Alfoxden on that day, but had resisted the urge to do so. This had partly been because he had known that he would not be welcome, but also because of an instinctive fear that far

235

from comforting her, his anger might have led him to say far more than was wise.

More than once, he had been tempted to excuse himself from the dinner, but he had decided against it. He did not want the disagreement with Theodora to become an estrangement. Now as he looked round the circle listening to the tragedy, he was glad that he had come, for the owner of the third name on the Duke of Portland's list was amongst the group gathered around Wordsworth on the grass.

When Coleridge had introduced 'my friend Thelwall, the radical thinker, from London' to the company in general, Alex had not recognized the man's face, but he was very familiar with the name. The man was indeed a radical as Coleridge had said. He had helped to form the London Corresponding Society, and was widely known as a Jacobin. He had even spent some time in the Tower of London on a charge of treason before being acquitted. Many still regarded him as being highly dangerous. Decidedly His Grace of Portland would want to know about this man's presence.

Looking across the garden, Alex recognized the spot where he had seen Theodora with Coleridge and was suddenly filled with disquiet. Did she know anything about the people with whom she was mixing?

Theodora had just finished changing when Dorothy knocked on her door to see if she was ready to go down. 'I must just wrap myself in an enormous apron, and make sure that Peggy is managing in the kitchen, then I shall join you all,' she said.

Coleridge was one of the first to step inside the parlour when the reading was over. 'My dear Theodora, how pretty you look,' he exclaimed, holding her by her hands at arm's length, then whirling her round until she was dizzy. 'What a pity that there is to be no dancing,' he went on. 'I am developing my dancing skills, and am quite a favourite with the young ladies in Stowey as a consequence.'

'You know that I cannot dance,' she replied, torn between hurt at what she perceived to be his insensitivity, and pleasure that he had noticed her new gown. She had decided that the dinner party at Alfoxden would be an appropriate occasion on which to dispense with strict mourning, and was clad in lilac, trimmed with floral braid in a darker shade of the same colour.

'I know that you *say* you cannot dance,' he responded. 'To my way of thinking, a great deal of dancing depends upon being temporarily off balance through skipping, hopping or twirling. It seems to me that dancing might be the very thing for you.'

'Oh, do you think so?' she asked, smiling up at him.

'Give me an occasion where there is to be some and I will prove it to you.'

'Good day, Theodora.' They turned round and saw Alex Kydd entering the parlour at the back of the group, his expression serious.

'Kydd!' Coleridge exclaimed. 'Do you not think that Theodora looks delightful?'

'Charming,' Kydd agreed, bowing, before coming forward to greet her.

'I've just been telling her that I think she should dance,' Coleridge went on. 'You must persuade her if ever you have the opportunity.'

'My experience of persuading Theodora to do anything that she has set her mind against has not been happy so far,' Kydd admitted ruefully.

She acknowledged him with cold formality. An awkward silence followed, during which they stood side by side, observing the assembling company, neither sure what to say to the other.

It was a noisy enough gathering, with Coleridge, Poole and Thelwall engaged in animated disputation, whilst Sara Coleridge chatted with her friends the Cruikshanks, and Dorothy occupied herself with some of the other guests, including Basil Montagu's father, also called Basil. Theodora had been at similarly animated gatherings before. Her brother Michael and his half-brother Gabriel could often be heard exchanging good-humoured banter over some matter. Lord Ashbourne, whilst maintaining his customary aloof stance, was not above getting involved, whilst Jessie, Evangeline and Gabriel's wife Eustacia were all ladies with minds of their own.

Theodora could well remember one occasion when some subject, now forgotten, was under dispute. Far more used to the quiet rectory, where there was usually just herself and her father, she had watched the animated faces and listened to the voices in wonderment, until Jessie had tucked a hand in her arm and asked her opinion.

Now she looked around at the assembled company. Do I really have a place here, she asked herself, listening to the merry hubbub, in which at that moment she was not included. Alex had turned to William Wordsworth to make some remark about his tragedy. Suddenly, for almost the first time since she had joined the Wordsworths, she felt lonely. She stared at Coleridge. Just now, he was the centre of a noisy circle, bearing his part with vigour, his blue eyes flashing, his hands raised to emphasize some point. Involuntarily, her gaze turned to Sara Coleridge, who had paused amid a lively conversation to cast a loving glance at her husband. From deep down within her, Theodora heard a voice say: *he is not yours, and he never will be.* She wanted to run out of the door and never come back.

'Have you heard from Michael recently?' Alex asked her gently, breaking into her reverie. She looked up with a start, not having noticed his return. For a brief moment, she almost took his breath away. The elfin winsomeness of her expression, tinged now with sadness, so struck him that he felt an almost overwhelming longing to pull her into his arms and to kiss away the shadows in her eyes. Then he remembered where he was, and how inappropriate were his thoughts. He was an engaged man, for goodness' sake.

'I had rather an entertaining letter from him,' he went on, determinedly bringing himself back to the present, as he described an amusing encounter that her brother had had with a group of bad-tempered geese. She had not heard the story before, and by dint of keeping her mind on Michael, she managed to grasp the point of the story, and rewarded Alex at the end with a laugh. 'That's better,' he said. He paused then went on, 'I've no desire to discompose you, so I shan't say very much about what happened the other day.' She made a little defensive gesture with her hand. 'I wanted to beg your pardon,' he continued, earnestly. 'I was unforgivably impertinent. You are under no obligation to explain your conduct to me.'

'I know you were only trying to be kind,' she answered, so softly that he could barely hear her.

'You are more generous than I deserve.' He paused. Then cautiously, he ventured, 'Dare I hope that we can still be friends?'

She glanced up at him. He was holding his head at its customary tilted angle, and a lock of hair was flopping over his brow as usual. Suppressing a sudden, quite unexpected impulse to push it back, she murmured, 'Still friends.'

'Thank you.' They were both silent for a short time. Then Alex said 'Have you met that gentleman before?' He nodded towards Coleridge's radical friend.

She shook her head. 'This is the first time that I have seen him.'

Alex grunted, and a moment later, dinner was announced.

The meal was every bit as lively as the conversation that had gone before it. The noisiest of the party by far were Coleridge and Thelwall. 'He is thrilled at meeting the gentleman at last,' said Theodora's neighbour, Thomas Poole. 'Thelwall is staying with the Coleridges at Stowey. Until this visit, they had not met in person.'

'I would never have supposed it,' Theodora replied, watching the way in which the two men debated together. The current dispute appeared to be to do with the religious upbringing of children. Thelwall, obviously an atheist, clearly believed that they should have none, and then be able to decide for themselves when they grew older. Coleridge took the opposite view. Thelwall was on his feet, excitedly making his point, obviously to the anxiety of the local man who was serving them.

'Tell me, have you taken a look at my botanical garden?' the grinning Coleridge asked the other man.

'Your botanical garden?' Thelwall echoed, puzzled. 'Where might that be?'

'At my cottage in Stowey,' was the reply.

'Why, it's full of weeds,' responded Thelwall. 'But what that has to do with my point . . . ?'

'Oh, nothing,' answered Coleridge. 'It's just that I thought I'd leave it for the time being. It can decide for itself later on if it wants to turn to strawberries or roses.'

There was a roar of laughter at this, in which Thelwall joined; but it was not long before he was on his feet again, making another point with unabated vigour.

After the meal was over, Dorothy led the ladies back into the parlour, where they sat conversing until the men joined them. Theodora found herself sitting next to Sara Coleridge, and asked her how Hartley was progressing.

'He is doing very well,' that lady replied. 'He is his father's pride and joy — and mine too, of course. How much longer are you to stay, Miss Buckleigh?'

'I am not sure. Dorothy is not anxious to lose me, but my stepfather and his wife will soon be returning home to Derbyshire from Lyme Regis, and I believe that they will want to take me with them.'

'Lyme is a very pretty place, and is starting to become fashionable, I'm told.'

'Yes indeed,' Theodora replied, smiling at the memory. 'Alex took me and we went out in a boat.'

Mrs Coleridge responded with some comments of her own about the local scene. Theodora knew already that Dorothy was inclined to despise her, but Theodora found her quite conversable. For the first time it occurred to her that in other circumstances,

Sara might have made a good friend.

A burst of noise outside the room gave notice that the men were about to return. Alex was conversing easily with John Cruikshank as he came in, but he soon made an opportunity to join Theodora.

'You have not lingered over your port,' she remarked. 'Was the conversation as noisy after we had left?'

'More so,' he replied. Then, turning to Mrs Coleridge, he began to ask her about the neglected garden, over which she raised her eyes to heaven, and in talking about gardening and related matters, the three of them passed the time until the tea tray was brought in.

Before he left, Alex approached Theodora once more. 'May I call upon you tomorrow?' he asked seriously. 'Not to upbraid you — I give you my word.'

'Very well,' she answered, glad to be on good terms with him again, although she would have been hard put to it to say why.

* * *

Alex had debated long and hard with himself whether to say anything, but had come to the conclusion that he could not reconcile it with his conscience to be silent. As he rode over to

Alfoxden the next day, he told himself that Theodora needed to know exactly what kind of people were members of the circle with which she had chosen to be associated. He doubted whether anybody there would have told her about Thelwall.

On his arrival, he was not surprised to discover that Coleridge and his guest had already made an appearance, and had borne Dorothy and Wordsworth off on a long walk. He was therefore free to spend some time with Theodora.

They went outside and began to walk about the grounds. After they had exchanged a few remarks about the previous evening's dinner, he carefully raised the subject that concerned him the most. 'What do you know about Mr Thelwall?' he asked her cautiously.

'Just that he is a friend of Coleridge, and that they have only known one another through correspondence until this visit,' she replied. 'Why?'

'You have not been told, then, that he was tried for treason?'

'Treason?' she exclaimed, much shocked. 'No. When was this?'

'A few years ago. He is, as Coleridge said, a radical. He has shown this through his political writings and his lectures. He has long been considered by the authorities to be

245

a dangerous man.'

'But if he was acquitted, surely he is innocent?'

'He is still being watched,' Alex replied. 'He is regarded with suspicion, and that means that all those who associate with him run the risk of being regarded in the same way. That includes your friend Coleridge.'

'Coleridge is not guilty of treason,' she said indignantly, her back straightening.

'I never said that he was,' he responded, carefully keeping his temper, even though her automatic championing of the other man irked him extremely. 'Coleridge, though once a radical, has retired from public life. What is more, I believe him to be loyal to his country and his God. But an outsider, seeing Thelwall at the centre of this circle, would make connections that might not necessarily be there, and suspect everyone involved. That would mean you, too, Theodora.'

She stared at him incredulously. 'That is absurd,' she said. 'If we are talking in that way, then it must also mean you, and someone as respectable as . . . oh, as Mr Poole.'

Alex grinned humourlessly. 'He, too, is regarded by some as dangerous.' When she stared at him, he added, 'His work with the Poor Men's Relief group is seen as being possibly seditious.'

She stared at him suspiciously. 'You seem to know a great deal about this.'

He sighed. 'Yes, I do, and I have probably said more than I should. But I could not reconcile it with my conscience not to warn you.'

'I see. I suppose I might have guessed that you would go to any lengths to extract me from Coleridge and his circle. When was Mr Thelwall acquitted of treason?'

'1794, but — '

'Three whole years ago! Can the man not be allowed to make a mistake? Must you come here and start spreading rumours about him?'

'I am not spreading rumours,' Alex replied, losing his temper. 'I am simply telling you what I know. Local opinion is very suspicious of all Coleridge's friends, including the Wordsworths.'

'Dorothy too?' she said incredulously. He nodded. 'Ridiculous!' she exclaimed, throwing up her hands. 'What you know appears to be gossip. Where have you heard this?'

'At the Globe in Stowey,' he admitted with a sigh. He had been there more than once and the gossip had not died down with the Wordsworths' departure, as he had hoped that it might. It had, if anything, become more virulent.

'So you are reporting the foolish speculations of men in their cups,' she said scornfully.

'You don't know what you are talking about,' he said hastily. 'My only intention was to warn you.'

'Well I wish you would not,' she retorted. 'All you have done since you came here has been to spoil things. Why do you not just go away?'

'And leave you to sigh over Coleridge, I suppose,' he said nastily.

She gasped and whirled round to leave him.

'Theodora, wait!' He exclaimed, already regretting his unkindness. He caught hold of her arm and pulled her back. The grass was a little uneven and, as she turned, she tripped, he caught her, and she found herself in his arms. Then, with an inarticulate exclamation, he lowered his head and kissed her on her mouth. For a brief moment, she stood still in his embrace, then struggled, pulling herself free.

'How dare you?' she cried, her voice shaking. 'You accuse me of all kinds of misbehaviour with Coleridge but he has never treated me as you have done! Never! Yes, I have been foolish enough to . . . to fall in love with him, but he has never forgotten that he is a married man. But you, as good as wed to Vivienne, behave like a . . . a libertine! How could you?'

'Theodora! Theodora, wait!' he said, but she did not. This was, perhaps, just as well, for had she done so, he would not have had the slightest idea what to say in his defence.

18

After parting with Theodora, Alex strode round to the stables, saddled his own horse with all the haste that he had been accustomed to using in his campaign days, and galloped off down the drive, heedless of how he was kicking up the surface.

It was not long before common sense prevailed. He slowed to a canter, then a trot. Before long, he was proceeding towards Bridgwater at a walking pace. His mind was in turmoil. He had been trying to conceal the truth from himself: now, he had to face it. He was in love with Theodora Buckleigh. His feelings for her had begun on the day he had met her, when she had turned that elfin face towards him and scolded him for his supposed insensitivity. Yet he had to confess, to his shame, that it had not really been until he had seen that she was in love with Coleridge that he had begun to think of her in a romantic light. What a waste, he had thought to himself. Fancy such a lovely girl sighing over a man who could never belong to her! So he had taken her to Lyme, and rowed her across the bay, all the while savouring the delight on her piquant little face.

Time and again, he had found excuses to visit, to linger when his work was done. Still it had not occurred to him why he could not tear himself away. He knew all along, of course that he was bound to Vivienne, but he had supposed himself safe, foolishly thinking that his feelings for Theodora must be brotherly. How ironic, then, that he should realize now that it was for Vivienne that his affection was fraternal. When he was in her presence, he felt none of the excitement, the desire, the longing to protect, that he felt when he was with Theodora.

However he felt, it was no use thinking like this. His sense of honour meant that he could not let Vivienne down in this kind of way. He hated to have parted with Theodora as he had done, and loathed himself for his boorish behaviour. But, in some ways, perhaps it was for the best. He would write her a civil letter, apologizing for his conduct and wishing her a pleasant stay for the remainder of her time at Alfoxden. Then he would devote himself to Vivienne and perhaps, with any luck, discover some kind of spark.

★ ★ ★

As Alex was making his way to Bridgwater, Vivienne was sitting sewing in a summer-house in her cousin's garden whilst Laurence Ormsby was reading to her. He had the book propped up on a small wooden reading stand, so that he could turn the pages with his single hand.

'What an entertaining tale,' she remarked, as he came to the end of the chapter.

'Another?' he suggested, putting out his hand to turn the page. By accident, he caught the edge of the book instead, and both book and stand went flying. 'Damnation!' he exclaimed, as he bent to pick them up. 'Forgive me. Such stupid clumsiness,' he murmured in a mortified tone, his head still bent over his task.

'No,' she said quickly, bending down to help him. 'You are not clumsy; you are gallant and brave. You cannot know how much I admire you for your determination and fortitude; your refusal to be beaten.' Their eyes met. 'Please, continue with your reading,' she said softly.

'Would that this privilege could always be mine.' Had the book not fallen, had his composure not been shaken, he would never have spoken as he did. He could have bitten the words back the moment that they were said.

'Don't,' she replied, turning her face away. When Laurence Ormsby had first arrived to visit her, she had been more delighted to see him than she had expected. She had known him before he had lost his arm, but at that time, she had not thought of him in any other light than as her brother's comrade in arms. Now, she found herself enjoying his company more and more, and hoping that he would stay for longer. She had not really known her heart, however, until Alex had appeared. To her horror, she had found herself wishing that he would go away so that she could enjoy Laurence's company undisturbed.

For his part, Laurence had always admired Vivienne. Had he returned from the war whole, he might have tried his luck. By the time he had recovered his health, Alex was engaged to her — Alex, his friend, who was certainly not in love with her and could never appreciate her as she deserved. He had been determined not to betray himself. But she had looked up at him and smiled; and he, still full of the romance of the story that they were reading, and disturbed by the small accident, had said too much.

'I beg your pardon,' he said. 'I should not have said anything. Or rather, of course, I should have been clearer.' He made a desperate effort to recover himself. 'I meant, of course, that I would be fortunate to be as lucky as Alex . . . to find someone . . . ' He looked at her face again. He leaned across and clasped her hands which were trembling on her lap. 'Oh Vivienne, forgive me,' he said unsteadily, getting up, and striding away towards the stables.

He had always been a superb rider, and the loss of his arm had not changed that. He called for his horse to be saddled, and was about to mount, when Alex appeared in the stable yard.

'Laurence,' Alex exclaimed. 'This is an unexpected pleasure.' His thoughts had been nothing but a torment. The sight of his friend offered a welcome diversion.

To his astonishment, Laurence did not pause, but leaped lightly into the saddle. 'You'd better treat her well, that's all I can say,' he declared almost with a snarl, before riding off at a smart pace.

Alex frowned after him, then gave his horse to the stable boy, and headed out into the gardens, where he was sure he would find Vivienne. He heard her before he saw her. She was in the summer-house, and she was crying. She looked up, saw him, and said involuntarily 'Oh no!'

Alex, who had been hurrying to comfort her, paused in his tracks. 'What's this?' he said, frowning. 'Has Laurence been upsetting you?'

'No, no, of course not,' Vivienne answered, pulling herself together and drying her tears. 'It's nothing. Forgive my . . . my opening remark. I do so dislike being found crying. So childish; but the story was very . . . very affecting.'

Had Alex not just discovered that he was in love with Theodora, he might have accepted this lame excuse. But having acknowledged his feelings made him more sensitive to the feelings of others. 'Let's sit down together until you feel better, shall we?' He suggested. After a few moments he took her hand. 'Vivienne, my dear, you know that I love you very much, don't you?' Her hand gripped his convulsively. 'In fact, I love you so much that I would hate it . . . *hate* it, if you denied yourself true love for the sake of the brother and sisterly affection that you and I have always had for one another.'

She stared at him, surprise and something that looked like dawning hope in her eyes. 'Alex . . . ?' she ventured.

'Would you like to be released from your promise to me?' he asked her gently.

'Of course not,' she protested, too quickly. 'Vivi.'

She turned back to him impulsively, at the sound of the old childhood name. 'Oh, Alex, it is as you have said. I love you very much but not . . . not in that way.'

He gripped her hands again, then released them. 'Look, I know I've only just arrived, but let me go and fetch Laurence, will you? I've a feeling that he might have something to say to you.'

An hour later, he sat in the same parlour of the inn in which he and Laurence had sat on a previous occasion. He had managed to catch the other man before he had done more than pour himself one glass of the bottle of red that he had opened, clearly intending to drown his sorrows. Now, with any luck, Laurence was proposing to Vivienne, and he, Alex, could drown his sorrows instead.

He was free. He could now approach Theodora; except that he couldn't. 'I have been foolish enough to fall in love with Coleridge,' she had told him. She loved someone else. He, like a fool, had shouted at her and insulted her, so that even when she recovered from this infatuation, he would probably be the last person about whom she would cherish romantic thoughts. He would be much better advised to go back to London, then to his estates, and put her out of his mind. She was as far out of reach as she had ever been.

Before he returned, however, he concluded reluctantly that he really ought to go back to Nether Stowey once more. He owed it to the Duke of Portland to give him an up-to-date report about what he had seen and heard in the vicinity. Besides, he was curious to discover what, if anything, the locals made of the notorious John Thelwall.

With that end in mind, he rode back to Nether Stowey alone, leaving his groom at Bridgwater, and once more took accommodation at the Globe Inn. He took the opportunity to walk about the village, and look at Coleridge's cottage. Not wanting to appear as if he was spying, he knocked at the door, but no one seemed to be there. Doubtless Coleridge was over at Alfoxden, entrancing Theodora with his delightful verse and his big blue eyes, Alex decided savagely.

He returned to the inn and tidied himself ready for his evening meal, which he ate downstairs in the public room. The landlord recognized him and, remembering him as a gentleman who knew how to pay his way, and reward good service with a little extra, welcomed him with a cheerful smile.

'Are you staying long this time, sir?' the

man asked hopefully.

'Just one night, I'm afraid,' Alex replied, remembering in time that he had assumed a slight West Country accent during his previous visit. Having consumed an appetizing but plain meal of meat pie, potatoes and cabbage, he settled down in the tap room, prepared to discover any fresh opinions on the subject of Coleridge and his circle.

He was not to be disappointed. As the locals drifted in, it was clear that Coleridge's new guest was the latest topic of conversation.

' . . . what the world's coming to,' one man was saying to another as they entered. 'Frenchies everywhere.'

'He's not a Frenchy,' his companion said.

'Who isn't?' asked a man who was already sitting with a glass in front of him.

'That foreigner staying at Gilbard's with Mr Coleridge.'

'If he's a foreigner, he must be a Frenchy,' contributed another man.

'That ain't so,' answered the man with the drink. 'He's not from these parts; he's from London, some do say.'

'Aye, and nearly got his head cut off for his wickedness,' put in a man who had not spoken so far. 'Not the sort we want around here.'

'I've heard him speak,' Alex ventured,

wanting to take some of the heat out of this conversation. 'All talk and no action is my opinion.'

A few of the men nodded sagely, but Alex overheard one say to another 'He's from London himself. What would he know?'

19

'I fear that I shall be obliged to leave you very soon,' said Theodora, opening a letter which had arrived for her that morning, and which William had collected from Holford along with the other post. 'My stepfather and his wife will be returning from Lyme Regis in the next few days. They will collect me and take me home.'

Dorothy looked disappointed. 'Are you sure that you cannot stay?' she asked. 'For my part, I would be glad to have you with us always.'

'You are very good,' Theodora replied. 'I have had a wonderful holiday but am now ready to go home.' As she spoke, she realized that it was true.

'Well there is this to be said for it; you *must* go, if you are to come again, as I hope that you will.'

'We will continue to write, will we not?'

'Of course,' Dorothy assured her. 'You will hear all the news.'

Both Wordsworth and Coleridge were sorry to hear that she was going; but with their continuing discussion about a possible joint publication of a book of poetry in the future, together with their own writing, Theodora knew that they would soon be occupied with other things.

Just a day before, she had received a letter from Alex. In it, he had stated that he was shortly to return to London. Then he went on in the following manner:

Forgive me for my ungentlemanly conduct. I am truly sorry for distressing you in the way that I did. I have very little to say in my defence. I was anxious about the presence of the gentleman whom we were discussing, and I became angry with you for not taking my concerns seriously. In my anger I struck out in an unmannerly way, which I shall always regart. Please accept my sincere apologies, and my best wishes for your continued health and happiness.

'Wretched man!' she exclaimed out loud, ripping his letter into four pieces, then instantly piecing it together so that she could read it again. 'I know why he is so keen to apologize. He doesn't want me to tell Michael about what he did.' She touched her lips with her fingers. That had been her very first kiss and, although he had been fierce and angry, he had not hurt her. Guiltily, she wondered what it might have been like had Coleridge kissed her. She closed her eyes to try and imagine it, but when she did so, it was Alex's face that she saw. 'Wretched, wretched man,' she said again, and this time ripped his letter into tiny shreds.

The arrival of Lord and Lady Ashbourne and her own departure almost came as an anti-climax to everything that had gone before. Coleridge had arrived, alone this time, and had taken William off for a walk. Dorothy had gone to Holford to collect the letters. It did seem for a time as if Theodora would have to leave without saying goodbye to anyone. She could see that both Lord and Lady Ashbourne found this very strange. Knowing by now the unconventional nature of the household in which she had been staying, Theodora did not think that anyone would feel in the least bit slighted if she were to leave without saying goodbye. For herself, however, if would have seemed dreadful to have to drift away without a word. She was, therefore, very thankful when, after she and her escorts had been waiting for perhaps twenty minutes, Dorothy reappeared, full of greetings and apologies.

'It has been such a wonderful visit,' Dorothy said, rather surprising Jessie by gripping both of her hands. 'We have been so pleased to have her with us. Do say that she may come again.'

'Her brother Michael is her guardian, so it is for him to say,' Jessie replied. 'But I think that he will be very pleased by the bloom of health in her cheeks.'

'You are looking exceedingly well, my dear,' Ashbourne put in, smiling at Theodora.

'May I offer you some refreshment before you go?' Dorothy asked them.

Theodora was longing for Ashbourne to say yes, as she was hoping that Wordsworth and more particularly Coleridge, might return so that she could say goodbye. She was not really surprised, however, when Ashbourne said, 'You are very kind but I fear that we must decline. We have a good deal of ground to cover. The nurse has gone ahead with our daughter and we must catch them up at Salisbury where we intend to spend the night.'

Theodora managed to keep her composure as she embraced Dorothy, but she did shed a few tears when Basil held up his chubby arms to press a sticky kiss upon her cheek.

Soon they were in the coach, Ashbourne had given the signal to go, and Dorothy was waving at the door. As Theodora was watching her through unshed tears, she saw her expression change; she paused in her waving, then stepped forward crying, 'Oh pray, stop, just for a moment.'

The coachman pulled on the reins and they came to a halt once more. A moment later, they heard the sound of running feet and Coleridge, flushed and breathless, appeared at the carriage door, clearly having run down the hill.

'Theodora!' he exclaimed. 'Leaving without a goodbye?'

'We have a long journey,' she answered, turning to glance at the earl and countess. 'I did not know when you would be coming back. Sometimes you and William are gone all day.'

'But not on the day of your departure,' he replied. 'We had things to discuss, but we came back so as not to miss you.'

As if to give veracity to his words, Wordsworth appeared, not running, but clearly having walked at a brisk pace. Briefly, he took Coleridge's place at the window. 'We wanted to see you off,' he said, with one of his rare smiles. 'Dorothy will miss you.'

'And I her,' replied Theodora truthfully. 'We have promised to write.'

'If you and your sister make a visit to your home county of Cumberland, do visit us on your way,' Ashbourne said politely.

'You may be sure that we shall do so,'

Wordsworth answered. He lifted Theodora's hand to his lips. 'Safe travelling, Theodora.'

'Thank you,' she answered. He had not proved to be the man of her dreams, but he had been a kind and conversable host, and although not wealthy, generous in sharing what he had.

He stepped back and Coleridge took his place at the window. Not content with kissing her hand, however, he lifted himself up by dint of putting one foot on the framework of the coach, leaned in, and kissed her cheek. 'Don't forget us, Theodora,' he said. Then, stepping down again, he drew a paper out of his coat. 'Do you remember when Sara scalded my foot and we sat outside under the lime trees? I've made you a copy of the poem I wrote.'

'Thank you,' she answered, barely able to hold back her tears. 'Goodbye; and . . . and pray send my greetings to . . . to Mrs Coleridge; and kiss Hartley for me.'

'I will. Goodbye; and God bless you.'

The coach moved off again, and Theodora waved until they were out of sight. Then, unable to help herself, she burst into tears, clutching her precious poem in her hand, whilst Ashbourne moved over to her side and pulled her gently into his arms, so that she could sob against his shoulder.

That evening, after they had arrived at the
inn in Salisbury at which they were to stay,
Ashbourne went for a walk around the town
to stretch his limbs, tactfully leaving Jessie
and Theodora together.

'Do you want to talk about it?' Jessie asked
her, when they were sitting together in the
pleasant bedroom that had been allocated to
Theodora. 'I'm a very good listener, and I
won't tell anyone; not even Raff, if you would
prefer it.'

Theodora nodded, but then seemed to give
the lie to that assent by looking down at her
hands which were clasped in her lap, and
saying nothing.

Earlier, after crying in Lord Ashbourne's
embrace, she had fallen asleep, whereupon
Jessie had gently removed the paper from her
fingers and, after a brief nod from the earl,
had read what was written upon it. 'It's quite
unexceptionable,' she had said in a low tone.
'Nothing improper. Actually, it's a very good
poem — very good indeed. That young man
has a way with words, there is no doubt about
it.'

'If he has been using his way with words, as
you put it, to damage my Thea, then I will
find a way to make him pay,' Ashbourne had

replied, his tone even, his grey eyes like chips of ice.

Now Jessie turned to Theodora, saying gently, 'When did you fall in love with him?'

Theodora looked up, startled for a moment, then smiled ruefully. 'From the very first, I think,' she answered. She described for Jessie how she and the Wordsworths had watched as Coleridge had leaped the gate and bounded towards them across the fields.

'Yes I can see that that must have made quite an impression upon you,' Jessie agreed. 'But surely — forgive me, I do not mean to sound critical — the fact that he was married must instantly have put you on your guard?'

'It would have done, had I known from the first, I think,' Theodora admitted. 'But I did not find out until . . . until . . . ' She broke off.

Jessie looked at her than said cautiously, 'I do not want to upset you further, my dear, but I have to say that I think it was very wrong of him not to tell you.'

'It was not his fault,' Theodora protested, looking more distressed than angry. 'There was no deliberate deceit on his part, or on anyone else's. Dorothy and William both knew about his marriage. I suppose that all of them just assumed that I must know.'

'So how did you find out?'

'Alex came to see me with his fiancée, Miss Markham. She was already acquainted with Mrs Coleridge and mentioned meeting her in Bristol.'

'Alex?'

'Mr Kydd, who escorted me to the West Country.'

'You saw something of him while you were staying with the Wordsworths, then.'

'Yes I did,' Theodora declared, 'and I must say that he is the most interfering, high-handed, judgemental person that I have ever met in the whole of my life.'

'Goodness!' exclaimed Jessie in surprise. 'What form did his interference take?'

'Oh, just acting as though he was Michael, and thinking he could tell me when I should be going home, and what I ought to think about some of Dorothy's guests,' she replied vaguely. She was well aware that over some matters — the business of being found lying on her back next to Coleridge for example — Jessie might well take Alex's part. They were quiet for a while. Then Theodora said, 'Jessie, how do you stop loving someone when it is hopeless?'

Jessie sighed. 'I am the very last person to ask,' she admitted. 'I was in love with Raff for years, and never dreamed that he would ever look my way. But then I was stuck in

268

Illingham, close to his estate, living with his sister and bound to see him from time to time. You are going far away from Mr Coleridge, into quite a different county, and amongst people who will have no connection with him. The memories are bound to fade. But you will have to try hard not to think about him.'

'I suppose so,' Theodora agreed with a sigh. But that night, she slept with his poem under her pillow.

PART THREE

Reality

20

'Welcome, welcome, my boy,' said the Duke of Portland. 'You come in a good hour. You'll take a glass of claret with me?'

'Thank you,' said Alex. After writing his letter to Theodora, he had travelled back to London by easy stages, eventually arriving at Bulstrode House. His grace greeted him in the same room in which they had spoken on his previous visit.

Their conversation ranged around various subjects for a time until Portland said, 'Now, do you have anything to tell me?'

Alex thought about how his whole life had changed since he had last stood in this room, but he decided that this was not what the duke wanted to hear. 'I visited a number of places in the West Country, but in particular concentrated my attention on Coleridge and his circle, as you desired.'

'And?'

'I think the man's harmless, sir,' Alex replied frankly. 'I've had conversation with him, and made enquiries in Bristol. While his views may be radical — although not by any means as radical as they were — he has largely withdrawn from public life. I saw no sign that he was seeking to stir the masses into unrest.'

'Hm,' the duke responded. 'Wait there a moment.' He left the room, but came back soon afterwards with a sheet of paper in his hand. 'I had this letter from one Dr Lysons in Bath. Apparently, a man who waited at table at a dinner attended by Coleridge and some others was much alarmed by the noisy vigour of the conversation, and by the radical nature of the sentiments. His anxieties got back to Lysons by a rather circuitous means, and he has written to me.' He tapped the paper. 'Thelwall was at the dinner, as was Thomas Poole, another radical.'

'Have you been given a full list of the guests?' Alex asked him.

'Not a full list, no.'

'Then you may not be aware that I was among the company.'

The duke looked up sharply. 'Indeed? For what reason?'

Reluctant to say anything about Theodora, Alex merely said, 'You asked me to keep an eye on things. I was introduced to Coleridge by chance, and made it my business to further the acquaintance. I happened to be in the vicinity when the dinner was arranged and was invited to attend.'

The duke looked at him with narrowed eyes. 'Would you have mentioned this circumstance had I not brought the matter up?' he asked.

'I had every intention of doing so,' Alex replied calmly.

The duke nodded. 'Very well. Give me your impressions, then.'

Alex gave the duke a broad outline of the conversation that had taken place at the table. 'My impression of Thelwall is that he is a spent force,' he concluded. 'What you have there, I think, is a group of intellectuals who are interested in politics, but who are as likely to be talking about religion, or poetry or nature instead. Yokels might find the vigour of their arguments alarming, but I would not have thought that they were of any danger to the realm.'

The duke nodded. 'No doubt you're right,' he agreed. 'Thank you for your views. Now, what of your own position? When are we to hear wedding bells?'

Alex looked rueful. 'Not for some time on my account, I fear. Miss Markham and I have agreed that we should not suit.'

The duke grunted. 'I'm sorry to hear that,' he said. 'Still, better to find out now than later, no doubt.'

'No doubt,' Alex agreed.

They conversed for a little longer on indifferent subjects, until eventually Alex took his leave, leaving his compliments for the duke's son and heir.

After the young man had gone, the duke stood looking after him thoughtfully before going to his study. He picked up a sheet of paper and re-read the message on it, which confirmed that his agent, one James Walsh, had been despatched to Nether Stowey. Perhaps Alex was right in saying that the group gathered in that region was harmless. Nevertheless, it would be useful to have a second opinion. Alex had spoken of a broken engagement. Perhaps half his mind had been elsewhere. He would not be the first to allow a broken heart to divert him from important business.

What was more, there had been something in Alex's tone which had suggested that the young man was partial. That was why the duke had said nothing of the plans that he had already put in place. It would never do for the younger man to decide to go back to Somerset and warn his radical friends of the agent's arrival.

★ ★ ★

276

Theodora was a little surprised that they should be returning to Derbyshire via London, until Jessie took her into her confidence. 'As you know, I'm increasing again,' she said one evening, 'and all in all, I don't feel very comfortable. Raff insists that I should consult his London physician, and I must own that I should be glad to do so.'

Theodora nodded seriously. Her own mother had died in giving her life, and she knew that Lord Ashbourne's first wife had died in childbirth. 'It would do no harm to be cautious,' she agreed.

Jessie's discomfort increased as the journey continued, so much so that on their arrival in London, Lord Ashbourne carried his wife upstairs in his arms and sent for his physician immediately. Theodora decided that the best thing that she could do would be to help to entertain little Leonora. The child was accustomed to having regular attention from her parents and, although she could not yet give voice to her feelings, clearly indicated as well as she could that she did not understand the situation.

'The doctor dresses up his remarks with fine language but he does not know what ails Jez any more than Leonora does,' Ashbourne told Theodora, his anxiety robbing him of some of his customary suavity. 'All he can say is that she must be allowed to rest and, above all, not travel. Would to God that we had stayed at Lyme!'

* * *

'I am very sorry for the way that things have fallen out,' Ashbourne said to Theodora after they had been in London for a week. 'You are now stranded in London in the middle of summer with nothing to do. Would you like me to arrange for you to be taken to Derbyshire?'

'Nothing to do?' Theodora replied. 'My dear Step-papa, I am thoroughly enjoying having Leonora to myself. When she has her nap, I manage to find plenty to entertain me.' Indeed, letters from Dorothy, Wordsworth or Coleridge arrived regularly, and were always answered without delay. There was also her correspondence with Michael to be maintained. She had half thought that Alex might write again, but there had been no correspondence from him after the letter that she had torn up. She knew that he had not left the area immediately after their stormy parting, for Dorothy had told her in a letter that he had been back to Nether Stowey. A servant of Thomas Poole had seen him in the Globe Inn and mentioned it to his master.

'You are very forgiving,' the earl replied. 'The truth of the matter is that I have removed you from your friends, only to leave you stranded here.'

'No no, it was time for me to come away,' she assured him. 'I do not repine.' The strange thing was, that she did not. She had needed a change from being protected and cosseted, and she had had it. Now, after a long holiday during which she had been left a good deal to her own devices, she found that a return to a close family atmosphere was just what she needed. It was quite strange to reflect that she was not related to Ashbourne and Jessie in any way.

Jessie had become increasingly uncomfortable after their arrival in London. On one occasion when Theodora visited her, Ashbourne having slipped out briefly, the younger woman could see that she was in a good deal of pain. An offer to fetch some warm milk was greeted with a feeble assent, so Theodora went to the kitchen to deliver the order herself, then took the cup back upstairs.

As she arrived at the countess's room, she overheard voices and realized that the earl was with her. Before she went in, she heard Jessie say, 'Raff don't leave me, will you?'

'Not for so much as a single night, I

promise you,' the earl answered tenderly.

Theodora went in with the milk, and found, as she had expected, that Ashbourne was sitting close to his wife, her hand in his. He got up, and took the milk with a smile and a word of thanks. She exchanged a few remarks with them, then left them alone. As she went back to her room, she remembered something that had happened in Nether Stowey whilst she had been staying there.

Coleridge and Wordsworth had been sharing some of their poems, and Theodora had had a chance to read a poem that Coleridge had written, entitled '*Sonnet, written on receiving letters informing me of the birth of a son, I being at Birmingham.*' She wondered how Sara Coleridge had felt, giving birth to David Hartley with her husband so far away. Ashbourne and his two sons both made it their business to be well within call when their children were being born. She recalled the occasion when Ashbourne and Coleridge had met and she had felt ashamed of her stepfather for his suavity and his perfect appearance. Now, witnessing his care and tenderness, she felt ashamed again, this time not of him, but of herself.

She was glad that she had remained in the West Country. To part from Coleridge before she had had the chance to see him in his home environment would not have done her any good at all. She would have continued to dream about him, with no reality to correct the dreams that she conjured up. A prolonged stay in Nether Stowey had done much to open her eyes. She still found him extremely appealing, but having seen the thoughtless way in which he often treated his wife — extraordinary for a man who noticed so much and felt so keenly — she was slowly coming to the conclusion that to be married to him might not be particularly comfortable. Nevertheless, he had been her first love. She retained an affection for him, and suspected that she always would.

They had been in London for almost two weeks, when Theodora was awoken one night by an agonized cry. Throwing on her dressing-gown she ran out into the corridor, only to bump into Jessie's abigail, who was just leaving her mistress's room. 'It's her ladyship,' said the servant in distressed tones. 'His lordship thinks she's losing the baby. He wants the doctor sent for at once.' That said, she hurried off to perform her errand.

Theodora paused in indecision, then after a few minutes she went to Jessie's door and knocked gently. The door was opened by the earl, his complexion ashen. 'What can I do?' she asked him.

He ran his hands through his hair. 'God knows. Go to Leonora, I suppose, and make sure she's not awake and afraid. And pray.'

Theodora did as she was asked. The little girl was fast asleep, her golden brown hair, so much like her mother's, spread out over her pillow, her thumb in her mouth. 'Poor mite,' said the nurse, tears coming to her eyes. 'God send she may not be motherless by the morning.'

It was the very thing that Theodora was thinking herself. Not giving voice to it, she said in as reassuring a tone as she could manage, 'There is no reason why she should be. Her ladyship is having the best of care, remember.'

'Yes, miss. Of course,' the woman replied, pulling herself together. 'Shall I heat some milk for us both?'

'Oh, yes please,' Theodora answered thankfully. 'I'm sure I shan't be able to sleep.'

'Nor I, miss.'

Nevertheless, after they had drunk their milk and shared in a little desultory conversation, the nurse's head began to nod. When she was asleep, and Theodora was sure that the little girl was as well, she tiptoed out and went down to the next floor to see if she could find out what was happening. As she arrived there, Lord Ashbourne came out of his wife's room, a dressing-gown thrown on over his shirt and breeches.

'Step-papa?' Theodora faltered.

'The doctor is with her, also her abigail and a midwife,' he said, his expression bleak. 'I've been told to go downstairs. Will you come with me, Thea?'

'Yes, of course,' she replied readily.

They went and sat down together in the book-room, where Ashbourne poured himself a brandy, offered one to Theodora, then recollected himself and said, 'Of course, you shouldn't be drinking this, should you?'

'I had a little from time to time in Somerset,' she confessed.

'Did you indeed?' he responded. Then, after a pause, he said, 'Tell me all about it — about him.'

Sensing that he needed to have his mind taken off what was happening upstairs, she began with the moment that she had seen Coleridge leaping over the gate, and told him everything, including the incident when they had laid on their backs side by side and looked at the clouds. 'He was the most wonderful man,' she concluded.

'When I first met him, I couldn't understand what you saw in him,' he replied.

'It was Jez who explained it to me.' He paused, and once again, his face looked anxious. 'Thea, what will I do if anything happens to her?' he asked, his tone one of quiet desperation.

A short time later, there was a knock at the door, and the doctor came in. Ashbourne sprang to his feet. 'My wife?'

The doctor smiled reassuringly. 'She is sleeping peacefully,' he replied. His expression became solemn. 'I fear that she has lost the child, however.'

'But she is all right?'

'She has lost some blood, but the bleeding has ceased. Rest is now the key to her recovery.' He paused. 'I am afraid that I am unable to tell your lordship yet whether she will be able to have any more children.'

'If she cannot, then I will regret it for her sake,' Ashbourne answered. 'For myself, I already have an heir, two other children and a delightful stepdaughter.' He looked briefly at Theodora, before turning back to the doctor. 'May I see her?'

'She is very tired, but she wants to see you,' the doctor answered. 'I will return in the morning. In the meantime, get some sleep yourself, my lord.' But he spoke to the empty air. Ashbourne was already out of the room and halfway up the stairs.

Knowing that she would find it hard to sleep, Theodora got into bed with her book of Coleridge's poems in her hand. Talking to Ashbourne about Coleridge had given rise to all kinds of thoughts, however, so instead of reading, she thought about the time that she had spent with him and the Wordsworths.

For the first time, it occurred to her that perhaps she had touched greatness. What if each of those two men was as singular as the other had supposed? What if in years to come, their poems were still being read long after they and all of their contemporaries had gone to dust? It was while she was mulling over this intriguing notion that she fell asleep.

21

To everyone's relief, the countess made an excellent recovery, and was soon chaffing at the instruction that she should keep to her bed. Ashbourne made sure that she obeyed orders, chiefly by remaining with her. Frequently, his lady would insist that he should get some fresh air, and on those occasions, Theodora sat with her. Sometimes, the two ladies read some of Coleridge's poems together.

'I do think that some of them are very fine,' said Jessie. 'Indeed, the poem which he wrote at the time of having to remain at home with a scalded foot I find particularly moving. It seems to speak to my own situation — trapped in this room.'

Jessie was beginning to look like a most unconvincing invalid. The glow was starting to return to her cheeks, and the sparkle to her eyes. Theodora suspected that this might have a good deal to do with the fact that that very morning, the doctor had declared that there was no reason why she might not have more children.

'I was there when he wrote it,' Theodora told her.

'You know, there is something rather compelling about gifted men,' Jessie said. 'It would have been very wonderful if you had not been attracted to him. The fact that you were no doubt proves your good taste.'

'Perhaps it does,' Theodora agreed. She was beginning to be able to think about Coleridge without longing or sadness.

That afternoon, Ashbourne and Theodora were downstairs whilst Jessie was having a nap, when the butler came in and announced that Mr Kydd had arrived.

Theodora went quickly over to the window to hide her suddenly hot cheeks. Since coming to London, she had heard something of the reputation of John Thelwall the notorious radical. She had also learned about Coleridge's own days of political activism, when he had stirred crowds in Bristol with his eloquence. She still felt that Alex had been rather high-handed, but she believed that she could understand something of his motives.

What had immediately come into her mind when he had been announced, however, had not been his motives or his high-handedness, but the kiss that he had pressed upon her mouth the last time that they had met. She almost felt as though the mark of it was still imprinted upon her lips.

'Lord Ashbourne,' she heard him say. She

had forgotten how deep his voice was. 'Miss Theodora.' He sounded surprised.

She turned around and made her curtsy. He looked tanned and healthy and she thought that his hair was a little longer than previously. He was dressed correctly for a morning visit, in a dark-blue coat with biscuit coloured breeches, a toning waistcoat with blue embroidery, and shiny boots. He was holding a large bunch of yellow roses.

'You are very welcome, Kydd,' said Ashbourne, courteously. 'In what way may I serve you?'

'I had just come into town, and heard that Lady Ashbourne was indisposed,' he said. 'I have brought her these trifling blooms.'

'That is very kind,' said the earl smoothly. It had not escaped his notice that Theodora had avoided the young man's gaze. Alex's expression when he had realized that Theodora was present had also been quite revealing. 'She has been resting, but I will see if she is awake and ready to receive a visitor. Theodora will entertain you whilst I am gone.' He went out of the room, very correctly leaving the door open behind him.

There was an awkward silence after which both of them began to speak at once. Alex signalled to Theodora that she might speak first, whereupon she found that she had no idea what to say. After a brief hesitation she said, 'Are . . . are you well, Mr Kydd?'

It was on the tip of his tongue to remind her that she had agreed to call him Alex, but he knew that he must tread carefully. No more than she had he forgotten what had happened at their last meeting. 'I am well thank you, Miss Theodora,' he replied.

Again, there was an awkward silence, broken by Alex saying 'In my letter — ' and Theodora saying 'Thank you for — '

As on the previous occasion, Alex signalled for Theodora to speak first. 'No, sir, it is your turn to begin,' she said.

'In my letter, I apologized for my conduct,' he said. 'I did not want to disgust you further by seeking another interview; but I fear that my letter did not convey the depth of my regret. I — '

'Oh pray say no more,' Theodora interrupted. 'It is over. Can we not forget it?'

'You are more generous than I deserve,' he said.

'I was angry at what you said, but I am prepared to believe that you spoke from the best of motives,' she went on. 'Over the past days . . . ' She paused, seeking to find the right words. 'Over the past days, we — my stepfather and I — have been dreadfully anxious about Jessie. It has made me realize that we should not be at odds with anyone, if we can avoid it. I would not be on bad terms with you, Mr Kydd — Alex.'

He smiled and took her hand. 'Nor I with you — Theodora.'

Neither of them mentioned the kiss, but the memory of it hung between them and there was a long pause as their eyes met.

The sound of footsteps in the hall broke the mood, and shortly afterwards, Lord Ashbourne appeared in the doorway. 'My wife would be glad to see you,' he said. 'Pray do not stay too long, though. She is still recovering.'

'Thank you.' He walked to the door with Ashbourne, then turned. 'May I take you out driving tomorrow?' he asked Theodora.

She looked doubtfully at the earl. 'I don't know whether I ought — ' she began.

'Some fresh air would do you good, Thea,' said the earl reassuringly.

'Thank you. I would like that,' Theodora answered.

'Then I will collect you tomorrow at about eleven, if that is convenient to you.'

After the men had gone upstairs, she stood for a moment, deep in thought. She had been aware for some time that the unhappy way in which they had parted had been on her conscience. Now she had been able to play her part in putting it right. It would be good to be on friendly terms with Alex again.

Suddenly she caught sight of her reflection in the mirror and realized that she was smiling. Take care, you foolish girl, she told herself. Coleridge was married; but Alex is engaged. Then she blushed at the train of thought that had made her link the one with the other.

★ ★ ★

The following day, Theodora was ready long before Alex arrived. Indeed, she had to prevent herself from running to look out of her bedroom window every time a carriage was heard. In the end she went to Jessie's room to wait. The countess was alone, Ashbourne having gone downstairs to speak to a man who had come to see him on a matter of business.

'You look lovely,' Jessie said.

'Do you think so?' Theodora had taken special care with her appearance that day. She was still getting used to the pleasure of wearing colours again after being in mourning, and had chosen to put on a carriage dress of sky blue, with a bonnet lined with matching silk and a pair of the specially made boots that hid her limp.

'Charming,' Jessie assured her. 'But take my word for it — don't go rushing down the minute he arrives. It doesn't do for a man to think that a woman is too eager.'

'I am not going to think of him in that way, Jessie,' said Theodora firmly. 'I fell into that trap with Coleridge and I am not going to do so again. He is an engaged man and out of my reach. He is a friend and that is all.'

'Perhaps,' Jessie agreed. 'But it does no harm to keep in practice, does it?'

Despite Jessie's advice, the moment that Alex arrived, Theodora hurried down the stairs and was ready to greet him in the hall. Ashbourne emerged from the book-room with his visitor at the same time. 'Very good,' he said. 'A wise woman knows that a man does not like to keep his horses waiting.'

'That is not what Jessie said,' Theodora replied, then blushed at the memory of the countess's words.

Ashbourne smiled. 'I can imagine what Jez said, but she does not know everything,' he drawled.

Alex helped her up into the phaeton with a steady hand, whilst his groom held the horse's heads. Theodora, recognizing the man said, 'Good day to you, Graves. I hope you are well?'

'Fair enough, miss,' the man replied, touching his hat.

In no time, Alex was guiding them through the streets at a smart trot. He was driving a matched pair of chestnut horses, his effortless skill showing a fine understanding of horseflesh. It reminded Theodora that he had been in the cavalry, and she mentioned the fact. 'Did you enjoy it?' she asked him.

'Yes — at least, I enjoyed the comradeship, the opportunity to work with the horses, train men into working together and so on. The violence of warfare didn't appeal to me.'

'Do you really think that war is necessary?' Theodora asked after a short silence.

Alex detected the influence of Coleridge, but wisely did not say so. 'I think it should be avoided wherever possible. Sadly, I do not think that that is the case with France.'

Their journey now took them through some streets which were very congested, so Theodora kept quiet to allow Alex to concentrate on his horses. She noticed how quietly confident he was, not alarming his pair by sudden movements or angry words or gestures as did some other drivers. She realized that she felt very much at ease with him, and thought that in view of how stormy their relationship had been at times, this was rather strange.

'How is Miss Markham?' she asked him once they had got to the park.

'I believe that she is well; however, I am not in any position to be able to give you any up-to-date news on her state of health. We have agreed to end our engagement, you see.'

'Oh dear! I am sorry,' she exclaimed in sudden sympathy. At the same time her heart gave a little skip that she would have been at a loss to explain.

'Are you?' he asked quizzically.

'Of course,' she responded at once. 'We may have had our differences, but I would never dream of rejoicing over your misfortune.'

'I do not think of it as misfortune,' he replied. 'We simply decided that we should not suit. We have known one another for too long, I think.'

'Is that possible in such a case?' she asked, looking at him and wrinkling her brow in a way that he thought positively adorable.

'I believe so,' he replied. 'Our relationship was essentially one of brother and sister. We love each other dearly and always shall, but it is only when another kind of love comes along that one knows the difference.'

'Yes indeed,' Theodora answered, recalling how she had only had to see Coleridge for a moment to fall in love with him. What a long time ago that now seemed.

'What are you thinking about?' he asked her, seeing her pensive expression.

'I was remembering Coleridge,' she answered immediately, then blushed. For a moment, he tugged on the reins, in a manner that was quite uncharacteristic of him. Then an acquaintance approached them, the subject was changed, and as they drove back later, they talked of other things.

'May I take you driving again?' Alex asked, when he returned her to Ashbourne's town house.

'If you like,' she answered shyly.

'I should like to very much,' he responded, his expression warm. 'You referred to the differences that we have had. I should like to think that they were now at an end.'

'So would I,' Theodora replied.

She watched from one of the upstairs windows as he swung himself up into the driver's seat and set off. He is free, she thought to herself. He is free.

★　★　★

They saw a good deal of Alex over the next few days. He took Theodora out driving twice more, escorted her to Hatchard's to change her books, and dined with them on the first occasion that Lady Ashbourne was permitted to come downstairs. Now that Theodora knew he was not engaged, she did not have to be guarded about her feelings and she found herself liking him more and more, particularly as happy memories of Salisbury and Lyme return-ed to her mind. They talked of almost everything and anything. They laughed at the same things, enjoyed the same books, and took the same pleasure in country pursuits. She had to wonder whether things would have fallen out differ-ently had he not been engaged when they had travelled down to the West Country.

On the occasion when he came to dinner, he was dressed in a midnight-blue coat with white knee breeches and stockings and a white waistcoat embroidered with silver. His dark brown hair had been brushed till it shone. He smiled at her and, for a moment, he took her breath away.

I'm cured, she thought to herself that night as she prepared for bed. I'm cured of Coleridge. As for Alex, she would not allow herself to think about what she felt for him just yet.

* * *

'Well, my lady, I am delighted to be able to say that you are completely fit,' the doctor pronounced one morning with a beaming smile, after he had examined Lady Ashbourne in her bedchamber. 'I see no reason why you should not return to Derbyshire.'

'Thank goodness for that,' her ladyship replied in a relieved tone. 'I have had quite enough of London for the time being.'

'Would you like me to inform the earl?'

'No, thank you. I would prefer to tell him myself,' was the answer. 'There is just one other matter on which I would like your advice, then I will let you go and visit some other patients.'

Needless to say, Lord Ashbourne was very pleased to hear his wife's news. He was, if possible, even more delighted at the answer to her further enquiry. 'Seeing you in bed and being unable to ravish you has been very trying to my nerves,' he drawled, leaning over to kiss her.

'There is only one thing that concerns me,' she said, after she had returned his embrace with enthusiasm. 'What about Theodora and Mr Kydd? I would not for the world put anything in the way of their romance.'

'An obstacle or two is good for romance,' Ashbourne replied. 'If Kydd is serious in his intentions, then he will pursue her to Derbyshire.'

'At least she is over Coleridge,' said Jessie,

leaning once more into his embrace.

Theodora told herself that she was delighted at the prospect of returning home. She longed to see Michael again, and was looking forward to discovering how much the babies had grown. There was no denying, however, that when she had received the news that they would soon be travelling north, she had experienced a hollow feeling in the pit of her stomach that was very much like dread. She had enjoyed seeing so much of Alex, and was not looking forward to parting from him. He was due to visit that day, she was not quite sure when. Would he feel the same way, or would he wave her goodbye without a qualm?

She was glad when a letter from Dorothy arrived to distract her. She must write and let her friends know that she would be going back to Illingham, so that she did not miss any letters. She began reading with a smile of pleasure on her face. By the time she had finished her letter, her expression was very different.

My dear Theodora

The most vexatious thing has occurred. We are to be thrown out of Alfoxden next year! It seems that there has been a spy in Nether Stowey, reporting on our various activities and painting them in the blackest possible light, giving the impression that we are traitors to our country! Word of this false report has got back to the lady who owns Alfoxden, and she has decreed that we are to be banished from Eden. Coleridge makes light of it, joking in his usual way, but I know that he is as disappointed as we are. You know how well he and William work together. We will just have to think of another scheme.

A spy! Who might that have been? Then she remembered, with a sensation of creeping horror, that Alex had been in touch with the Duke of Portland, the home secretary. He had spoken against Coleridge's views and warned her, Theodora, about the radical nature of some of the company at Alfoxden. He had been to Bristol where, she knew, Wordsworth and Coleridge had first met. He had visited Nether Stowey again without telling anyone about it. Could he be the spy? Had he even been trying to find out more about Coleridge on the day when he had taken her to Lyme? The idea was too repulsive to be borne.

While she was still standing with the letter in her hand, the butler announced Alex. He walked in smiling, but his smile faded as he took in the look on her face. 'My dear Theodora, what is it? Is it bad news?'

'I do believe it is,' she replied coldly. 'Tell me Alex, did you pass on information about Dorothy and William and their friends?'

'What is this about?' he asked her, honestly puzzled at first.

'You tell me,' she responded. 'I am not the one who makes mysterious visits to Nether Stowey without telling anyone.'

He flushed slightly. 'It was not mysterious,' he said. 'A man does not have to speak about every visit that he makes everywhere, surely.'

'For goodness sake Alex, stop playing games!' she said in an exasperated tone. 'Can you not be honest about this?'

He sighed. 'Very well,' he said. 'I did visit Nether Stowey, and I did want to find out what was being said.'

'And then you reported it to your paymaster, and I have now discovered the consequences of your spying.'

'I was not spying,' he said.

'Did you tell your employer the Duke of Portland about what my friends were doing?' she demanded. 'Well? Did you?'

'He is not my employer,' he answered. 'Yes, I did, but — '

'Would you like to know the consequences?' she asked him, ignoring his last remark. 'My friends have been given notice to quit. Yes, you may well stare,' she continued, in response to his expression of astonishment. 'They were happily settled at Alfoxden, where William and Coleridge could work together. They had made a home for themselves, and for little Basil. Now, thanks to your tale-bearing, that home is being snatched from them, and they have done nothing wrong — nothing at all.'

'Theodora, I assure you — '

'Did you make notes after that dinner party, so you could pass them on? I cannot believe that you could sit at someone's table and then behave in so underhand a manner. How could you be so vile?'

'Theodora, I — '

'Oh go away, go away and never come back! I never ever want to see you again as long as I live. It makes me sick even to look at you.'

Alex's face had taken on an ashen hue. Now, he took a step backwards. 'If that is what you think of me, then I have no alternative but to withdraw. Pray accept my best wishes for your future happiness, and my assurances that I never meant to . . . to — '

'Just go,' she repeated, turning her back so that he would not see the tears streaming down her face.

22

London — Spring 1798

Strangely enough, coming to London this time had not seemed to Theodora to be nearly so much of an ordeal as it had the previous year. Then, she had been shy and morbidly fearful of being stared at. Time spent with the Wordsworths and Coleridge had changed her way of looking at the world. She would never be as careless of appearances as were they — no one connected in any way to Lord Ashbourne could possibly be that — but she was much less concerned with the opinions of strangers. She had found her voice and if she disagreed with people, she was not afraid to say so.

Lord Ashbourne's town house was more crowded this year than it had been the previous autumn, for in addition to the earl and countess, Michael and Evangeline were in residence, visiting London for the season. This suited Theodora very well. Although more confident than she had been, she still did not relish being the focus of attention. With the blond, beautiful and curvaceous

302

Evangeline in the vicinity, there was no danger of that. Michael and his wife had also brought their son Paul with them, and with two year old Leonora on the premises as well, the house was anything but quiet.

Theodora loved being at the heart of the family. If at times she thought with regret that she did not have anyone special of her own, she did not do so for long. Love had contained too many unpleasant pitfalls. She would not make that mistake again.

She had not heard from Alex in many months. After she had given him his *congé*, he had attempted to contact her in person at first. She had steadfastly refused to see him, telling Lord and Lady Ashbourne that his conduct had been too intolerable to be borne. He had written to her as well, but she had returned his letters unopened, and after a while they had ceased.

Ashbourne had enquired whether he ought to teach the young man his manners. This offer had turned Jessie's face pale. She had reminded him that the last duel that he had fought, which had been over her, Jessie's honour, had nearly been the death of him. Theodora, alarmed, had made haste to assure them that Alex's bad conduct had in no way affected her reputation. More than this she would not say. As they had by no means set their hearts on her making a match with the young man, they had allowed her to cut the connection without further explanation. She told herself firmly that she had intervened, not because she cared two straws about Alex; rather it was Lord Ashbourne's welfare that concerned her.

She had dreaded that Michael, who was closer to him, might ask to know more, but evidently the earl and countess must have warned him, for he said nothing of the matter. Later, he casually mentioned that Alex had gone abroad on a diplomatic mission of some kind. 'More spying and poking his nose in, no doubt,' Theodora had remarked nastily. More than that she would not say, however much Michael might stare. As far as she knew, Alex was still abroad and she was glad of it. She had no wish to encounter him again.

Dorothy and William were long since resigned to leaving Alfoxden in the summer. Indeed, Dorothy had written to say that they and Coleridge were all making plans to go to Germany in the autumn in order to study there. Dorothy referred to their times spent together with great affection. Her last letter had contained some sentences that had leaped out at Theodora from the page.

Have you ever considered visiting Germany? I am already looking forward to the visit with pleasurable anticipation, but my pleasure, I know, would be all the greater if Theodora were there. Coleridge and William have both spoken about how we all enjoyed your gentle company. Will you not consider it?

Germany! She could not deny that she was tempted. Yet could she really afford to be in Coleridge's vicinity again? She had overcome her infatuation. Would it be rekindled if she were in his company? She was soon to find out.

She was sitting alone in the drawing-room one morning, writing a letter to Eustacia who, being in daily expectation of delivering her second child, had not come to London. Jessie and Evangeline were out paying calls, and Lord Ashbourne had gone to his club, whilst Michael was in the book-room. She was just trying to think how to phrase her next comment when the butler opened the door. 'Mr Coleridge is here, miss,' he said.

'Coleridge!' she exclaimed, flushing a little. 'Thank you, Rook. Please ask my brother to come through, will you?'

The butler withdrew. She put her hand to her heart. It seemed quite steady. What was

305

she feeling? She scarcely knew. Moments later, the butler announced her visitor, and there was Coleridge, hurrying in impetuously, a broad grin on his face as he exclaimed 'Theodora! Dear friend!'

All hesitation was at an end. She ran towards him, threw herself into his arms and he swung her around before setting her on her feet and planting a kiss upon her cheek.

She smiled up into his face and laughed, her eyes filled with happy tears. 'Dear friend indeed,' she echoed, and found that she meant it from the bottom of her heart. 'This is wonderful. What brings you here? Are you settled in London? You will have some wine?' She rang the bell.

'In reverse order, yes, no, and I am visiting the Wedgewoods, my kind sponsors, in Surrey, so have taken the opportunity of coming up to Town.'

'Is Mrs Coleridge with you?'

'No, indeed. She remains in Somerset. I think I told you in my last letter that she has made me a happy father again.'

At this point, Michael entered, and Theodora hurried over to him. 'Michael, I believe that you have heard me speak of my friend, Mr Coleridge. Coleridge, this is my brother, Mr Buckleigh.'

Michael had been very uncertain about

how he would feel on meeting Coleridge, for although Theodora had been very discreet, he could not but be aware of how much heartache the young man had caused his beloved younger sister. Nevertheless, he said pleasantly, 'I'm pleased to meet you, Mr Coleridge. I've read some of your work in the *Morning Post*. Your poem *France: an Ode* I thought particularly fine.'

'You are very good,' Coleridge responded.

'Are you making a long visit to London, sir?' Michael asked when they were seated, echoing Theodora's earlier question.

'Only a very brief one,' the other man replied. 'I needed to pay a visit to the offices of the *Morning Post*. Then someone told me that Theodora was in London, and I made haste to come and see her.'

'Coleridge has been reminding me that his wife has recently given birth to another child,' Theodora said, as Rook came in with wine.

'Then we must drink to your family,' Michael answered. 'I do trust that mother and baby are doing well?'

'Exceedingly well, I thank you.'

The conversation proceeded on courteous lines, with the two men finding a good deal in common, especially when Michael was reminded that as well as being a poet and journalist, Coleridge was also a preacher, with a strong Christian faith.

'Will your commitments to the Wedge-woods permit you to dine with us?' Michael asked. 'We have no engagements this evening, if you are free. And Mrs Coleridge of course, if she should be with you.'

'Mrs Coleridge is in Somerset,' he replied. 'For my part, I should be delighted to accept.'

'I didn't expect you to invite him,' Theodora said frankly, after Coleridge had taken his leave. 'Step-papa did not like him at all.'

Michael grinned. 'Now, why does that not surprise me?' he said. 'The thought of the two of them meeting is quite entertaining; Father, as usual, looking as if he had stepped straight out of his dressing-room, and Coleridge dressed all by guess.'

Theodora laughed. 'When they met for the first time, Jessie and Step-papa arrived in the rain, and his boots were still without a single speck on them. Then Coleridge appeared, soaking wet, and remarking that he wished he could shake himself like a dog.'

Michael laughed. 'I don't wonder at your liking him, little Sister,' he said. 'He's most refreshing company.' Then, after a pause, he added, 'That *is* all it is now, isn't it?'

Theodora nodded. 'He is a dear friend,' she replied simply.

If Lord Ashbourne was less than pleased at Coleridge's being invited to dinner, he did not show it, and Jessie, for her part, said that she would be delighted to meet him again. 'I have sought out his poems over the past nine months, and I think that he is a young man with something to say,' she remarked.

So that Coleridge's presence would not look too particular, Michael invited a gentleman whom he had met at his club, and with whom he had a number of mutual connections. The gentleman arrived that evening with his wife, and Theodora was astonished to discover that Mrs Ormsby was the former Miss Markham.

'Good heavens!' she said blankly, taken by surprise, then colouring at her rudeness, as she begged the guest's pardon.

'Not at all,' replied Mrs Ormsby, colouring herself. 'Laurence has been most unhelpful, telling me only that his new acquaintance was a son of the earl of Ashbourne, at whose house we were to dine. Had he but mentioned the name Buckleigh, I would instantly have understood, and then I should have been able to warn you of my arrival.'

'I knew that your engagement to Mr . . . Mr Kydd was at an end, but I had not realized that you had been married. May I wish you every happiness; or am I too late?'

'By no means,' answered the lady who was, Theodora realized, dressed far more fashionably than she had been on the occasions when she had seen her before, and looking very much younger. 'We were only married in January, and it is all still very new to us. But you must allow me to present my husband to you.'

Laurence Ormsby, who had been conversing with Michael, turned to meet her. 'Miss Buckleigh,' he said smiling. 'At last.'

'That is a curious expression,' remarked his wife.

Ormsby smiled. 'It is simply that I have heard about Miss Buckleigh from you, my dear and . . . ' He paused almost imperceptibly, then went on smoothly, 'I wanted to meet her for myself.'

Theodora expressed gratification at this disclosure, but she had the strange feeling that he had been going to say something else. Shortly afterwards, Coleridge arrived, correctly dressed for evening, but looking, as usual, just a little dishevelled. Theodora had been wondering with some concern how friendly Lord Ashbourne might be, but the earl was perfectly cordial, partly owing to two circumstances. The first was that Ashbourne himself remembered the gentle courtesy that Jessie had experienced at Coleridge's hands when she had nearly tripped at Alfoxden. The second was that Michael had spoken to the earl and disclosed the fact that Theodora was definitely no longer in love with the radical poet.

'I understand that you have recently become a father again,' said Jessie on greeting him. 'May I offer you my heartfelt congratulations?' She was smiling, but there was a hint of sadness in her eyes.

'You are very generous, my lady,' was all that he said, but his blue eyes were full of sympathy as he gripped her hand.

She almost began to cry and Ashbourne, as they prepared to go into dinner, asked concernedly in an undertone if she was all right. 'Oh yes, yes indeed,' she told him in a similarly low tone. 'But he is so very kind.'

Lord and Lady Ashbourne took the head and foot respectively. Coleridge was on Jessie's right. As he was Theodora's special friend, she was seated next to him on his other side.

'So you are planning to go to Germany, Mr Coleridge,' said Jessie. 'Is this with some particular purpose, or simply for pleasure?'

'Certainly not for pleasure, although the consequences will please me,' he replied. 'I have been fortunate enough to secure some generous patronage, and I intend to use some of it to complete my education at a European university. I hope to study Schiller at least; but I also have it in mind to walk in the mountains.'

'Coleridge is an indefatigable walker,' Theodora put in. 'He thinks nothing of walking twenty miles a day.'

'I wouldn't think much of it either,' Laurence remarked, making the company at that end of the table laugh over this small sally.

'It will be agreeable to have Dorothy and William accompanying you,' said Theodora.

'They are not able to stay in Alfoxden, so it was a logical decision,' he replied.

Noting that Jessie was now giving her attention to something that Laurence Ormsby was saying, Theodora said regretfully, 'I feel much to blame for that.'

'Why should you feel any such thing?' Coleridge responded. 'It was all the fault of Spy Nozy.'

'Spy Nozy?' Theodora echoed hollowly, thinking of how she had accused Alex of poking his nose in where it did not concern him. She loathed what he had done, but did not want to hear it recounted.

'Why yes,' Coleridge responded, leaning back in his chair, conscious now that others were listening. 'Apparently, a special agent was sent down to discover what the rascals at Alfoxden were up to. And I have to hand it to the fellow, he was nothing if not persistent.'

'You were aware of his activities,' said Ormsby. 'Not a very good choice of tool, then.'

Coleridge laughed. 'No indeed. He trailed us all over the place, no doubt burrowing through the undergrowth on his belly, for all the world like an Indian tracker. I wonder whether he had been warned how far Dorothy and Wordsworth and I walked in a day.'

'I trust he was given extra for shoe-leather,' Michael put in.

'It would be only just,' Coleridge agreed. 'There was a time, at the beginning, when I understand he thought he'd been rumbled. He overheard us talking, you see, and believed that we were referring to him as Spy Nozy. The explanation was quite different. We were talking of Spinoza!'

The whole table erupted with laughter at this. Theodora joined in, although she was still more than a little confused. This man to whom Coleridge was referring was certainly not Alex. Where did Alex fit into this scheme of things?

'Not an educated spy, then,' Ashbourne drawled, confirming Theodora's opinion.

'No; nor a very well favoured one,' Coleridge agreed. 'His nose matched the description admirably.'

'Where had you this information?' Ormsby asked.

'Oh, the landlord of the Globe is an old acquaintance of mine,' Coleridge replied. 'When asked to confirm what had been said before the magistrate, he could only declare that he knew nothing of any unpatriotic dealings amongst our company. All he could say about your humble servant, apparently, was that I was a poet who would make the town famous.'

'So Spy Nozy returned to town with his tail between his legs,' suggested Ormsby.

'I assume so,' Coleridge responded.

'But however inept the man, the consequences were serious enough,' Michael said. 'Your friends are obliged to quit Alfoxden.'

'That is indeed vexatious,' Coleridge agreed. 'But perhaps it is for the best in the end, as it has spurred us all on to make plans to go to Germany.'

The conversation moved to other subjects, in which Theodora bore very little part, other than the occasional smile or nod of assent. Her mind was busy with all that Coleridge had said. Soon the ladies rose to leave the gentlemen to their port, Jessie leading the way. Once the drawing-room was reached, Theodora found herself conversing with Vivienne Ormsby, whilst Evangeline and Jessie discussed the following day's arrangements for an outing for the children presently sleeping upstairs.

'Where are you living, now that you are married?' Theodora asked.

'Laurence has a house in Wiltshire, but we are in Town for the season,' Vivienne replied. She smiled ruefully. 'I always thought that I was a country girl at heart, and I still believe that that is true. I have discovered, however, that even a country girl can enjoy London fashions and lively Town gatherings.' She paused briefly. 'Have you seen Alex?' she asked.

Theodora shook her head. 'Not since last autumn,' she confessed, colouring a little at the memory of her harsh words, some of which at least she now suspected were unmerited. 'I was told that he had gone abroad to — ' She was going to say 'to spy' but altered her words to 'serve his country'.

'Yes, that is so,' Vivienne agreed. 'I saw him just before he left.'

'You saw him?' Theodora echoed.

Vivienne nodded. 'We parted upon good terms,' she replied. 'Our relationship was one forged upon friendship, but without the added ingredient that is necessary for marriage. He left England determined to do his duty as he saw it. It seemed to me that he had hoped to have a reason to stay, but that he had been disappointed — perhaps in love.'

'Not over you, Mrs Ormsby?' said Theodora a little anxiously.

'No; decidedly not over me.'

At that point, the gentlemen joined them and, as Vivienne's eyes met those of her husband, it seemed to Theodora that their relationship definitely had the certain added ingredient that had been lacking between Miss Markham and Alex.

Jessie rang the bell for the tea tray to be brought in, and when the tea had been poured, it was Coleridge who brought Theodora her cup. 'I've just been thinking,' he said, his blue eyes sparkling. 'You could come to Germany with us.'

'To Germany?' she said, astonished. Although Dorothy had already written of it, she had dismissed the idea from her mind.

'Yes, why not?' he answered. 'Think of what a splendid time we would have, together as we were at dear Stowey and Alfoxden. Dorothy would love it. Do say you'll at least consider it.'

'I . . . I don't know,' she answered. 'This is such a surprise. I must think about it.'

'We aren't going until September, so there's plenty of time,' he told her.

'Will Mrs Coleridge be coming?'

'I think it unlikely,' he replied. 'With two little children, it would be too difficult for her to manage abroad.'

At this point, Theodora, looking around, realized that no one else was listening to their conversation, so she said quickly in a low tone, 'Coleridge.'

'Thea, my dear?' He also lowered his voice.

'Did it ever occur to you that Spy Nozy might not have been the only spy?'

He leaned a little closer to her. 'Why, whom do you suspect?'

'Alex,' she said. 'I thought it was Alex . . . ' To her horror she could feel her voice breaking on his name.

Coleridge laid his big hand on hers. 'Don't discompose yourself,' he said. 'Say no more. I'll write to you.'

★   ★   ★

'Michael, dearest, are you perfectly sure that she has got over that slovenly poet of hers?' Evangeline asked her husband that night as he was brushing her hair before they retired. Although Evangeline's maid was perfectly capable, it was a task that he always

317

reserved to himself.

'Why do you ask, sweetheart?'

'Tonight, after we had all come into the drawing-room, they were sitting close together and at one point he was holding her hand.'

'I'm sure,' he answered. 'She told me so. Indeed, I had had hopes of Alex. I don't know what came of that, but I think that they quarrelled.'

'Lovers do, I believe,' she said, turning as he put down the brush so that he could kiss her.

'Yes indeed,' he agreed, obliging her. 'Perhaps we'll find out soon. Alex is in Town. Ormsby told me so this evening.'

★ ★ ★

Theodora found out about Alex's arrival on the same morning when a letter came for her with her name written upon it in Coleridge's distinctive writing. The letter was brought to her at the breakfast table, but she did not open it until she was alone in her room.

I could see how anxious you were to discover the truth, but fearing to distress you in front of the company, I thought it best to tell you what you wanted to know in a letter. Your friend Alex, I do believe, is innocent of any connection with the eviction of the 'foxes' from their 'den'. On hearing what had happened, he wrote to me expressing his regret, and admitting that he had promised the Duke of Portland that he would look into our activities. Having done so, however, he went back to his grace to give the assurance that he saw no harm in us, even in Thelwall. The duke obviously chose to send another instrument and believe information from other sources.

Theodora put her letter down, stared into space for a time, then picked it up, and read it again slowly. There was only one possible interpretation of all this, which was that Alex was innocent of every accusation that she had hurled at his head. She tried to rekindle her anger by reflecting that he had certainly offered to find out about her friends for the Duke of Portland, but it couldn't be done. The country was at war. The duke was right to be concerned about those who might threaten the realm. Alex, a loyal Englishman, was right to offer to do what he could. Even Coleridge, a stalwart opponent of the war, at least for a time, did not seem to blame him for that.

She thought about the friendship that they had enjoyed when they had both been in

319

London, a friendship that might so easily have ripened into something else. She had thrown all of that away. Now, he was abroad, risking his life in goodness knows what enterprise, and he was thinking all the time that she believed ill of him. What was she to do? She had no idea where he might be or of how to communicate with him.

She was thinking about the problem as she came downstairs when she heard Michael speaking to Evangeline in the hall. 'If I see Alex, I'll ask him to dinner,' he said. Theodora halted on the stairs as if she had been turned to stone. Michael's words could only mean that Alex was back in England. What was more, he was in Town. If he came to dine, what could she say to him to make up for the angry words that she had hurled at his head? Would he ever forgive her? Suddenly, it seemed terribly important that he should.

23

Despite the fact that Theodora took extra care with her appearance that evening, Alex did not appear. Perhaps he had been invited, but had made his excuses because he did not want to see her. It was not a very cheering thought.

They were dining a little early because Jessie wanted to attend the opera. Lord Ashbourne had his own box, so they were assured of being able to watch and listen in the greatest comfort. Jessie had invited Coleridge to join them, but he had declined. 'I am not at all sure what my plans may be,' he had said. 'You must offer some other person my place.'

'If you do chance to come to the theatre, you must visit us in our box,' Jessie had assured him.

In the event, they were just five: Lord and Lady Ashbourne, Michael, Evangeline and Theodora. Theodora was torn between wanting to stay at home, in case Alex might call, and going out to some frequented place, like the opera house, where he might be present. In the end, because it took less explanation, she opted for the latter course. She was in a gown of pink, which had been chosen for her by Evangeline. Her sister-in-law had a good eye for colour, and an unfailing sense of style, so the gown became her very well indeed.

Theodora had now attended the opera more than once, so managed to refrain from gaping at the impressive interior with her mouth open. She also managed to avoid staring at all the other people in the boxes. This was considerably more difficult, for she did not want to miss seeing Alex if he was there. What was more, she did not want him to catch sight of her before she had seen him.

Despite her state of mind, the beauty of the music provided an excellent distraction. She had not visited the opera so frequently that it had ceased to be a real pleasure to her. Although other members of the audience continued their conversation unabated, therefore, she gave all of her attention to what was taking place on the stage. Then the act came to an end and the curtain came down. She turned her head, intending to look at Lord Ashbourne, but before she had completed the movement, as if fate had intended it, her eyes met those of a dark-haired man in a nearby box.

Years after, she would say, with Dorothy,

that she never forgot the first time she had seen Coleridge. When he had come bounding up to them through the field, her heart had done an extraordinary series of leaps, and had then started beating rather fast. A similar thing happened just now, as her gaze locked with that of Alex.

Try as she might, she could not look away whilst Alex, for his part, continued to return her gaze, his face solemn, even stern, whilst he executed a polite bow. Theodora inclined her head and, greatly daring, ventured a small smile. He did not return it, but turned to leave the box which he was sharing with a couple whom she did not recognize and a very pretty girl of her own age, in a fashionably cut pale-blue gown. Could he be coming to see her, Theodora? She sat up very straight and waited.

Michael murmured something about fetching some refreshment, but he had only been outside the box for a moment or two before he popped his head back in and said 'Look who has discovered us!'

Theodora turned eagerly then, with a surge of disappointment that would have astonished her nine months before, she realized that it was not Alex but Coleridge. 'I was in the pit, and spotted you,' he said.

'Then you must join us,' said Ashbourne

urbanely. 'Come, sir, take a seat. Michael, ask for an extra glass.'

Coleridge grinned down at Theodora and, because he was her friend and she was genuinely pleased to see him, she smiled back. Alex, pausing to ask if anyone would like wine, saw them together, immediately forgot what he was going to say and resumed his place. The next time Theodora saw him, he appeared to be enjoying a light-hearted flirtation with the girl in the blue gown which, Theodora could now see, was rather insipid. She looked away and gave all her attention to Coleridge, who was anxious to share his impressions of the evening's performance. Alex, after glancing briefly at her once more, turned back to his companion, giving no sign that his thoughts were miles away.

Coleridge left before the start of the second act. 'I am expected elsewhere,' he said. 'But I shall be in Town for a little longer, so doubtless I shall see you again.'

'I will look forward to it,' Theodora said. Inside, however, all she could think was that Alex had seen her in the box, but he had not come, preferring the company of his own party. The next time she looked in their direction, however, it was to discover that Alex had gone. She could not avoid the conclusion that he had not forgiven her for what she had said.

It was only after she had got ready for bed and was settling down for what she felt sure would be a sleepless night that she suddenly sat bolt upright. Of course he had not forgiven her. She had not told him that she was sorry! He still thought that she believed the very worst of him. Now that she knew that she had been mistaken, she must try somehow to inform him of the change in her sentiments. Then, perhaps, there might be a chance for her.

She held that thought in her mind and considered it. A chance for what? She closed her eyes, and saw his face, as it had been on many occasions, alight with laughter, that dark-brown hair flopping over his brow. Oh for the right to push it back, then pull him down and kiss the portion of his brow exposed thereby, only to have the same thing happen again. Then they would laugh about it, as lovers do.

Lovers! There; she had actually framed the word in her mind. Now she was forced to acknowledge the truth: that she was in love with Alex. This was not a foolish dream, like her ideas about William Wordsworth, nor an impossible infatuation like the feeling that she had once had for Coleridge. No, this was real love; and it had been growing since their visit to Lyme. Had she not been so befuddled by her infatuation, she might have realized it sooner. Now, it might be too late. She thought about the young woman with whom he had been flirting at the opera. What if he was in love with her instead? All she knew was that if the man she loved could not return her feelings, then the hurt that she had suffered over Coleridge would be as nothing to what she would feel over losing Alex.

★　★　★

'You know that I do not care for dances,' Theodora told Jessie in the carriage the following evening. Michael and Evangeline had been invited to dine with some old friends, so Theodora, the earl and the countess were travelling together to another engagement.

'It's not a formal dance, and it's not going to be a large event,' Jessie promised. 'It's a musical evening with some other items.'

The home of Mr and Mrs Buchanan was just outside London, in Surrey. It was a neat, attractive house about fifty years old, set in its own grounds. To Theodora's relief, as Jessie had promised, the company was not too large. The plan, Mrs Buchanan explained, was to have a little entertainment by way of singing, playing or recitation, followed by refreshments, then dancing. 'We are very fortunate,' Mrs Buchanan gushed. 'We have that celebrated writer Mr Coleridge to recite his poems for us. He is staying with our neighbours, the Wedgewoods and they have brought him this evening.'

Theodora smiled. 'I am acquainted with Mr Coleridge, and will be glad to hear him,' she said.

Coleridge was already there, and he came bounding over to her, catching her hand with delight. 'Theodora! This is splendid.' He made his bow to Lord and Lady Ashbourne.

'You are to recite this evening, I believe,' said Theodora.

'Why, so it seems,' he agreed, before asking her permission to introduce her to his friends.

The rooms began to fill, and Theodora took her place next to Jessie, with Coleridge sitting the other side of her. 'You'll dance with me later,' he said. 'Do you remember I promised to dance with you one day?'

'Yes I do. I also recall that I did not commit myself.'

The music was just beginning when Alex came in at the back of the room. He had planned to come with the Ormsbys, but Vivienne had fallen victim to a nasty cold, and Laurence had stayed home to bear her company.

'I'll give your apologies,' he had said. He hadn't wanted to go alone, but could not be so discourteous as to deprive Mrs Buchanan of three guests.

'I fear there may not be any places,' Mrs Buchanan whispered to him.

'That's all right. I'm happy to stand,' he replied. Had he not been standing, he might not have caught a glimpse of Theodora's ash-blond hair, gleaming in the candlelight. Then inevitably, he recognized the dark head that was close to hers. Coleridge! He set his teeth together. He could not decide whether it would be more painful to go or to stay. He looked along the row and saw that she was accompanied by Lord and Lady Ashbourne.

He remembered his earlier suspicions about the earl; suspicions that he now acknowledged were unworthy and untrue. All the same, Lord Ashbourne might now be a reformed character, but he had at one time been a great rake. Could it be that he had encouraged his step-daughter to believe that an irregular liaison with Coleridge would be acceptable? Alex could not believe it; yet when he saw the dark head and the blonde one close together, he was so filled with jealousy that he would be prepared to believe almost anything.

Following Theodora's dismissal of him, he had written to Coleridge, assuring him of his innocence in the matter of spying. Then, after a number of unsuccessful efforts to see her, and the return of several of his letters to her unopened, he had offered himself for a very difficult and delicate mission upon the Continent. He had desperately needed something else to occupy his mind, and this plan had achieved its purpose in part, as he had needed to keep alert every waking hour. But when he lay down to sleep he thought about her, and she haunted his dreams. Now, back in London, here she was again, and apparently as much in love with Coleridge as ever.

A round of applause reminded him of where he was, and he stood waiting for the next item. With a sense of awful inevitability, he heard Mrs Buchanan refer to 'one of our literary lions', and then invite Coleridge to come forward.

'This is a poem which I wrote in June of last year,' he said. 'Some friends came to visit me in my cottage in Stowey. Hardly had they arrived, than a most unfortunate accident meant that I was so disabled, I was unable to walk for their entire stay. One evening, after they had left me to go for a walk, I composed this poem in the garden bower. I would like to dedicate the recitation of my poem, *This Lime Tree Bower My Prison*, to a most charming and delightful young lady, Miss Theodora Buckleigh.'

Theodora flushed with pleasure. At the back of the room, Alex barely repressed a snarl, turned on his heel, and went to find a bottle with which to drown his sorrows.

After the final item, a piece on the pianoforte played by Mrs Buchanan's niece, the company was invited to go into another room where a sumptuous buffet had been laid. Coleridge was immediately surrounded by a crowd of admirers, so Ashbourne escorted Jessie and Theodora to a table, then went to procure refreshments for them. While they were waiting for him to return, Theodora became conscious of someone staring at her, and looking across the room, she saw Alex, his dark hair flopping across his brow, his expression insolent. He began to straighten from the pillar against which he was leaning, and for a moment, she thought that he might approach her. Then Ashbourne returned, followed by a footman with a selection of delicacies and some plates, and he settled back into his former position.

Theodora sat up, and tried to give the impression of one who was enjoying herself hugely. She was not entirely successful, for after a short time, Ashbourne asked her what was the matter.

'Oh, nothing,' she answered, trying to adopt an airy tone. 'These lobster patties are . . . are . . . '

Ashbourne turned his head, and caught sight of Alex, looking in their direction. 'Young Kydd seems to have had a little too much to drink,' he drawled. 'I wonder whether I ought to suggest that he take some fresh air.'

'Oh, pray do not,' said Theodora. While she was still speaking, Alex inclined his head and turned away. 'See, he is probably going to do that very thing.' They did not see Alex again in the refreshment room, but Theodora found that her appetite had gone, and she could do little more than play with what was on her plate. She was never a big eater, but Jessie, observing her concernedly, asked whether she was quite well and if she would like to go home.

'No, no, I forbid it,' said Coleridge's voice from just behind them. 'Did I not say, Theodora, that we should dance?'

'Well, yes, but — '

'Come, then,' he declared, catching hold of her hand. He turned to Raff, 'By your leave, my lord?'

Ashbourne made a gesture of assent, and

soon Theodora and Coleridge were facing one another on the dance floor. The dance was a country one of some vigour, and Coleridge was nothing if not vigorous, his dancing demonstrating energy rather than grace. At first afraid that her limp would be glaringly obvious, Theodora soon found that everyone else was more interested in their own steps than in hers. She relaxed and began to enjoy herself, forgetting all about her limp and laughing up at Coleridge when they made a mistake.

When the dance was over, he led her to the side of the room nearest to them, which was opposite to where Jessie was sitting talking with friends. Someone addressed a remark to him, and while his attention was diverted, Theodora took a couple of steps away and immediately found herself face to face with Alex.

'You're enjoying yourself, I see,' he said unpleasantly.

'Alex; it's good to see you,' she replied, looking up at him. He wasn't really drunk, but his eyes gleamed recklessly, and his stance was a little more careless than usual.

'I wouldn't have thought that my presence would have made any difference to you one way or the other,' he replied. 'I know you said you never wanted to see me again, but I really am entitled to attend social occasions. Although after what I've witnessed tonight, I'm not sure whether I really care for them.'

'What you've witnessed tonight?' she asked him, puzzled.

'You're quite obviously still in love with him,' he said. Looking round and seeing that no one was watching them, he pulled her through the nearby doors which led out onto the terrace.

'Whatever are you talking about?' she asked him, allowing him to lead her outside rather than make a scene.

'Coleridge!' he declared. 'Anyone can see by the way that you look at him.'

'No, no, you are quite mistaken,' she said, anxious to convince him, but not wanting to give away her feelings.

'Don't pretend, Theodora,' he answered. 'You told me yourself that you were in love with him. Tell me, what does Sara Coleridge think to this little expedition?'

'Why should she think anything about it?' Theodora asked him. 'I am not responsible for Coleridge's presence in London. I did not even know that he was here.'

He laughed humourlessly. 'A likely story! Does she know that you are seeing her husband? Or have you convinced yourself that the stepdaughter of Rake Ashbourne does not need to live according to ordinary people's standards?'

She slapped him hard across the face. 'How dare you?' she demanded. 'How dare you say such things? And to think that I was going to tell you that I was sorry for the things that I thought about you! That I . . . I . . . ' Her voice failed and she dashed a hand across her eyes. 'Let me tell you, Mr Kydd, that your mind is infinitely more grubby than mine. You must allow me to excuse myself. I can manage without the pollution of your company.'

She turned to leave. 'Wait,' he said in quite a different tone, catching hold of her arm just before she went back into the ballroom.

'Well?'

He closed his eyes briefly. 'I hardly know what I'm saying,' he said, rubbing his hand across his brow. 'Seeing you with Coleridge — I was wrong to say what I did.'

'Yes, you were,' she agreed coldly. 'May I go now?'

'No; wait.' There was a pause.

'For what purpose? So that you might insult me again?'

The musicians were just preparing to play another tune, whilst dancers were moving onto the floor ready for the allemande. 'Dance with me,' he said urgently.

'I beg your pardon?'

'You did with Coleridge,' he said.

Theodora knew the steps of the allemande. She had even practised it in private; but the dance would be too slow for her to bear her part with dignity. Even were she not still angry with Alex, she would never attempt such a dance in public. She shook her head. 'You must excuse me,' she said. Then, not wanting to leave him without an explanation she went on. 'You see, I — '

His face took on a set expression. 'Oh, enough,' he snarled, interrupting her. 'I can see where I am not wanted. Your pardon, madam, and good night.' He bowed, and stalked off in the opposite direction.

★   ★   ★

When she came back into the ballroom a little while later, looking rather pale, Coleridge was waiting for her. 'There you are,' he said. 'I must leave now, as my hosts are waiting for me. I may be returning to Stowey tomorrow or the next day. However, before I leave, I wanted to ask you whether you had given any further thought to accompanying us to Germany.'

'Germany?' Theodora's mind was still taken up with the scene that had just taken place between herself and Alex.

'Dorothy would be so happy if you would come,' he said.

'I'll think about it,' she said, and she meant it. What was there for her in England now, after all?

24

'I wish you weren't going,' Evangeline complained. 'I don't know why you want to go to Germany.'

'It will be interesting to visit another country,' Theodora replied. 'I have never been outside England before. And besides . . . '

'Besides?' Evangeline prompted.

'Never mind,' Theodora answered brightly. 'At least it's a lovely day.'

'For now,' Evangeline agreed ominously.

Theodora had been escorted to Great Yarmouth by her brother and sister-in-law, having said goodbye to the rest of the family in Derbyshire. Coleridge and his companions had planned to travel by mail coach from London to Norfolk, and Theodora had originally intended to join them in the capital. This Michael would not by any means permit.

'I will take you to Yarmouth myself and see you safely on board,' he had declared. 'I do not know Norfolk at all and neither does Evangeline, so it will be a new experience for us. We will visit Norwich on the way back.'

As they travelled to the docks in Michael's

carriage, Theodora reflected that she had been lucky that no one had forbidden her to go. She owed this restraint to her peculiar circumstances. Michael was her official guardian, but his wife Evangeline, who had been rather spoiled in her youth, did not permit him to be too authoritarian. No one else felt that they had any right to interfere. She was free to go to Germany with her very dear friends. She just wished that she felt happier about it.

Alex had made no further attempt to contact her after the musical evening at the Buchanans', either in London or after she had returned to Derbyshire. He knew now that she no longer thought badly of him, for she had told him so. She had tried to mend matters, but they had only hurt one another again by ill-considered words. Obviously, there was no future for them. No doubt he was even now dancing attendance on the insipid girl from the opera box. That being the case, she might as well be in Germany as anywhere else.

They stopped at the docks and Michael got down to make enquiries concerning the whereabouts of the ship.

'Are you sure?' Evangeline asked her sister-in-law for perhaps the tenth time. 'It is not too late to change your mind.'

'I'm sure,' Theodora responded. 'It won't be for ever.'

'I've found out where it is,' said Michael, climbing back into the carriage. 'It's a little further on.' Michael and Evangeline engaged in desultory conversation in which Theodora took neither part nor interest. She was thinking about Alex. As she looked at the grey North Sea, she recalled how they had visited Lyme. How happy they had been on that day! Would he know that she had left England? Would he care?

When the carriage had come to a halt, Michael got out and helped them both down. Theodora looked up at the ship tied alongside, and had a moment's panic. If either Michael or Evangeline had said anything about going home at that moment, she would have turned around and gone with them, but neither of them did. Filled with a rush of affection, she turned and embraced them both. 'I'll miss you,' she said, with tears in her eyes.

'I'll just go and make sure that your luggage is properly stowed,' said Michael, walking up the gangplank with the grace that character-ized his and his father's every movement.

Impulsively, Theodora turned to Evange-line. 'If by any chance Alex should ask where I have gone — '

'You want me to tell him?'

'Yes — I mean no.'

'You *don't* want me to tell him?'

Theodora turned away in wretched indecision. 'I don't know.'

Evangeline, from her superior height, looked beyond Theodora to where a man was approaching with hasty steps. 'Fortunately, to save me from saying the wrong thing, he appears to have come to find you.'

'What?' Theodora turned again, to see Alex standing before her, dressed for travelling, a cloak bag in his hand. 'Alex? Where are you going?'

He sighed. 'Ah, well, that's a question without a quick or easy answer. May we go somewhere private?'

'Use our carriage,' said Evangeline helpfully, gesturing behind her. 'Leave your bag here with me. It will be quite safe.'

Theodora turned towards her. After the first rush of happiness at seeing him, she had recalled all that had gone before. 'I am not at all sure that I want to be private with this gentleman,' she replied.

'Theodora please,' said Alex. 'I've been such a fool. Give me a chance to explain. If you don't like what I have to say, then I promise you I'll go, and never trouble you again.'

Theodora glanced again at Evangeline, who nodded briefly. 'Very well,' Theodora replied, shaking off all but the barest minimum of assistance from him as she climbed into the carriage. He sat down opposite her, his hands clasped between his knees.

'Well?' she said, sitting up very straight.

'I don't really know where to begin,' he said.

'You could start by apologizing for getting drunk and insulting me at the Buchanans',' she suggested. 'You could also apologize for your disgusting inferences about members of my family.'

He flushed darkly. 'That is an evening that I do not care to recall,' he said in a mortified tone, 'and yet some of the events that took place are burned into my memory. I neither acted nor spoke like a gentleman, and I ask your pardon for it.' There was a long pause. 'Theodora, will you forgive me?'

She shook her head, and for a moment, he felt quite sick with disappointment. Then she said in puzzled tones, 'I just do not understand why you behaved in the way that you did.'

He looked at her, an arrested expression on his face. 'You mean you really don't know?' He took a deep breath 'Very well, then. The

French have a proverb which says that to understand everything is to forgive everything.' He closed his eyes briefly. 'I've taken plenty of risks in my time, but none of the consequences of them mattered to me as much as this.' He paused again. 'It was because of Coleridge.'

'Coleridge?' she echoed, surprised.

'Yes, damn him!' Alex ground out. 'Coleridge, with his energy and enthusiasm and dazzling intelligence, and his big blue eyes and unblemished face. The man you are in love with, remember?'

'But Alex . . . ' she began. She very much wanted him to know that she was no longer in love with Coleridge, but felt too self-conscious to say so.

'I saw you smile up at him, and laugh with him. Then you danced with him and my jealousy overcame me.'

'Jealousy?' she murmured, hardly daring to hope.

'That's how you feel when you're in love,' he told her intensely. 'I'm in love with you, Thea. I fell in love with you the first time I saw you, I think, only I was too stupid to understand my feelings at the time. It was in Hatchard's, if you remember. You caught me staring at you and you thought that I was staring at your limp. I told you that it was

342

because I had recognized the colour of your hair. In truth I was staring because you were the most exquisite thing that I had ever seen. Of course I was engaged to Vivienne at the time, and determined to think of you only as the sister of a college friend.

'Then I saw you falling for Coleridge and I found that I was seized with the most horrible clawing jealousy. I told myself that it was just anger at your loving a man who was not free to marry you, but that wasn't true. I wanted you for myself. When you told me that you were in love with him, I was wretched indeed.'

He sat looking down at his clasped hands, Then, to his surprise, a small hand placed itself over his. 'I *was* in love with him,' Theodora admitted. 'I fell in love with him before I knew that he was married. But now he is just a dear friend.'

He looked up at her face. 'Are you sure?' he asked her, hardly daring to hope.

She nodded. He was about to ask whether there might be any hope for him, when he noticed the way in which her eyes were shining. Suddenly, he realized that incredibly, he did not need to ask, for his hopes had become reality. Gently, cautiously, he raised her hand to his lips, closing his eyes in thankfulness. Then, he moved to sit beside her and clasped her head between his hands with infinite gentleness. Slowly, he lowered his head towards hers, and their lips met in a long tender kiss.

'You love me?' he murmured, after an interval.

'I love you,' she agreed, blushing. She had thought that she might love Wordsworth; she had been in love with Coleridge for a while; but it was the first time that she had ever said the words out loud to any man.

'I can't imagine why,' he said frankly. 'I said all manner of wicked things to you — unforgivable things which I bitterly regret. I can understand why you fell in love with Coleridge. For one thing, he does not snarl at you and throw accusations at you as I do.'

'No, he doesn't,' she agreed, nestling comfortably against his shoulder as he put his arm around her. 'But you do yourself an injustice. Even when you were lecturing me or trying to make me go home, I knew that you were acting out of real consideration for what you thought was my good. And we were always friends, were we not?'

'Always,' he agreed. 'Particularly when you came to London from Devon. By then my engagement was over and I was a free man again. You were away from Coleridge's influence and I really began to think that there might be a chance for me. Then you accused me of spying upon your friends and told me that you never wanted to see me again.'

'I know now that that was not true,' she told him guiltily. 'Coleridge told me all about the man who had really done the spying, and that it had not been you at all. At the Buchanans' musical evening, I wanted to say sorry for the things that I had said, but then you . . . you . . .'

'I saw you with Coleridge again; remember? Then you danced with him, but you would not dance with me. Why wouldn't you, Thea? Was it to punish me?'

'Partly, I suppose,' she admitted honestly. 'You had made me very angry. But the real reason was that you asked me to partner you in an allemande. That demands a grace of movement that I don't have. I danced a country dance with Coleridge. My limp does not show in those kinds of dances.' She looked down at her feet. Her tone was subdued.

He caught hold of her hands. 'I wish you would believe that I really don't notice it,' he said. 'Don't you realize how beautiful you are?'

She looked up, then, and saw all the love in his eyes. 'Beautiful? I?'

345

'Like something from fairyland,' he said. 'The story of Beauty and the Beast, for instance.' He gave an awkward little look and turned away, his scarred cheek hidden from her gaze.

'What do you mean?' she asked him.

'I just wish I was a little prettier for you, that's all,' he answered. He paused. 'I was engaged to another woman before I went to war, as I think you know. After I returned with this, my betrothed told me that she could not endure being wed to such a horror.'

She caught hold of his chin and turned his face so that he was looking directly at her. Then she pressed a kiss to his scar. 'You really have no idea, do you, how dashing I think this makes you look?'

'Dashing?' His tone was incredulous.

She nodded. 'There is no other word for it.'

'In that case, then, will you dance with me?'

'When?'

'I'm hoping, perhaps at our wedding breakfast?' he said diffidently. 'That is, if you can bear to marry me after the way that I have behaved?' The willing way in which she returned his kiss assured him that she could indeed bear to do so. 'I do hope that you are not going to insist that I wait to marry you until your friends return from Germany,' he said eventually.

She shook her head. 'I do not know how long they will be away,' she admitted. She went on a little more slowly. 'I hope that you will not mind that they will still be my friends.'

'No, I don't mind,' he replied. 'That was one of the hardest things for me. Even when I was most jealous of Coleridge, I couldn't help liking the man.'

'He is very likeable,' Theodora agreed. 'But not, I think, a very good husband.'

'Well I intend to be an exceedingly good husband,' he replied, this time pulling her onto his knee so that he could kiss her with considerably more thoroughness than hitherto.

'Alex, how did you know to come here today?' she asked him, as soon as she was able.

'Coleridge wrote to me,' he said.

'Dear Coleridge,' she murmured in a teasing tone, prompting him to kiss her again.

'I won't rise to that bait, because I'm too grateful to him,' he answered. 'He suggested that if I came to find you here I might discover something to my advantage.'

'And why did you have a bag with you?'

'I couldn't think of anything to my advantage except that you might be prepared to forgive me. That you might even love me I

347

didn't dare to hope. I had decided that if there seemed to be any spark of a chance for me, then I would beg to be allowed to go to Germany with you. If you had been as angry with me as ever, well, I was simply going to find the next boat and sail to wherever it might be going; I didn't much care where.'

'And now?' she asked him, her head on his shoulder, her hand tucked in his.

'We go wherever you want — Germany, Spain, the Antipodes, anywhere.'

She smiled up at him, and he leaned over and kissed her tenderly. 'Let's go home,' she said.

Epilogue

Coleridge watched from the deck as the shore receded. Michael had found him, when he had come on board to make arrangements for Theodora's luggage.

'I doubt she'll be travelling with us, though,' Coleridge said, pointing to where Theodora and Alex were getting into the coach.

Michael smiled, then after a brief moment, he said, 'Do you mind?'

Coleridge looked directly at him. 'We shall all miss her,' he said. Michael nodded and wished him well, before disembarking.

The coach had left the harbour by the time they sailed. Coleridge stood on deck, looking back at the shore, thinking of Theodora returning to the heart of her family. Sara, he thought to himself with a sudden tug of anguish. My babes!

'Col,' said Dorothy, breaking his chain of thought. 'Are you going to stay up here?'

'I thought I might,' he answered, then turned to look at her. She was very pale. 'Good Lord!' he exclaimed, trying not to laugh.

'William is worse,' she said. 'I really think I ... ' She put a handkerchief over her mouth. 'Pray, excuse me,' she said behind it in muffled tones, before fleeing below. Once she had gone, Coleridge chuckled. Then laughing out loud, he tossed his hair and relished the sensation of the wind whisking through it as he gazed back at the disappearing shore.

Author's note

During the course of this novel, Theodora Buckleigh's life becomes entwined with those of Dorothy and William Wordsworth, Samuel Taylor Coleridge and others. This process begins when she meets Dorothy in Halifax.

Dorothy and her brothers were orphaned in early life, and were brought up by various relatives, some of whom lived in Halifax. Dorothy continued to pay visits to these relatives from time to time. However, it was always Dorothy's ambition to share a home with William, and this ambition was at last achieved when they moved into Racedown in Dorset. From then onwards, they were never really parted until Dorothy's death in 1855.

Wordsworth and Coleridge met in Bristol in the late summer of 1795. At that time, Coleridge was a leading light amongst the intellectual community in Bristol. He had also gained some fame, if not notoriety, through the delivery of a number of political lectures, during which he made no secret of his anti-Pitt sentiments.

It was also in Bristol that Coleridge met Sara Fricker, whom he married at St Mary

Redcliffe on 4th October 1795. The young couple settled initially in Clevedon, then after a period of time spent in Bristol, they went to live in Nether Stowey in the winter of 1796–7.

Coleridge was a great walker, and it was not at all unusual for him to undertake the walk from Nether Stowey to Racedown in two days. Dorothy and William Wordsworth were working in the garden at Racedown on a summer day in 1797 when he appeared on the other side of a gate across a field about 100 yards from their house. He did indeed leap the gate and gallop across the field to meet them. Brother and sister both remembered the event many years later, each separately describing him as 'a wonderful man'.

This meeting was the start of a very productive period of writing for both men, which continued until their estrangement some years later. Dorothy Wordsworth was a significant figure in this arrangement, sharing her notebooks and insights with her brother and his friend. Letters passed amongst the group with great frequency, often enclosing new poems for comments, and it would not be at all unusual for a letter to be written and sent on the day following a visit.

Alex and Theodora are both creations of

my own, but when including real people in my book, I have, wherever possible, used real situations. So it is that Theodora is present when Coleridge leaps the gate. She witnesses the moment when Wordsworth and Coleridge share their plays, and she is in the gig when Coleridge drives his visitors 'over forty miles of execrable road'.

She also witnesses the occasion when Sara Coleridge spills a pan of hot milk over her husband's foot, and is present when, obliged to forgo an outing with his friends, he is inspired to write 'This Lime Tree Bower My Prison'.

Coleridge was very keen to gather all his friends together at or near Nether Stowey, and John Thelwall, the radical, was already acquainted with him, although only by letter. The dinner party at Alfoxden really did take place, with fourteen sitting down to dinner (although the identity of all the guests is not known.) It was at this dinner that Thelwall's eloquence alarmed a local man who had been brought in to serve at dinner. He shared his fears, which were passed on to Dr Lysons in Bath, who, in his turn, passed them on to the Duke of Portland, the Home secretary. This resulted in an agent being sent down to look into the activities of Coleridge and his circle.

Coleridge makes light of the whole matter

in *Biographia Literaria*, but at the time it must have been a distressing business for the Wordsworths to be told that they would have to leave Alfoxden. However, no doubt their plans to travel to Germany, must to some degree have softened the blow.

Coleridge was fortunate in having the Wedgwoods for his patrons, and he was indeed visiting them at the time when Theodora was in London. Finally, we are told that as he and the Wordsworths left England, he alone was unaffected by seasickness, but was afflicted by sudden anguish at the thought of leaving his babes behind. Indeed, the younger of the two, Berkeley Coleridge, whose birth he announced to Theodora, died whilst he was on the continent.

Where possible, I have attempted to give real characters their own written words to say. When I have given them words of my own creation, I trust that I have not been disloyal to the spirit of the people that they were. I have taken as my touchstone Coleridge's description of imagination as 'that willing suspension of disbelief', trusting that my readers will be ready to exercise that similar faculty.

Bibliography

The Friendship: Wordsworth and Coleridge by Adam Sisman (Harper Collins 2006)

Coleridge and Wordsworth in the West Country by Tom Mayberry (Alan Sutton Publishing Ltd 1992)

Coleridge: Early Visions by Richard Holmes (Flamingo Harper Collins 1999)

Coleridge by Katharine Cooke (Routledge and Kegan Paul Ltd 1979)

Coleridge: The Clark Lectures 1951–52 by Humphrey House (Rupert Hart-Davis 1969)

Dorothy Wordsworth by Robert Gittings and Jo Manton (O.U.P. 1985)

Letters by Samuel Taylor Coleridge ed. Ernest Hartley Coleridge (Houghton, Mifflin & Co 1895)

The Complete poems by Samuel Taylor Coleridge (Penguin 1997)

We do hope that you have enjoyed reading this large print book.

Did you know that all of our titles are available for purchase?

We publish a wide range of high quality large print books including:
Romances, Mysteries, Classics
General Fiction
Non Fiction and Westerns

Special interest titles available in large print are:
The Little Oxford Dictionary
Music Book
Song Book
Hymn Book
Service Book

Also available from us courtesy of Oxford University Press:
Young Readers' Dictionary
(large print edition)
Young Readers' Thesaurus
(large print edition)

For further information or a free brochure, please contact us at:
Ulverscroft Large Print Books Ltd.,
The Green, Bradgate Road, Anstey,
Leicester, LE7 7FU, England.
Tel: (00 44) 0116 236 4325
Fax: (00 44) 0116 234 0205

JILTED

Ann Barker

When Eustacia Hope is jilted at the altar, her parents send her to stay with her godmother Lady Agatha Rayner, a clergyman's widow. Her mother warns her to shun Lady Agatha's brother, the notorious Lord Ashbourne and his son Lord Ilam. And she soon discovers that her godmother isn't all she seems either. Then Eustacia meets Lord Ilam and the two are attracted to one another. But it is only after the arrival of Eustacia's estranged fiancé and the unexpected appearance of Lord Ashbourne that matters can be resolved in a way that is satisfactory to all parties.

CLERKENWELL CONSPIRACY

Ann Barker

When Captain Scorer died in action, his wife Eve was obliged to seek refuge with her cousin Julia. Treated as a poor relation and pursued by Julia's admirer, Eve is thankful when escape is offered through the bequest of a bookshop in Clerkenwell. She has no knowledge that Colonel Jason 'Blazes' Ballantyne, her husband's commanding officer, has been ordered by William Pitt to make enquiries concerning a codebook that has been left in the bookshop by French spies. When certain incidents and rumours convince Jason that Eve has a dubious reputation, it doesn't prevent attraction flaring between them . . .

LADY OF LINCOLN

Ann Barker

For Emily Whittaker living in Lincoln, the closest thing to romance is her lukewarm relationship with Dr Boyle. But a new friendship with Nathalie Fanshawe brings interest to her life. Then Canon Trimmer and his family move into the cathedral close. When Mrs Trimmer's brother, Sir Gareth Blades visits them, he seems a romantic figure, and apparently attracted to Emily. But she finds a mysterious side to Sir Gareth with the arrival of Annis Hughes, not to mention his connection with Mrs Fanshawe . . . Is Sir Gareth really a gallant gentleman or would Emily be better off settling for Dr Boyle after all?

THE OTHER MISS FROBISHER

Ann Barker

Elfrida Frobisher leaves her country backwater and her suitor to chaperon Prudence, her eighteen-year-old niece, in London. Unfortunately, Prudence has apparently developed an attachment for an unsuitable man, which she fosters behind her aunt's back. Attempting to foil her niece's schemes and prevent a scandal, Elfrida only succeeds in finding herself involved with the eligible Rufus Tyler in a scandal of her own! Fleeing London seems the only solution — but Prudence has another plan . . . Elfrida yearns for her quiet rural existence, but it takes a mad dash in pursuit of her niece before she realises where her heart truly lies.